NODAWAY TRAIL

By David R. Lewis

Nodaway Trail
Copyright: 2012 David R Lewis
Published: Ironbear, LCC
ISBN: 978-0-9969038-7-5
Cover Design: Jack W. Davis
JackDavis.com

This is a work of fiction. Names, characters, places, and incidents either are the product of the author's imagination or are used fictionally; and any resemblance to people, living or dead, business establishments, events, or locales is entirely coincidental.

All rights reserved. No part of this publication may be reproduced, stored in a retrieval system, or transmitted in any form or by any means, electronic, mechanical, photocopying, recording or otherwise, without express written permission from the author.

Titles by David R Lewis

Nosferati Series
BLOODTRAIL
BLOODLINE

Crockett Series
CALL ME CROCKETT
GRAVE PROMISE
SITUATIONAL FLEXIBILITY
ABDUCTED
WITNESS REJECTION
UNDERCOVER
BEHIND THE BADGE (coming in early 2017)

Trail Series
DEER RUN TRAIL
NODAWAY TRAILCALICO TRAIL
PAYBACK TRAIL
OGALLALA TRAIL
KILLDEER TRAIL
CUTTHROAT TRAIL
GLORY TRAIL

Stand Alones:
COWBOYS AND INDIANS
ONCE UPON AGAIN
ENDLESS JOURNEY (nonfiction)
INCIDENTS AMONG THE SAVAGES

You can read the first 3 chapters of **CALICO TRAIL by David R Lewis** at the end of this book!

This story is dedicated to the memory
of Louis L'Amour
and all of us who miss him.

CHAPTER ONE

I was settin' in front of the Sheriff's Office thinkin' about gittin' me somethin' to eat when he come ridin' in on that big ol' ugly blue roan a his. I watched him git off an' wrap a rein around the rail. He favored his back some. The roan got busy with the trough an' he clanked his way up on the boardwalk, them Mexican spurs a his lettin' a fella know evertime his boots hit. I hadden seen him in over a year, not since me an' Miss Harmony got hitched. He eased down in a chair beside me an' I noticed a scar on his left cheekbone that warn't there afore. His big droopin' mustache had gone near total gray. He put a ankle on a knee an' squinted at the street for a minute.

"Sheriff," he said.

"Marshal," I said.

We set there for another minute afore he grinned an' slapped me on the knee.

"Ruben, gawdammit!" he said, "Are ya all right?"

"I believe I am, Marion," I said. "How the hell are you?"

"I'm trail tired, boy," he said, "and that there is the straight of it. What's the Sweetwater got on special today?"

"Are you so feeble ya cain't even walk over an' find out?" I asked him.

"Mebbe you outa come with me in case I fall over and cain't git up."

"Maybe I should," I said. "We got laws agin folks layin' around in the street in this town."

Marion grunted an' stood up, then walked off down toward the corner on them godawful long legs a his. As usual, I followed along behind.

* * * * *

We took a table near the back, an' the owner, a fella name a Hershel, come over.

"Rube," he said. "Marshal. We got some extra nice catfish today with green peas an' fried potatoes or chicken stew an' cornbread."

We both took the catfish an' stayed purty quiet until after we et an' got more coffee. Marion stirred a little brown sugar inta his.

"Miss Harmony all right, is she?" he asked.

"Fixin' to have a baby," I said.

"The hell she is!"

"Yessir. Miz Clary says it'll be a spell yet. Prob'ly November sometime."

"Ain't that fine. You got a kitchen built on that place a your'n yet?" he asked.

"Nossir," I said. "After Harmony said she was gonna have a baby, her daddy wanted us to move into his place down at the livery. Nice big house, plenty a room. Even got that pump from the cistern right there in the kitchen. So we done it. I help out with the stock an' on the forge some. So does Harmony. Cain't git her to quit. We give my place to Arliss, it bein' right behind his shop an' all."

"Nice of ya," Marion said.

"Ol' Arliss has been plumb good to me. Least I could do."

"How's the sheriffin' business goin' for ya?" Marion asked me.

"Them two fellas that Homer sent over has worked out real good as deputies. Town's mostly quiet these days. Got a fair council an' Elmo McCoy's the mayor now. How's the Marshalin' trade doin'? I notice ya got a new scar."

Marion touched his cheek. "There was nine of 'em, Ruben," he said. "But I got all of 'em with five shots."

"It took ya five?" I said. "You must be slowin' down some. Ol' age, ya reckon?"

Marion grinned at me. "Last fall," he said, "I was over in Gasconade tryin' to keep Homer on the straight an' narrow. I was standin' out by the rail in front of the Sheriff Office next to that jug headed roan a mine when a horsefly or somethin' got up in his ear. He tossed his head my direction an' the shank a his bit smacked the hell outa me. Knocked me on my ass. The doc had to put seven or eight stitches in the damn thing. Said it give me a concussion. I doan know about that, but I had a helluva headache for a couple days."

"Homer all right?" I asked.

"He was then," Marion said, "but I doan know about now. I swung through Gasconade on the way here, but he was off chasin' somebody somewheres. Horse stealer, I believe it was."

We set there for a spell, quiet-like, while I waited for him to git to the point. Marion doan git in a hurry much, unless it's called for, then he gits around right smart. Putry soon, he spoke up.

"You reckon them deputies a your'n could take care a this town with you gone for a spell, Ruben?" he asked me.

"I reckon," I said.

"An' Miss Harmony," he went on. "You s'pose she'd be all right if you left for a while?"

"That baby ain't fixin' to be here afore November," I said. "She's with her daddy, Verlon. Harmony's tough, Marion. Whatcha need?"

"Quite a spell ago," he said, "even afore the war most likely, come a feller up by the Missouri north a Saint Joe in Atchison County name a Clovis Waxler. Set hisself up a ferry business gittin' folks across the river. Rumor has it he had two sons an' some of his wife's kin hangin' around a few years later. Now an' then, a couple a folks an' their wagon would disappear or some little pole boat wouldn't show up down river when it was supposed to.

"Eight or ten year ago it was believed that two a his nephews, last name a Siebert, held up a bank over by East Saint Louis. The Pinkertons got after 'em but lost 'em in the Missouri Breaks. After a year or so, they give up. That whole mess was supposed to be hangin' around up near where that ferry usta be, out in the sticks runnin' between Atchison and Nodaway Counties. Month or two ago, his sons, Jack an' Jim, is believed to be the two men that got with a couple a whores in the Blue Island saloon on the north side a Saint Joe, kilt one of 'em with a knife, an' cut the other one's ear or nose off, an' sliced her up here an' there.

"Some County Sheriff formed a posse an' took off after 'em. Like most possies, once a couple a them fellers got shot, they lost heart an' give up the chase when the bunch run for Nebraska or Ioway. When shit like that happens, the mess falls to fools like me. You done good when you come with me an' Homer when we went after that Duncan bunch. You've done yerself proud here. I could use ya, Ruben. I hate to wade into this mess all by myself. A course, you'd be a deputy marshal."

"When do we leave?" I asked him.

CHAPTER TWO

After we et, Marion went by the gunsmith shop to visit with ol' Arliss Hyatt a spell while I walked down to the livery. Verlon waved at me from the forge. Harmony was in the kitchen poundin' on a pile a dough to make bread. She set the dough aside under some cheesecloth, wiped her forehead with her apron, an' come over an' give me a kiss. I thumbed some flour offa the end of her nose an' grinned at her.

"Been snowin' in here?" I asked.

"One of us has to work a little bit," she said, throwin' a grin back at me. "What brings you home in the middle of the day?"

"Marion's in town," I said.

"Oh! Well ask him over for supper. We haven't seen him since we got married."

"I will if ya want me to," I said.

"Why wouldn't I want you to," she asked. I followed her to the outside stove where she checked the fire an' oven.

"Well," I said, "he wants to borrow me for a while."

"What for?"

"He's got some business to take care of over north a Saint Joe a ways," I said, "an' he wants me to ride along. He figgers that two of us would be some better than one a him."

"The two of you would be better than four or five of most men," Harmony said. "If he needs your help, of course you have to go. You wouldn't feel right if you didn't."

"I don't want ya gittin' worried about me an' all," I said.

"Ruben Beeler, my worries are my worries," she said. "There is nothing you can do about them, and precious little that I can. You don't need to worry about me worrying about you. Marion needs you. You go ahead along with him. Hank and Emory can take care of things here."

"You don't mind it if I go?" I said.

"Yes, I do," she said, "but not as much as you'd mind it if you didn't. Understand?"

"I reckon I do," I said.

She smiled at me. "Then I reckon," she said, "that I don't want to pound that dough out again. Get out of my way. Ask Marion over for supper. Arliss, too, if he wants to come along."

* * * * *

On my way to Arliss' shop I run across Hank Buford an' told him I'd be leavin' for a while in a day or two an' that if he needed help to git aholt a Arliss or Verlon Clarke to fill in. He said he would an' he'd make sure to tell Emory in case I missed him. I went on then an' found Marion in the shop talkin' to Arliss.

"Marion tells me you an' him is takin' to the trail, Rube," Arliss said.

"Whenever Marion wants to go," I said.

"I'm restin' up for a day or so, Ruben," Marion said. "Take a day to git what truck you need in shape and some chuck for us. You still got that packhorse?"

"Still do," I said.

"Good," Marion said. "I'd just as soon stay on the trail as much as we can. We'll leave enough tracks as it is without ridin' through ever town we see."

"Suits me," I said. "Harmony would be right pleased if'n the two of you would care to set with us for supper this evenin'. Last I seen her, she was fixin' to stick a couple a loaves a her sourdough in the oven. The ones she puts a little cinnamon in an' glazes with honey. Verlon's got a ham or two in the smokehouse that should be about ready. Might be a hard meal to miss."

"'Bout half-past five seem good, Rube?" Arliss asked.

"Make it six," Marion said. "I need to git Miz Clary to do a little laundry for me, an' I'd like to git down to the barbershop for a haircut and a tub a hot water. Might be a while before I can git to that kinda thing."

* * * * *

The next day I set to cleanin' my guns an' lookin' after my horses an' tack. Verlon trimmed up my packhorse an' put fresh shoes on him. I put a new cinch on my saddle as the ol' one was gittin' a little thin. I'd had one break on me once, an' I didn't care for it. It was deep spring an' Willie was gittin' a little grass fat. A trip would shape him out an' drop some weight. I went over to the general store an' got some flour an' cornmeal, some dry beans, some salt-cured bacon, half a dozen cans a peaches, coffee, one a them plugs a dried tea, some jerky, brown sugar for Marion, some peppermints an' four a them little boxes of Gayetty therapeutic papers. Harmony always kept 'em in the outhouse an' I'd got some used to 'em. They was a luxury shore enough, but they was a damn site more useful than a corncob or a handful a moss an' leaves.

I stopped by an' seen Elmo at the dry goods store an' got me a nice pair a buckskin chaps. If we was gonna be ridin' the river any, I wanted somethin' to turn briars an' thorns. I also got me a new slicker as mine was leakin' at the seams, a wax-treated ground cloth, an' a spool a stage line in case we might need to string us up a shelter a some kind.

I was fixin' to go collect the buckboard to pick up all my truck, when I seen Verlon comin' down the street in his wagon with some bags a feed. I flagged him down an' loaded up my stuff an' he saved me a extra trip. Back at the livery I packed up my panniers, added my three pound axe to the load, an' finished up gittin' what we needed for the trail.

That night, Harmony didn't have a lot to say an' hung onto me quite a bit while she slept. It was worrisome an' kept me awake more that I mighta liked, but I let it go. I knowed she was some upset I was headin' out with Marion an' all, an' I didn't feel no need to add to her discomfort none. She did fix us a big ol' breakfast a ham an' eggs an' fried potaters, an' sourdough biscuits an' gravy. I didn't figger I'd git that good a breakfast for a while, so I et as much as I could hold an' still swing a leg over a horse.

I had them panniers strung up on my pack saddle an' was putting a skillet an' coffee pot in one of 'em when she come out with a sack a them biscuits for us. I got everthin' closed up, an' was tossin' a blanket on Willie when Marion caught up his roan an' saddled up. Arliss was on hand, claimin' that if he was thirty years younger he'd go with us. We said goodbye to him an' Verlon, Harmony gimme a kiss an' a hug, an' about a half hour after daybreak, me an' Marion took out. We warn't more than a hour gone when clouds gathered, the wind picked up, the temperature dropped, an' it come to rain.

I wonder how come it is that a fella can feel wetter in the rain than if'n he jumped in the durn river? It never did rain terrible hard, but the wind kindly drove it at us, turnin' some of it into a mist that snuck down collars, up sleeves, an' into eyes an' ears 'til the two of us was shiverin' from it. It warn't but the middle a the afternoon afore we come on this little creek an' got down next to it up agin a high bank that cut the blowin' from the northwest an' give us a windbreak. Marion rooted around in some brush that had collected in a bend at high water, lookin' for some dry wood while I hobbled the horses an' strung that groundcloth to give us a little roof to set under. Between the saddles an' the panniers offa my packhorse, I fixed us up a place to lean back out the weather an' dug a pine knot out the pack about the time Marion showed up with a armload of small stuff that warn't too wet. That pine knot got them sticks goin', an' purty soon we had us a fair camp an' fire. I got some water outa the crick an' put coffee on an' a pot to boil an' handed Marion a peppermint stick.

"I thank ya, Ruben," he said, leanin' back an' puttin' that stick between his teeth. "Ain't it fine how a stick a peppermint can take the edge offa unfair day like this 'un. It's the little things that can make the biggest difference, I guess."

We'd set there a hour or so an' I'd put some beans in the pot an' a piece a bacon when Marion had to go piss. He durn near fell down tryin' to git up. It embarrassed him I believe, an' he limped off a little ways. When he come back, he grunted when he set down, an' screwed his face up some. He beat his hat on his knee a lick or two to git the water offa it, put it back on an' stared into the fire.

"Now before you even ask, boy," he said, "me and the roan took a fall this past winter over by Sikeston. There was a foot a snow on the ground, and I speck that softened up things some, but I hurt my back down low a little. Wasn't long afore I had some shootin' pains down my ass plumb to the back a my right knee that was worrisome. Got to where it kept me up of a night and I couldn't hardly walk. I went to a doctor over that way, and he rolled me around on the floor pullin' on that leg and pushin' on my butt four or five different times. Felt right foolish, but it helped quite a bit. I git around all right with it now, 'cept once in a while it hangs up on me. Wet weather seems to aggravate it some."

"I believe that horse a your'n has had all a you he wants," I said. "First he slaps you upside yer head an' knocks the hell out of ya, then he tries to cripple ya fallin' down. Maybe ya oughta git a mule."

Marion rolled that peppermint sick around a minute afore he spoke up.

"I believe," he said, rockin' his head a little from side to side like he usually done when he was gittin' cocky, "that little tin star you been wearin' for a spell has turned you into about three-quarters of a smartass."

I grinned at him. "Anything's possible," I said.

Marion rooted around in a pocket under his slicker for a minute.

"Well," he said, "I reckon this'll only make matters worse."

He tossed somethin' silver at me, an' I caught it. It was a U.S. Deputy Marshal badge.

"Do you swear to uphold and the rest of all that?" he asked me.

"Yessir, I do," I said.

"All right then," he said, sinkin' a little lower into his set. "Good to have ya along, Ruben. Doan let the fire go out."

He pulled his hat down low over his eyes an' sighed, what was left a that peppermint stick twitchin' a little.

* * * * *

I woke up afore daybreak the next mornin' an' freshed the fire. The rain had stopped overnight, but it was still cool an' windy. By the time Marion got up, I had coffee hot an' bacon on to go with Harmony's biscuits. Marion headed out to do his business an' I give him a box a them Gayetty therapeutic papers. He looked at 'em, quizzical like.

"What the hell's this?" he asked me.

"Well, it ain't a handful a wet leaves," I said.

When he come back, he didn't say nothin' about them papers, but he didn't give 'em back neither.

CHAPTER THREE

Our third night on the trail we camped four or five miles outa Saint Joe. The next mornin' Marion left me at camp an' rode to town. I had me a cup a tea an' brown sugar, an' et all but the last two a them biscuits, then squared everthin' away so we could git on without much fuss. While I was waitin' on Marion, I took a little ride down toward the river an' found a couple a boys fishin'. I got offa Willie an' tied him to a saplin' an' walked down the bank to where they was.

"You boys doin' any good cuttin' down on the fish population?" I asked.

The little 'un spoke right up.

"We got us some catfish, mister," he said. "Five of 'em."

"The heck ya do," I said. "Lemme see."

He pulled on a rope they had tied off to a root, an' shore enough, they had three mudcats, a little channel, an' about a five pound flathead.

"Would ya sell that flathead?" I asked.

The little fella studied on me for a minute, squintin' in the sun. "How much?" he said.

"You got the product," I said. "You set the price."

He thought that over an' said, "two-bits."

"You got change for a dollar?"

"Neither one a us got any money, mister. You ain't got two bits?"

"All I got is a dollar," I said.

He studied on me' afore he spoke up.

"If'n you ain't got nothin' to eat," he said, "I'll give ya that channel so ya don't go hungry."

I grinned at him. "How 'bout I trade you my dollar for the flathead," I said.

He blinked at me. "A whole dollar?"

"Take it or leave it," I tolt him.

He took it.

* * * * *

I rode back to camp, freshed the fire, an' put a chunk a bacon fat in the skillet to cook down. While that was sizzlin', I took out my Barlow an' cleaned the fish, throwin' the guts an' skin away from camp 'cause a flies. I dipped that catfish in some a the cornmeal an' had just laid him in the skillet when Marion come back.

"Ain't no town law on hand," he said, pullin' a little slack in the roan's cinch. He walked over an' looked down at the fire. "Catfish, ain't it?" he asked.

"It is," I said. "Flathead."

"Where the hell did you git a catfish?"

"You ain't noticed that big ol' river just west of us?" I asked.

Marion thought that over for a little bit, but he didn't let no question git away from him. He didn't let none a his half a that catfish git away from him neither.

* * * * *

After we et, we rode around Saint Joe an' come back at it from the north side. I went on in with the packhorse an' run across the Blue Island Saloon on the edge a town. It was a rickety buildin', long an' narrow, with a floored tent attached to it on the east side servin' fatback an' potaters an' such. I hooked that little shotgun on my belt, made sure my badge was covered up, an' went in.

There warn't hardly but six or seven fellas in the place. A couple a hayshakers was takin' turns drawin' cards an' hollerin' at each other at one a the tables. I went up to the bar an' this heavy set fella come up an' asked me what did I want.

"Shot a whiskey," I tolt him, "an' it better be in the bottle it come in."

"You'll git what everbody gits," he said, reachin' under the counter.

I smiled at him. "Mister," I said, "if I figger it come outa a tub in the backroom, you'll git a bath in it afore I leave."

He stopped his reach an' took a bottle offa shelf behind him, poured a shot, an' set it down.

"Two bits," he said.

"Thank you," I said, an' dropped the money on the bar just as Marion walked in, his badge showin'. He took up space about six or seven feet from me. I ignored him. Them two fellas playin' cards quit they yellin' an' got quiet.

"Yessir, Marshal," the fat fella said. "What can I do for ya?"

"You had a couple a whores in trouble a while back," Marion said. "One kilt an' one with her nose or ear cut off, I hear."

"One was kilt," he said. "Bled out. The other'n had her nose an' face sliced up some an' got beat on or somethin'."

"Know who done it?" Marion asked.

"I wasn't workin' that night," the fat fella said.

"I didn't ask if you was workin' that night," Marion said. "I asked if you knowed who done it."

The fella licked his lips. "Nossir," he said, "I don't. Some folks talked, but I doan remember what they said."

Marion smiled at him an' leaned his elbows on the counter. "You think maybe," he asked, "if you was on this side of the bar you might have a little better idea?"

The fella started to take a step backwards an' Marion had him by the shirtfront, just as quick as that. "Do ya?" he asked.

"I doan know, Marshal," the fella said, kindly shrinkin' down some.

"Let's see," Marion said, an' just hauled him over the bar like he warn't no heavier than a loaf a bread.

Marion, as calm as you please, stood there, holdin' that fella like he was one a them kids on the river. "Now then," he said, "how's yer memory?"

"Honest, Marshal," the fella said, "I wadden here. But I heer'd it said it was them Waxler boys, Jim an' Jack. They took off an' the sheriff over in Nodaway county set after 'em with a posse, but two or three fellers got shot. The Waxlers an' them are a wild bunch. They purty much used to own Atchison an' Nodaway counties. That's all I know. Honest."

Marion turned loose a him then. "Thank you for your cooperation, sir," he said. "That cut up lady here today, is she?"

"Yessir, she is. Upstairs. Room four. Nobody with her that I know of."

"Reckon I'll go up an' have a talk with her an' anybody else I care to," Marion went on. "I doan speck to be bothered none. That all right with you?"

"That's fine, Marshal," the fat fella said, wipin' some sweat off his face with a sleeve.

Marion turned away then an' climbed them steps. If he had a bad back, I shore couldn't see it.

As soon a Marion got outa the room, them two hayshakers lit a shuck. I sipped on that shot for a spell an' finally Marion come back down an' walked out. I finished the shot an' got another one. I waited a couple a minutes, took the shot an' stepped outside. Soon as I got on the off side a Willie I spit that whiskey in the dirt, mounted up, grabbed the packhorse's lead rope, an' set off. Marion would be waitin' for me on down the line.

* * * * *

I stopped at a livery on the way out an' filled our water bags from their cistern, then kept Willie at a easy canter an' caught up to Marion in about three miles.

"There was two fellers in there flippin' cards," I said. "They lit out when you went upstairs."

"Musta got tired a playin'," Marion said.

"Oh hell yes!" I said. "That's what I figured. Ain't no chance them fellas might be on the way to tell somebody we're out here lookin' inta a killin'. When we camp tonight, let's build us the biggest fire we can so anybody that gits ta lookin' can see it from ten miles away. Maybe hire some ol' boy to hang around an' play the mouth harp or the fiddle. What the hell do we havta worry about?"

Marion smiled. "Settle down, Ruben," he said. "You'll git a sour stomach."

CHAPTER FOUR

We hit some heavy brush for a while, but it broke up after a ways. I rode up beside Marion.

"Was that lady hurt some?" I asked him.

"Quite a bit," he said. "She's healed up most a the way, but she ain't never gonna be right. Nobody took a knife to her. A feller did cut on the other one's neck an' she died from it, but the one I talked to got hurt tryin' to help her friend. She come at the ol' boy with the knife an' his sidekick flung her across the room. She went face first inta a lookin' glass on a dresser agin the wall. That glass busted up inta splinters when she hit it. She ain't but about twenny years old. Doan know if she ever was purty, but she damn shore ain't now. Said her name was Charity. Wasn't no charity in what that feller done to her."

"She know the names a who done it?" I asked.

"Says she don't," he said. "Said they was just a couple a hard cases she'd never seen afore, and she'd only been in town for a couple weeks. May be true. She's plumb broke down about it, though. Scared right through. This other gal I talked to claimed it was boys from that Waxler bunch, but she wasn't sure which ones. That's just what she heard a couple a the other whores say. None a them other girls would talk to me."

"This Waxler got a ranch up this away?" I asked.

"He's got somethin' up this way," Marion said. "I doan know if the old man is even still alive. Way I heer'd it, he never was mor'n a pirate on the river anyway. Shit, boy. He prob'ly come up here afore the war. This was some rough country in them days. Oglala injuns was still raidin' this far south an' east of their territory. Cheyenne was burnin' out settlers. Dakotas was raisin' hell west a here a ways. Wadden no law a hardly any kind. Couple a big ranches tryin' to get started, raisin' horses though, not cattle. Homesteaders an' squatters scattered around. It was frontier. Waxler an' some a his kin show up an' purty much just take what they want an' hold onto it with a gun. In them days, Nebraska City was a piss-pot. Lincoln wadden much better. Hell, Omaha wadden mor'n a wide spot on the trail, saloons an' whores. Liquor an' humpin' has always paved the way for the rest a the herd, Ruben. Neither one a them things is exactly whatcha might call polite society. Folks that come up through that time, an' profited from it, got no plans to change anythin' unless they is give a real good reason. Kinda like a pack a wild dogs. They got their territory. As a rule, ya cain't just wade in there and gentle 'em down so they'll trail along behind the wagon. Most times ya gotta run 'em off or shoot 'em."

"You think them fellas that took outa that saloon was some a the bunch?" I asked him.

"You ever watch a pack a wolves?" Marion asked.

"Nossir."

"There's usually a dog an' a bitch in the middle of it," he said. "Them two purty much run things. Everbody else sucks up to 'em. Then ya got the rest a the pack. They got a order to 'em. Rank an' file, just like the goddam army or somethin'. Like generals an' colonels an' majors an' captains, right on down to privates an' new recruits. Everbody down the line wants to move up the line. To do that they gotta git noticed doin' somethin' by command an' prove they do a good job. Sometimes in a wolf pack there'll be one or two strays hangin' around the edge a things, tryin' to figger a way into the bunch so they doan havta go it alone. Could be that's what them fellers was at the saloon. If I recall, they was fair young. Might be they seen a chance to go runnin' to a captain or a major with the news that I'm out here sniffin' around, an' git themselves noticed some."

"If that's the case," I said, "somebody's gonna know we're comin'. Then maybe somebody on up the ladder might wanta come look us over."

Marion smiled. "Or do somethin' to get a boost on up another step or two," he said.

"Well, ain't that just fine," I said.

"Be some easier if they was three of us," Marion said.

"Be some easier if they was thirty of us," I tolt him.

He thought that was kindly funny an' chuckled a while. "Ol' Ruben," he said.

"You spent time watchin' wolves?" I asked.

"Some," he said. "When I was yer age, back afore the war, I spent time watchin' injuns. Them an' wolves operated along the same line. Them injuns didn't have to be taught rank an' file like our boys. They was born to it. That's why we never could whip 'em in a fair battle. We could out gun 'em, but we damn shore never could out fight 'em. I never did feel sorry for no injun. That don't make no more sense than feelin' sorry for the wind. But I damn shore feel sorry for what we done to 'em. Seems to me like preachers an' politicians cain't never leave nothin' alone. Hell, Ruben, we even give 'em bad blankets an' such so they'd git the fever or the pox an' die from it. We done the same thing to the injuns that we done to the bufflers. Them big shaggies never stood no real chance neither. Injun or buff, mebbe it was just their time, but the way it come about was terrible wrong. Damn shame, Ruben. Damn dirty shame."

* * * * *

We stayed on the trail all day, never mor'n a mile or two from the river, chewin' on jerky now an' then. Later that afternoon we come on a open flat for a ways, studded up with new growth river birches an' thorn bushes an' such, nothin' mor'n four or five feet high. Marion turned toward the river then an' stopped next to a gravel bar in grass about a foot tall. Willie flushed a rabbit an' my packhorse took exception an' got to dancin' around some an' give me a little rope burn through my shirt. Marion swung down an' looked up at me.

"You git done playin' with them horses," he said, "why doan you go ahead on an' make camp?"

"Some early ain't it?" I asked him.

"Lemme borrow your rifle," he said.

I pulled the Yellaboy outa the scabbard an' handed it to him.

"Tend to the roan for me. I'm going for a stroll," he said, an' walked off down our backtrail.

I pulled saddles an' packs an' hobbled the horses after I led 'em down for a drink. They went after that grass like it was under gravy. They was some dry wood above the high water mark an' I carried a bunch of it in an' built a fire. 'Cause we had enough time, I put on a pot a beans an' got the flour out for fry bread. We still had two or three hours a good light left when them beans started to boil. I tossed in some bacon an' salt, then added a little molasses an' let 'em bubble.

It was a purty place. Had a nice breeze from the south, hardly no cloud in the sky. I got one whiff of a skunk from God knows how far off. Unusual that was, gittin' skunk scent in the daytime. I set there an' watched a big ol' heron along the river bank, now an' then grabbin' a little fish an' slidin' it down that long neck. I coulda easy had us a rabbit, but I didn't wanna fire off no gunshot, Marion someplace out there like he was an' not knowin' I was only shootin' at a critter. Instead, I opened one a them cans a peaches, leaned back agin my saddle an' et half of it, puttin' the rest aside for the marshal.

Musta been a couple a hours go by when Willie tossed his head an' looked off toward the south, twitchin' his ears. He snorted once, then relaxed an' went back to the grass. Marion was comin' back I figgerd, or Willie wodden a been so calm about it. Sure enough, a few minutes later he come walkin' into camp. It come on me then that I didn't hear them Mexican spurs a his. I took notice an' seen the rowels was tied up with little pieces of rawhide. He leaned the Yellaboy agin the backside a my saddle an' grunted as he set down.

"Beans an' bacon in about a hour," I said. "Half a can a peaches open for ya. Coffee's hot."

"Thanks, Ruben," he said. "If they come in, them three fellers might git here in time for the beans."

"Three fellas?" I asked.

He nodded. "A mile or so south. I figger they trailed us from town. I was them, I'd circle an' come in from the north. That way my horses could git scent first an' not be shy, an' it wouldn't be so plain I'd been trailin' nobody."

"Whatcha reckon they want?" I asked him.

"See who we are. Maybe try an' git the bulge on us. They most likely know why I was in town. I speck two of 'em was the fellers in the saloon. They got any guts, they'll come in to size us up. If'n they don't, they might come at us after dark. If the third one is like them other two, they ain't nothin' but kids. Kids usually ain't got a lotta experience. They git nervous an' maybe figger they got somethin' to prove. They is more hazardous than dangerous. Hazardous can shore enough put a feller in the ground, though."

Marion got up an' moved his saddle farther away from where I was settin', fetched that can a peaches, an' stretched out.

He et a peach an' grinned at me. "Wanted to put a little more distance between us," he said. "Wouldn't want one a them fellers to hit me just 'cause he was tryin' to shoot you."

* * * * *

They come in outa the northeast after we et, an' it was gittin' on toward sundown. Three of 'em. Number one was a big fella with a black slouch hat an' a black, kindly holey beard. He was carryin' a silver-lookin' Colt with a gold hammer an' shiny white grips in a crossdraw. Number two was kindly heavy-set wearin' a ol' gray hat with a ragged brim an' a string comin' down around his neck from it. He was packin' another Colt in a side holster by his left hand on a gunbelt lined with bullets. The third fella didn't have no hat. He was little an' skinny with wiry carrot hair, freckles, an' light-colored, quick eyes. He had what looked to me like a ol' Colt's Dragoon shoved down in his pants. That revolver musta weighted five pounds. If it hadn't been converted, it was a cap an' ball. They horses warn't much. I eased my scattergun down beside my leg. Marion didn't move at all. When they got close, number one spoke up.

"Howdy," he said.

Marion nodded to him.

"Me an' my frens had a long day. Could you spare a cup a coffee for some travelers?"

"Wodden turn no man away from coffee that had his own cup," Marion said. "It's on the fire. Help yerselves. That little bag layin' there has got some brown sugar plug in it, if'n you got a taste for sweet."

"Thank you, sir," number one said, gittin' down a collectin' a cup from his saddlebag.

The other ones got down, an' number two got his cup. One an' two poured coffee an' squatted across from us, number three just stood behind 'em an' watched. They was all young, none of 'em older than me.

"Where you fellers headed?" number one asked.

Marion yawned an' scratched his neck. "Omaha, mebbe," he said.

"What's in Omaha?"

"Hell, boy," Marion said, real cheerful like, "they's a whole bunch a shit in Omaha. Ya ever been there?"

"Nossir, I ain't," number one said.

"I recommend it," Marion went on. "If'n I was you, I'd finish my coffee an' head up that way. Ain't hard to find. Just go back the way ya come an' keep on goin'."

"You sayin' you want us to leave?" number one asked.

"No," Marion said. "I'm just sayin' that it might be safer for ya in Omaha than it is here."

Number two spoke up. "Well, yer about a hard ol' stump, ain't ya?" he said.

Marion smiled. "Son," he said, "I was twenty-three year old the last time my daddy kicked my ass. It was a lesson of value. It taught me to never confuse age an' ability. Might save you some grief if you was to take heed. Omaha is lookin' better for you boys all the time."

It was then that number three went for his gun. Marion shot him before he even cleared his belt. He fell over backwards an' I raised the scattergun an' leveled it at them other two. Neither one of 'em moved a inch. The one on the ground commenced to wheeze an' twitch. Number one spoke up.

"You sonofabitch!" he hollerd. "Yew shot Bucket!"

"Who?" Marion asked, his Colt pointed between the two that was left.

"Bucket, Goddammit!"

Marion grinned at him. "Safe to say," he said, "that there bucket is leakin' some. He'll settle down an' git quiet in a minute. Meantime, I'd appreciate it if you two boys would take out your revolvers an' toss 'em, real gentle like, over to this side a the fire. A course, ya doan have to. My pard over there can easy git both of ya with that little shotgun a his. Doan make me no never mind. The more the merrier. I ain't gonna dig no holes anyway."

Them guns come over the fire in short order. Marion picked up the shiny Colt an' looked it over while I kept the scattergun on them two.

"This here is a nice piece," he said. "Pearl handles, all engraved, nickel plated with a gold trigger and hammer, 'bout a eight inch barrel." He looked at number one. "This your'n?"

"You know damn well it is," number one said.

* * * * *

"Bullshit," Marion grunted, gittin' to his feet. "Ain't no way a web-footed river rat like you ever had half the money in one spot to git a fine piece like this. You took this offa somebody, most likely after you backshot him." He stepped over the fire, grabbed number one by the throat an' lifted him up on his tippy-toes. "Mebbe I oughta give this Colt back to ya an' let ya come at me with it, boy," he growled. "You want it? You want yer smokepole back, you chickenshit sonofabitch? You wanna drag leather agin somebody who's facin' ya?"

Marion held him there for a minute, eye to eye, an' then just kindly tossed him away. Number one hit the ground gaggin' with snot runnin' outa his nose an' wheezin'. Marion looked at number two. Two was terrible pale an' shakin' some.

"Pick up that dead bucket over there an' tie him to his horse," he said. "Then you an' that coward mount up an' git out. I ever run up on either one a you agin, I'll shoot ya. My name is Marion Daniels, boy. I am a United States Marshal. I can see like a hawk an' scent like a hound. Anybody in that bunch you'd like to run with wants to try me on, tell him to bring a shovel an' a friend to use it. You got two minutes to git that snot-covered asshole up an' git out a here. Doan forget to take that redheaded bucket a shit with ya. I doan want him stinkin' up my camp."

* * * * *

Them boys got real busy then, pickin' up that one that got shot an' tyin' him to his horse. It warn't long afore they was on their way.

We watched 'em ride off, an' Marion tossed another piece a wood on the fire.

"Hey, Ruben," he said. "We got anymore a them peaches?"

CHAPTER FIVE

I didn't sleep too good that night. I'd seen ol' Marion git after it a time or two an' truth be tolt, he was so sudden that it put me off some. I warn't scared a him or nothing like that. He an' me was friends. But when his blood come up, Marion was near extra human or somethin'. He was terrible fast with a gun, like nothin' I'd ever imagined, much less seen, but that ain't what jarred me. I ain't sayin' he was like a cat or nothin' 'cause he warn't, but he had that same kinda cat single mind when his ruff come up. If ya ever seen cats fight, there ain't nothin' else in the world important to 'em right then. Nothin'. Like the time he run down that slope into them Duncan Brothers an' their bunch. There warn't nothin' else in the world to him right then but puttin' a stop to that mess. You coulda stuck a elephant in his way an' he woulda ducked right under it an' kept on goin', givin' it no mind at all, 'cause it warn't part a his world right then. Homer tolt me once that Marion thought some of me, an' that if Marion thought some of a fella, that fella shouldn't oughta waste it. I didn't want to, but I was kindly scairt I might. That's what kept me up, I reckon. Thinkin' about what he would do, an' what I could do. Anyways, my lack a sleep made me a little late gittin' up the next mornin'. It was full light when I come around, an' Marion was pokin' at bacon with a stick, turnin' it over in the skillet, an' there was some leftover frybread warmin' on a rock set in close to the fire.

"Mornin' Ruben," he said. "Thought I'd letcha sleep some. I noticed how you was a little restless last night."

"I tossed an' turned a mite," I said.

"Killin' a feller, or watchin' one git kilt, ain't easy," he went on, "special if that feller was fixin' to kill you if he could, and woulda if you didn't git him first. Truth is, it doan never git no easier, neither. Best you can do is lock it away in the back a your head somewheres an' git on down the trail. I've put a few ghosts back in that space and most times they stay there. Once in a great while, special if I've had too much whiskey, one or two of 'em might sneak out for a spell, but I git 'em shut back up. It bothers me a helluva lot less than if I just let 'em all run loose. A feller has got to protect hisself from what he's had to do, son, or it can eat him up. That's the straight of it. You can do it. If I thought ya couldn't, I never woulda took you after them Duncan brothers, much less brung ya out here. Puttin' that kinda stuff away where it cain't git at ya is what they call a acquired skill. The more ya do it, the better at it ya git. Like playin' the mouth harp or shootin' a gun. If it come easy, it wouldn't be worth a durn."

I didn't know what to say to him about all that, but I kindly felt like I should say somethin', him talkin' to me about it like he done, so I nodded at him an' said, "all right."

Smilin', Marion turned back to pokin' at the bacon an' I went off to take care a business.

* * * * *

When I come back, Marion was gone an' his coach gun was layin' where I'd left my Yellaboy. I et that bacon an' frybread an' went to cleanin' up, thinkin' about what he'd said to me. I packed up, saddled the horses, an' was kickin' out the fire when Willie throwed his head an' snorted. Purty soon, Marion come walkin' in.

"You all right?" he asked me.

"Yessir," I said. "I appreciate you talkin' to me 'bout everthin'."

He walked over to my horse an' stuck my rifle in the saddle scabbard.

"Them boys circled an' went back toward St. Joe," he said. "Could be they ain't part of the bunch. Just assholes lookin' to git what they could."

He went to his saddlebags an' took out that fancy Colt with them pearl grips. He fussed with it a little, clickin' the cylinder an' checkin' the barrel an' such, then looked at me.

"Be a good replacement for that Schofield," he said.

"Would be if a fella wanted to git rid of his Schofield," I said.

"Thought I'd offer," he said.

"Reckon I'll refuse," I said.

He smiled an' stepped away a piece, then that gun went off three times, faster than I could count. I swear I doan know how anybody could cock an' fire as quick as he done. It was a mystery to me. He come walkin' back an' stuck that Colt in his saddlebag.

"I believe ol' Arliss can do it some good down in his shop," he said. "Think maybe I'll keep it."

"Terrible fancy," I said.

Marion grinned at me then. "Ain't I just," he said.

* * * * *

We followed the river a ways an' run onto a little feeder crick comin' in from the east. It had a shallow an' purty easy bottom, so Marion got down in it an' we followed it to the northeast for a couple a hours 'til it kindly run out in this muddy an' low spot, across the way from a stand a woods along the bottom of a slope from some low hills. There was some activity goin' on along the edge a the trees an' we headed over.

We come on a half-dozen or so fellas an' a couple a freight wagons. They was sawin' an' splitin' red oak offa two or three downed trees, an' stackin' that wood in them wagons. One of 'em walked over to Marion, takin' off his hat an' wipin' sweat.

"Howdy," he said. "Names Higgins, Marshal. Met ya five or six year ago at a hangin' in Saint Joe."

"I remember ya," Marion said. "You developed a hatred for squirrels?"

Higgins grinned at that, an' Marion swung down. I did the same.

"Supplyin' wood for riverboats," Higgins said. "Cut down a mess a these big ol' oaks five year ago. Come back ever year, cut down some more, then cut up the ones that's been layin' out for a spell. Wood gits purty dry after two or three years. Haul it down to a spot a little south a here where I got me a ramp down to the river. Them boats pick up what they need an' leave the money at a livery in Saint Joe for me. I give the smith a little cut for takin' the payment. He cheats me some, but not enough to ruin the deal."

"Doan sound too bad to me," Marion said.

"It ain't. I hire these kids for four-bits a day an' work 'em purty hard. I pay a little tribute for takin' trees now an' then, but I make out."

"Tribute?" Marion asked.

"Yessir. To the bunch that claims they own this land. Couple times a season, four or five riders'll come in an' I give 'em twenty dollars or so for the rights to cut this wood."

"What if ya don't pay?" Marion asked.

"They's a rough herd, Marshal. I never considered not payin' as a option."

"Who are they?"

"They're part of that Waxler bunch, I guess. Mostly they run north a here a ways, but they'll come down thisaway if it means money."

"I ain't looked at no records or nothin'," Marion said, "but it wouldn't surprise me none if nobody has ever filed on this land, or paid nobody else for it that has filed. I believe this is open country. You always paid these fellers?"

"First year I got this big idea, I come down to the river with a mess a green cedar to build my ramp. Four or five ol' boys showed up 'bout the time it was finished an' said it'd be a good idea if I was to offer 'em a little somethin' for permission to do what I'd done. I told 'em that I didn't need no permission, this was free country. They went off. A couple a weeks later I come up here with some hired boys an' cut a mess a downed wood. When I took the wagons over to the ramp, the ramp was tore up an' no good. We rebuilt it in a week or so an' got back to haulin' wood. Some fellers showed up to see how we was doin' an' admired that new ramp. Wondered how long it would stand. Be a shame to lose the ramp an' all that wood we'd worked so hard to cut an' haul. They was right full a sympathy for me. I give 'em twenty dollars, an' they went away. That's how it started."

"Bunch runs north a here a ways," Marion said.

"Yessir."

"Speck I should go up that way an' talk to these boys," Marion said, gittin' back up on his roan.

Higgins looked up at him. "Oughta be careful," he said.

"Damn right they should," Marion said.

CHAPTER SIX

We rode most a the rest of the day an' turned back toward the river to make camp where the horses could git to water. We set up on a little gravel runout into the edge a the river. They was plenty a dead wood dry enough ta burn. 'Bout a mile on the flat afore we got there, we flushed some pheasants that flew on ahead a us a ways. Marion switched shells from buck to number six shot in that coach gun a his an' went ahead on foot. We hadn't gone a quarter mile afore he flushed a cock an' two hens. He busted both a them hens. I skint 'em while he made camp an' started a fire. Most folks like skin on a bird. To tell the truth, so do I, but not enough to pluck two pheasant hens to git it.

Marion found some young sage an' a couple a wild onions down the bank a ways, an' I stuck 'em up inside them birds. Then I fixed up a spit outa some green willow an' strung them birds on it, up above the fire. I opened a can a peaches, an' we 'et em. I put about half the brown sugar we had left in the juice an' stirred it up in a slurry. While them hens was cookin' I used the skillet to make flour an' cornmeal frybread in bacon grease an' poured a little a that peach slurry on them hens now an' then, kindly spreadin' it out with my fingers. Long about dark, we each took a hen an' got after it. I swear, I ain't never cared near as much for pheasants as I have chickens, them bein' bred for eatin' an' all, but them pheasants, tastin' a sage an' onion from the inside out, an' peach an' brown sugar from the outside in, was as good as anythin' I ever deserved. Marion kept makin' gruntin' noises while he chewed on his bird. When he finished, he drunk quite a bit from a water bag, an' got a bottle a whiskey outa his possibles. He come over an' set down, took a pull offa that bottle 'an passed it to me. I took a drink an' passed it back.

"By God, Ruben," he said, "I have et a mess a meals around a campfire, but I ain't never had nothin' like that. You oughta open yerself a café or somethin'. All you'd need is brown sugar, peach juice, and pheasants. Boy, you'd git rich."

"As long as all my customers had been in the saddle three or four days," I said.

"Miss Harmony know you can cook like that?" he asked me.

"I never had the need to show her," I said.

"It's a secret worth keepin'," he said. "She finds out the truth, you'll be in a apron an' she'll be out here with a gun on her hip."

The thought a that tickled me some, an' I got to laughin' a little bit. When I quit, he handed me the bottle' an' I took another drink. I handed it back to him. Then, outa my mouth come stuff that never went through no part a my brain at all, I don't think.

"Marion," I said, "how come you go at things like ya do?"

"Whatdaya mean?" he said, takin' another drink.

"Well," I went on, "like them Duncans when you run off down that hill into the middle a things like ya done. Or them fellers that come to our camp. You set there with 'em for a minute, nice as ya please, then you just went at 'em. Wound up havin' to shoot that little one. An' now, you're fixin' to go after this Waxler bunch with just the two of us. You really gonna do that?"

Marion chuckled an' handed me back that bottle. "Well," he said, "I ain't gonner git in no gunfight with the whole damn mess at one time, Ruben. That'd be foolish. When I was a kid, we lived about a mile outside a little ol' town over in the bootheel. Now and then dad would send me walkin' into town to git something. On the edge a town was this place that kept a big ol' yaller dog on a rope out in the yard. Evertime he'd see me, he'd git to roarin' at me and hittin' the end a that that rope. Scared me to death. I had nightmares about that damn dog. One mornin' I was walkin' by the place and that terror come chargin' at me on the rope the way he done, and that damn rope broke. Here he come across that yard like a cougar on wheels. I couldn't think a nothin' else ta do, so I hollerd and run right at him, screamin' for all I was worth. That's when he made a mistake. He thought about me for a second. Then I had the bulge on him. I just kept comin'. When I got right up on him, I slapped his face. He turned off and went up on the porch.

"That dog coulda chawed me up and spit me out in a minute, but he didn't. The reason he didn't was because I come right at him. It was unexpected behavior. Unexpected behavior makes some folks give up or run away or hesitate enough to give a feller a edge. Like that kid I shot. He was the hard one. He give it away when he didn't set down with them other two. He give it away agin when he wouldn't let his eyes be still. He warn't nervous as much as he was edgy. He was figger'n to shoot one or the other a us when they got off their horses. When I come at his partners like I done, he paused. Then I had my edge. Plus I knowed you was settin' there with that scattergun a your'n. Ever since I tangled with that dog, I've purty much come right at trouble. More now that I'm gittin' older, I speck. I never could understand why ol' folks is always so careful. A man a sixty has got a lot less to lose than a man a twenty. Seems to me a sixty year old oughta be more fearless than most of 'em are. Plus, when ya go right at somethin', ya got better focus. When yer focused, ya got a little edge, too."

I took a drink an' passed the bottle back. "So when you tangled with that dog, bein' focused made ya brave?" I asked.

"No," he said, "bein' scared made me desperate."

"You was desperate?"

Marion chuckled. "Musta been," he said. "I walked another fifty yards afore I noticed my pants was all wet."

* * * * *

We was late breakin' camp the next mornin'. I had a headache that didn't wear off for a while. Marion seemed to set the saddle a little stiffer than was usual. About the middle a the mornin' we hit a faint wagon track an' took to it. A little ways into the afternoon we come up over this low rise an' seen a place down in a shallow valley. It looked like it mighta started out as a soddy. Clapboard that was rottin' away at the ground was most of it, with a shallow roof covered with leaves an' some moss, 'cause of a big ol' oak that shaded one side. It had been built onto some on the other side an' had windas, but with open shutters an' no glass. They was runoff from a little spring up the slope behind the place than come down the far side an' into a big pen that was full a mud an' hogs. You could smell the pig shit. There was a couple a ratty sheds on the near side, an' a horse an' a mule tied to a rail out front.

"Pig farmer," I said.

"And wore out whores," Marion said. "We could use some clear water for the bags, though. Let's go in."

He turned the roan down the slope an' I moved out a few yards to his left an' kept pace. We was maybe fifty yards from the place when the barrel of a rifle showed out the winda next to the front door, an' a voice yelled from inside.

"Yew sonsabitches go ahead on now," it yelled. "I give ya money last goddam month, an' yew know it! Yew come any closter, an' I'll knock at least one a y off his horse, gawdammit!"

Marion stood up in his stirrups an' lifted off his hat. "Hold on now," he yelled. "We ain't who you think we are. We doan want none a your money, but we could use a little water from your spring if them hogs can spare it."

"Who be ye?" come another shout.

"We're United States marshals," Marion yelled. "My name is Marion Daniels."

"Who?" the fella hollerd.

"Marion Daniels!" Marion roared.

"Name Cliffton Kensey mean anythin' ta yew?"

Marion grinned. "Wife killer," he yelled. "I shot him in the ass back in seventy-two over by Blue Springs. They eventually hung him I believe."

The gunbarrel disappeared an' a barefoot fella in long handles an' blanket pants come out the door an' onto the porch.

"He was my uncle," the man said, "an' no dirtier bastard ever drawed breath. Come ahead on, Marshal. You et?"

By the time we'd got off the horses, three women had come out on the porch with him. Two of 'em was in their night clothes. They was all kindly dirty an' nasty like. One of 'em kept smilin' at me an' rubbin' on herself. It didn't put me at ease much. Marion jawed with the fella fer a spell then turned to me.

"Why doan you go out back and fill them bags up," he said.

I took the bags offa the packhorse an' walked around back with 'em. About twenty feet behind the house there was a little rocked-in open cistern that the water flowed into afore it run off into the hog pens. I knelt down beside it, an' started fillin' the first bag. That woman that'd been grinnin' at me come out the back an' stood on the stoop.

"How you doin' today, sweetie," she said.

"Fine, m'am," I said, tryin' to git the stopper outa the second bag.

"Whatcher name, honey," she asked me, rubbin' on herself'.

"Arlo Stucky," I tolt her, 'cause I'd gone to grammer school with a kid by that name an' he was a asshole. I shoved them bags down in the cistern an' wished they'd hurry up an' fill.

"My name's Lulu, Arlo," she said. "I ain't busy right now. I could git busy with a nice young man like you, though. Four bits an' you'll remember me for a long time."

"I gotta git these here bags full m'am," I said, "then I gotta be goin'."

"Two bits, honey," she said, "an' you'll be on your way in five minutes. You doan have to come inside. You don't have to come in the house, neither." She giggled then, an' that last bag finally filled up.

I stuck thet stopper in on the second try an' stood up. "No thank you, M'am," I said. "I gotta be goin' now."

I hustled around front as Marion was stickin' a cheesecloth bag in one of the panniers. I hung them water bags an' hit the saddle.

"Thanks for the information," Marion said to the fella. "Maybe I'll be able to settle things down some."

He turned the roan an' we went back up the hill. We was plumb over the top afore I felt I could draw breath.

"Hey, Ruben," he said, "you make a new friend?"

I touched Willie, put him at a lope, an' left Marion behind. But I could hear him laughin'.

CHAPTER SEVEN

It commenced to storm that night. We didn't have no warnin' neither. We was both sound asleep when that first strike a lightin' hit a tree a little ways from where we was layin'. It was so close, it durn near throwed us both offa our rolls. You could smell it, both the scent of the lightnin' an' that dog shit odor a new red oak. I come up terrible confused an' didn't know what was goin' on, except for the awful noise still in the air. My ears warn't workin' too good neither. I set up an' looked around, tryin' to figger out if hell had broke loose. It was black as pitch except for some spots glowin' red on what was left a that tree. Lightnin' flickered' an' I seen Marion gittin' to his feet. He hollered at me an' his voice come to me like he was a hunnerd yards away. He was yellin' at me to git the horses down.

The lightnin' was comin' purty regular then, an' I grabbed the rope off my saddle an' run to Willie. He was scared an' shied away from me, fightin' his hobbles, but I got a loop around his offside rear, an' pulled. That put him off balance leanin' away from me. I threw myself agin his near shoulder with everthin' I had an' over he went, me crashin' on top of him. I got up on his head an' neck then. A hunnerd pound woman can hold a fifteen-hunnerd pound horse down if she can git on his head. Willie was thrashin' around some. I got to talkin' to him an' he settled a little. In one lightnin' flash I seen Marion layin' across that roan's head, his hat gone somewhere.

Them clouds come alive with flashes an' streaks, flickerin' plumb from one side of the heavens to the other overhead an' outa the west. It warn't dark no more. It was then that I was tryin' to figger out how the hell I could keep Willie down an' git to the packhorse. He was maybe twenty yards from me, tryin to buck agin his hobbles. I was lookin' right at him when that lightnin' hit. It was so bright that I went kindly blind for a spell, but I remember when it took him. He was in the middle of a buck, his ass end up in the air, with just his front feet on the ground. I seen it hit him at the base a the tail, then my eyes kindly quit on me, them clouds opened, an' the most terrible rain a my life come pourin' down. I hung onto Willie an' just took it. There warn't nothin' else a fella could do.

It was awful. Thunder rumbled all the time, vibratin' the ground with hardly no stop to it. I could see them flashes of the lightnin', but nothing else for quite a spell 'cause a lookin' at the packhorse when he got hit, I reckon. The rain had weight to it, pressin' down on me like, an' holdin' me to the ground. I'd never been through nothin' like it in my life. I doan know how long it went on, 'cause I doan rightly know when it started. In the middle a somethin' like that, a fella cain't hardly judge no time anyways. I hung on to Willie as much for my sake as his. He fought with it for quite a spell, but then just quit. It kindly hurt my heart some when that little buckskin just give up like he done. I thought a lot of him, an' when that godawful storm broke him, it damn near broke me, too. It might have, I believe, if it hadn't a been for Marion. In the middle a all that crashin' an' bangin' an' flashin', with that rain poundin' down on everthin' the way it was, I heard him now an' then, through all the noise. He was singin' at the top a his lungs. It was a hymn, I believe. Somethin' about folks gittin' together by the river. He went right at that storm with it, throwed it up in the face a all that thunder, beller'd it in the teeth a all that lightnin', hammered it agin the heft a all that rain, an' he didn't quit until things begin to settle down some. I swear, they ain't but one Marion Daniels on the whole earth, an' there damn shore wouldn't be room for two.

* * * * *

The lightnin' quit in early daybreak an' I got up offa Wille. He didn't wanna git up much, kindly locked up, layin' there in the mud an' all. I come at him real gentle, coaxin' him an' talkin' to him. Purty soon he tossed his head an' snorted, kindly comin' back to hisself. He rolled up on his chest then an' commenced to lookin' around an' I knowed he was gonna be all right.

"Are ya alive, Ruben?" Marion said to me.

He was up an' standin' with the roan. I could just barely see him through the rain.

"I'm drawin' breath," I said.

"That buck all right?"

"He's gittin' over it," I said, watchin' Willie git up an' shake. Then I heard Marion cuss.

"Oh, gawdammit to hell!" he hollerd. "Would you look at that?"

He was pointin' to the ground where that roan had been layin', an' there, flat as a pancake, was his hat. At that instant, Willie farted.

I purty much crossed the border then, settin' straight down on the ground an' laughin'. I really didn't have no choice. Marion come splashin' over, knocked my hat offa my head, stomped on it, an' set down with me. In a minute, the two of us was layin' flat on our backs in that cold rain, howlin' like a couple a fools. There warn't nothin' else we could do.

* * * * *

By the middle of the day, I had the ground cloth strung up over some branches a that downed oak, an' some other ones chopped outa the way so we had us a little cave like to set in. We'd pulled the panniers an' pack saddle offa the dead packhorse moved them under cover. Everthin' we had was wet an' it was still rainin'. We huddled under that ground cloth without no fire an' et jerky an' peaches. I stuck my hat on a exposed branch an' let the rain beat some a the mud off it, then tried to reshape it. It was too damn wet everwhere to make any difference. We spent the night. The next mornin' we shoved all our truck an' possibles up under the oak an' piled more brush on it. Marion saddled up an' got a rope on the packhorse an' drug him off a ways. Then we took off, tryin' to find a little civilization. It just kept right on rainin' like that was all it was ever gonna do.

* * * * *

Late mornin' the next day we come on a wagon track an' slopped our way along it for a spell 'til we run up on a little town. There was a livery on the outskirts an' we stopped. A fella in a derby hat come outa the back to greet us.

"You boys look a mite damp," he said. "C'mon in an' dry down some."

"I doan believe we can stay for two weeks," I said.

"You shore look like you been up against it. Four bits an' I'll keep yer horses inside an' grain 'em. Hell, I got some mash for 'em. They ain't in no better shape than the two a you."

"That'd be right nice." I said. "You got any horses for sale here?"

"I got a big sorrel colt near seventeen hands that's green broke, an' a mare that's purty old an' not terrible thrifty. But that's it right now. What you boys need?"

"My packhorse got hit by lightnin' durin' that big storm," I said.

"Oh, Lord," he said. "That didn't do him no good, did it?"

"Nossir. Not one bit."

"That's a durn shame, ain't it," he said. "I hate ta see a horse git kilt like that. I'm sorry for ya, son. I am."

"You got a roomin' house or somethin' like that around here?" Marion asked.

"Nossir," the fella said, "we ain't. But you boys can bunk up in the loft if ya care to. Toss your rolls out on some straw. It's dry. No charge for sleepin'."

"Kind of ya," Marion said. "What town is this?"

"Tarkio is what they named it. We just got our plat last year. Brand new."

"Got a general store?" Marion asked.

"Right down Main next to the barber shop," the fella said.

"How 'bout somethin' to eat?"

"We got that, too," he said, "on the other side a the barber shop. You boys probably ain't had a hot meal in a day or two, have ya? No fire either, I bet."

"Nossir," I said, "we ain't."

"You fellers just go on now an' git warmed up an' full. I'll drop them saddles an' brush yer horses out for ya an' feed 'em good. I'll shake yer rolls out an' let 'em dry, too. When yer ready, just take 'em up in the loft an' settle in. The convenience is right out back when ya need it."

* * * * *

That barbershop had a bathtub. We went to the general store an' got new shirts an' pants an' such, then I went to eat while Marion took his bath. I had two pieces a pie after my chicken an' dumplins, then got a haircut an' a shave. Then I got in the tub while Marion got his haircut an' shave an' went to eat. We left our clothes with the barber who said his wife would wash 'em for us an' we could git 'em the next day. By the time we got all that done, it had actually stopped rainin'.

* * * * *

When I woke up in the loft the next mornin' the sun was shinin'. I went outside, an' the livery fella was out there finishin' working on our saddles an' tack with Neatsfoot oil.

"Mornin'," he said. "That buckskin a yours is a real sweet little feller, ain't he?"

"Yessir," I said, "Willie does all right. Didn't expect ya to clean up our leather."

"You boys is marshals, ain't ya?" he asked me.

"We are," I told him.

"Nice to have you around. We ain't got no law in this town, an' not much of a sheriff in the county. Things git some rank now an' then. Got some fellas come through here once in a while that ride purty roughshod."

"That Waxler bunch?"

"I reckon that's who they are," he said. "They mostly stay north up toward Ioway I hear, but they grace us from time to time. Lowlifes. You know the type."

"Yessir, I do."

He smiled at me then. "I see ya got some new duds an' been to the barber."

I grinned back at him. "I have," I said.

"What happened to yer hat?" he asked me.

"It met with unfortunate circumstance," I said.

He laughed at that an' held out his hand. "I already tangled with yer partner's," he said. "Gimme that."

I did, an' he stuck it down in the trough to get it wet, then used a curry brush on it for a minute, then put it on my head an' fussed with it for a spell. "There ya go," he said. "Good as new. No charge."

Marion come walkin' up from around the back then, an' I headed out to take my turn. When I come back, Marion had our gunbelts laid out an' the fella was workin' on them while he cleaned the hardware. I jumped in an' started on that little scattergun. The livery fella took notice.

"That there is what ya might call a dangerous weapon," he said.

"Sure would be if ya dropped it on yer foot," I told him.

"That Waxler crowd what brings you men up this way?" he asked.

"Thought I might git the chance to have a little chat with some of 'em," Marion said.

The fella studied on him for a minute. "That there could be one hell of a conversation," he said.

* * * * *

After everthin' got cleaned up, we walked back down by the barbershop to the café for a bite. I doan believe I ever had ham an' eggs that tasted any better. A fella there sent us on down to the other side a town to a smith that maybe had a horse we could git. That smith was a short fella with big ol' arms an' shoulders. If he was half as stout as he looked, he could pick up a railroad car.

We jawed with him a spell an' he admitted he didn't really have no horses that'd be useful for a pack animal, but then he brung out a mule.

"I got this mule around ten years ago," he said, "when he was a yearlin' for my daughter to ride. Wanted somethin' that was steady of foot for her. She an' him got along good. Then, when she waren't but fourteen, she run off with a shithead an' I ain't seen her since. This mule has just been eatin' grass for two years."

I looked him over. He was a little thing, maybe just thirteen hands, with them floppy ears an' slanted eyes on him. Sorta looked to me like he was fixin' to bite somethin'.

"He nippy?" I asked.

The smith grinned. "Looks like it, don't he?" he said.

"He does," I agreed.

"Not a bit," he said. "He ain't got no attitude at all. He doan git excited, he doan git skittish, he don't balk, he don't kick. He does what ya want him to do an' not one durn thing more or less. Sound a foot an' frame. Keeps easy an' don't bray. Gits along with horses an' women. Doan think much a dogs, though."

"How much?" I asked him.

"Ten dollars for the mule, a dollar for the halter an' lead rope."

I paid him an' we started back, Marion up on the boardwalk, tryin' to hold onto his grin, an' me, walkin' out in the street, leadin' a durn mule.

We stopped by the general store an' got what supplies we could easy tote on horseback, picked up our clean clothes from the barbershop, then went back to the livery an' saddled up. The feller there didn't want hardly a thing for what he'd done. Marion give him five dollars, an' we headed out, back toward where we'd left our truck an' possibles. Marion, me, an' a little ol' mule I decided to call Arliss.

CHAPTER EIGHT

I noticed that critters had been at the packhorse some when we passed by where he was layin' on our way back to where we started out. Marion got to gather'n things up while I put the packsaddle on Arliss the mule. He took it like he was used to it. Them loaded panniers didn't fret him none neither. We started off an' he come right along, not pullin' on the rope none at all. We got down near where that packhorse was' an' I seen a couple a coyotes settin' off a ways, grinnin' like they do. I ain't over fond a 'yotes. I took out my Yellaboy an' cranked a round off at 'em, but they was too far off for me to be any kinda trouble to 'em. They went slippin' away in that shufflin' trot they got, knowin' they was safe enough at the range they was. That mule never even took notice a the gunfire. He just kept right along like nothin' had happened. I swear, by the time we'd gone a mile I think I coulda took that lead rope plumb offa him, an' he still woulda follerd us anywhere we went.

We stayed in the bottomland a the river basin the rest a the day. Late in the afternoon, the low hills come closer to the river an' we come on a little cabin on a low rise, an' a fella with a team a mules an' a single bottom plow cuttin' soft furrows in the muddy ground a little ways in front a the place. Marion drifted over that way an' I follerd along. When he seen us, he stopped them mules an' took the reins from around his shoulders. Up at the cabin, a woman come out on the porch with a rifle an' watched us close. We both set easy an' kept our hands in plain sight. The fella was tense, but when he noticed that mule was packed up, he eased hisself a mite.

Marion nodded at him. "Some better with a team than just one mule, ain't it?" he said.

"Yessir, it is," the fella said.

"I'd appreciate it," Marion said, easin' his vest back so his badge would show, "if you'd ask yer wife not to shoot at us none. Makes my horse nervous."

The fella smiled then, an' raised his ol' hat offa his head. The lady at the cabin lowered that rifle an' two young'uns come out to look at us.

Marion innerduced us to him then, an' we found out his name was Spence.

"I know it pays to be cautious, Mister Spence," Marion said, "an' I shore doan blame nobody for not takin' any chances. You folks had trouble around here?"

"They's some lowlifes come by this way a while back," Spence said. "Hard men. They stopped to water their horses from our cistern, an' took two hams I had in the smokehouse with 'em when they left. Five fellers. A couple of em' paid close attention toward my wife, but they went on."

"Which way'd they go?"

"They come from down toward Tarkio," Spence said, "an' headed on north. Probably on the way to the hole. It's on up about ten mile or so an' then on east a ways, up outa the bottoms."

"The hole?" Marion said.

"Was a sort a town once," Spence went on, "called Tyler or Taylor, but a lot a folks left it back when the boats took over most a the shippin' between Omaha an' Saint Joe. Now it's just a few tents, a ol' saloon, an' whores. What wagons an' such that still make the runs stops there, I guess. Field hands an' stock riders an' the like."

"You know the Waxler bunch," I asked him.

"Everbody around here has heer'd of 'em. They usta ride the river some, but I ain't never had no real trouble with 'em. I reckon them boys that took my hams was maybe part of 'em. Ain't no law here. That attracts men a low order."

Marion looked at the turned earth. "Whatcha puttin' in?" he asked. "Corn?"

"Yessir," Spence said. "Corn grows real good here in the bottom. The river come up some early this spring. That happens an' it grows extra good. Got a turnip patch up by the house. We keep a few hogs. Turnips an' corn does well by 'em. Wife's got a little garden for beans an' such, there's a arbor behind the place for grapes, an' we got a milk cow an' try to keep a calf to butcher. This spring I managed to git a few hens an' a rooster. So far, the 'yotes ain't got to 'em. The girls is four an' six. They help with the grapes an' chickens an' garden already. Once in a while I knock down a deer an' I trap some in the winter. We git by purty fair."

Marion smiled. "Looks to me like ya do," he said.

I reached back in my saddlebag an' fished out two a them peppermint sticks. "Mister Spence," I said, "if you doan mind, I believe them young ladies might enjoy a little treat. I'd appreciate it if you'd see they git these here compliments a the U.S. Marshal Service."

He was some got. He took them peppermints an' come over almost shy like.

"Thank ya, sir," he said. "Lou Anne an' Sue Anne doan git much a this kinda thing. They'll be durn near as pleased as I am. That's right nice of ya, that is. I'd like it if you boys would wait a minute."

He hustled off toward the house then, an' come hurryin' back in just a few minutes carryin' a small cloth sack that was bulgin' some.

"There's four eggs in there, wrapped in dry grass," he said. "Handle 'em careful."

We thanked him an' went on then, an' I waved toward the house as we did. The littlest a them two girls waved back.

* * * * *

We took up offa the bottom a hour or so later an' went up into the edge a the hills to make camp. I fixed bacon an' frybread for supper, an' fried up them eggs in that bacon grease. One of 'em had two yolks.

* * * * *

I took special care that night puttin' hobbles on Arliss the mule, 'cause I figgerd he might git loose an' head off home. Mules is like that. The next mornin' when I got up an' stirred the fire, that mule was layin' flat out on his side like he was dead. He raised his head an' looked at me, then got to his feet an' shook hisself. I found his hobbles layin' a little ways away. I walked off some to do my business, an' he come with me an' follerd me back when I was done. It was right peculiar.

Marion had coffee on when I come back, then he walked off a ways. Arliss the mule come up an' stood a little back from the fire, head down like he was half asleep. I spoke to him then, an' he switched his tail. That got me grinnin'. I said somethin' else to him, an' that tail switched agin. How he knowed I was talkin' at him an' not just talkin', I doan know, but he did. Marion come back in a minute an' squatted down outa the smoke. The wood was a little wet. He looked at me.

"Who you talkin' to?" he asked.

"Arliss the mule," I said.

"By God," he said, lookin' at the mule, "I doan think I ever been so much in need a conversation I ever talked to no damned mule."

I grinned at him. "I talk to you, doan I?"

"Boy," Marion said, "you are gittin' a little close to offerin' me a insult."

"Ain't no insult to it," I said. "A fella finds a good listener someplace, he's bound to take advantage of it."

That mule was just standin' there like he was the only thing in the world.

"Ain't that right, Arliss?" I said.

Durned if he didn't switch his tail.

Marion kindly give a little hitch. "Naw," he said, "I doan believe that."

* * * * *

We had coffee an' some stale frybread an' broke camp. We headed a little deeper inta them hills at a easy walk. Marion didn't seem to be in no kinda hurry. Early afternoon we struck a wagon path an' took to it for a ways. Afore too long we crested a rise an' seen a little sloped valley with a crick runnin' through it goin' on down into the bottoms. On either side a that crick was a little settlement. They was what was left of a few buildings that had wore down an' most likely been stripped for firewood. There was a barn an' a couple a sheds still standin' that had a few horses in a pen, a low rock buildin' or two, a well weathered two story place with a false front an' a ol' sign that usta have a name on it, an' several tents, a couple of 'em good size with wood floors, the rest of 'em small cabin style. Might a been a dozen or so horses an' a wagon or two tied out in front a some a the places. As we walked on down the slope, Marion took off his badge an' pinned it to the inside a his vest an' well outa sight. Takin' his heed, I took mine offa my belt an' pinned it up by my collar so my kerchief covered it up, then I lifted that little scattergun offa my saddle horn an' snapped it up over my belt on the left side in a crossdraw angle.

Some a them small tents had ladies standin' in front of 'em that spoke to us as we rode in. One of 'em, a big ol' fat gal, hollerd at me an' called me sonny boy, offerin' me company a some sort. Marion seemed to git a little kick out that. We crossed over a narrow wood bridge at the crick an' Marion stopped in front of a big tent with a sign on it that said "Good Eats" a couple a doors up from the saloon. We got down, tied off the horses an' Arliss the mule, an' walked in. There was five or six fellas in there, skinner types an' hayshakers, eatin' gray lookin' fatback an' boiled potaters with greasy gravy for two-bits a plate. My appetite took off on a high lope.

"Nossir," I said.

Marion nodded. "Let's try the saloon," he said, an' we went back out. There was two fellas outside lookin' at Willie. I walked over.

"Howdy," I said.

The big one looked at me. He had on a flat brim hat with a tear in the crown. Tobacco juice had stained his beard an' the front a his kettlecloth shirt. He wore a Colt Navy conversion in a crossdraw on a wide black belt an' canvas pants tucked into knee-high heavy boots. He smelt like whiskey an' damp root cellar.

"This here buck your'n, boy?" he asked, a little juice slippin' past his lower lip.

"Yessir," I said, lookin' up at him. "He is."

"What's he worth to ye?" he asked me.

"Ten thousand dollars," I said.

He kindly drawed back on hisself an' glared at me. "Bullshit," he said. "Ain't no gawddam horse in the world worth nothin' like that."

"Sir," I said, "it is plain to me that you do not appreciate the value of superior horseflesh. You hand me ten thousand dollars cash money, an' you kin ride him on outa here today, if he'll let ya."

"The hell you mean if he'll let me?"

"Well sir," I said, "this horse is unusual. He's got a nose like a bloodhound an' he is some particular about what gits close to it. You have a good afternoon."

I collected Willie's reins then an' walked off toward the saloon, Arliss the mule comin' along behind.

Marion joined me at the rail, tied up the roan, an' grinned at me.

The saloon warn't much. The bar was boards nailed together on top a three or four barrels. They was some tables an' chairs scattered around an' maybe a dozen fellas in there. They was just a open doorway to git inside. Me an' Marion walked up to the boards on them barrels an' a skinny fella with a heavy limp come over an' looked at us.

"Two shots," Marion said.

The barkeep set us up an' took his four bits.

"Any place around to git somethin' to eat?" Marion asked.

"Couple doors up," the fella said, jerkin' his head the way we come.

"Any place without mold an' maggots?" Marion asked.

"That there is all they is," the fella said, an' shuffled off.

They warn't no lookin' glass behind the bar like they was in the Red Bird or the Houston House back in Deer Run, so Marion turned his back to the bar an' leaned a elbow on it. I done the same. We was a some interest to a lot a the fellas in there, an' ignored 'em as we sipped our whiskey. It burned quite a bit. Marion throwed his down an' made a face.

"Drink up, Ruben," he said. "It's a little close in here. I speck we're gonna need some space afore all this is over."

I warn't quite sure what he meant, an' I looked at that little glass. To be honest, I warn't terrible certain if I put that whiskey in my mouth I'd be able to swallow it. 'Bout that time four fellas come in, that big ol' boy that was lookin' at Willie puffed up at the front of 'em. I felt Marion put a little distance between us just as that big fella seen me. He come heavy footin' it over to where I was.

"Boy," he said, "I'm gonna give you forty dollars fer that horse."

"Sorry, sir," I said. "I told you the price."

"Now you listen here, pup," he said, leanin' in on me, "I'm makin' ya a—"

I tossed what was left a that shot a whiskey in his face an' he squalled an' reeled backwards. I heard Marion say "stand easy, boys" an' I waded in. It took me two steps to git back to that big fella. I took that Colt Navy outa his holster an' smacked him in the teeth with it. That drove him back some more an' he hit a table an' fell across it crashin' to the floor. He was game an' struggled to git up, blood sprayin' some as he puffed. I used his gun', this time on a full swing at his ear, an' that purty much done it.

I turned around an' Marion was still standin' there at the bar, only now he had a Colt in his right hand an' was smilin'. Them three other fellas was real still, their eyes shiftin' between me an' the marshal. I looked at 'em.

"When he wakes up," I said, "you tell him I appreciate his offer but it was a little light. You kin also tell him that if'n he wants to discuss this further, I'll shoot him an' anybody that comes with him."

There was no fight in them boys, an' me an' Marion walked on out an' mounted up. I tossed that fella's gun in the dirt. Marion looked at me an' grinned.

"Ol' Ruben," he said.

* * * * *

We made a cold camp that night an' took turns settin' guard, but nobody showed up. Mid mornin' the next day we was ridin' down along the edge a the bottoms when we seen six or seven riders on the top of a ridge to our east. They follerd along a little while, then turned their horses our direction an' come at us on a run. I yanked my Yellaboy an' got off Willie while Marion put the reins in his teeth an' pulled both his Colts. Them riders was comin', about two hunnerd yards away, when the lead horse fell an' rolled. From the south of us, I heard a gunshot.

Them fellas slowed a mite then, an' another horse fell an' another gunshot arrived. They pulled up an' scrambled around some, pickin' up one rider, an' scattered back up an' over that ridge. Marion got down an' we stood an' waited. In about five minutes, Homer Poteet come up on that gray a his with the bad ear, an' looked down at us.

"By God, boys," he said. "Are the two of ya scairt?"

CHAPTER NINE

"How the hell are you?" Marion asked Homer. Both of us was kindly surprised to see him.

"I'm fine," Homer said, "me bein' a hero an' all, savin' you two from death an' destruction like I done. Mebbe now you boys'll be a little nicer to me."

"Maybe now," Marion said, "granny'll stop suckin' eggs, too. Yer eyes gittin' so bad you gotta shoot horses?"

"You ain't gonna git no information outa no horse," Homer said. "They left one a them boys behind. If you think you can git up on that ugly-ass roan, mebbe we outa go see if he's still drawin' breath."

We mounted up an' Homer looked at me. "You doin' all right are ya, Rube?" he asked.

I grinned at him. "Nice to see ya, Homer," I said.

"How's that good lookin' wife a your'n?" he asked. "She still off her feed 'cause I left town?"

"She's gonna have a baby," I said.

"Doan that throw the cat in the well?" he said, a big ol' grin takin' over his face. "Pappy Rube. Now ain't that got a nice ring to it?"

"Sounds about as good as Uncle Homer," I said.

"Congratulations ta me, boy," he said, an' reined that gray a his toward the slope.

* * * * *

Halfway up the hill we come on a dead bay horse. A little ways away was that same fella I tangled with in the saloon. His face an' ear was all swole up an' he didn't have no front teeth. He was settin' in the grass holdin' his left arm. It had a crook in it a little ways up from the wrist where there shouldn't a been one. He looked up at us an' took notice a Homer.

"Whar the hell you come from?" he asked.

"Indiana," Homer said, "but I'm startin' to like it here."

Marion got down an' walked over to that fella. "Yer one tough sonofabitch," he said, "I'll give ya that. You know Jack an' Jim Waxler?"

"Ain't never heered of 'em,' the fella said.

"Here's the deal," Marion said. "I ain't got no more use for you than a pile a dogshit. You an' yer friends come out here to kill us an' steal our horses an' possibles. That means I can leave you dead as a hammer an' have no extra thought about it. As it is, you ain't hurt so bad you cain't walk outa here an' git to some help. How you think you'll do if'n I take yer boots an' four or five of yer toes? Think you might be able to hike back afore ya give out an' a mess a coyotes showed up?"

The fella had sand. He looked square up at Marion. "You wodden do that," he said.

"Naw, he wouldn't," Homer said. "But I would. Better yet, how 'bout I just toss a rope over ya an' drag you the first mile or so a yer journey?"

He shook out a loop then, an' dropped it over the fella. Then he turned that gray an' just walked off. That loop come tight around the fella's shoulders an' off he went draggin' across that grass behind Homer an' his horse. Homer touched the gray into a trot, an' that fella come to bouncin' along behind him for a little ways afore he started yellin' for Homer to stop. Marion an' me went over to where he laid an' I got down offa Willie. Homer loosed the rope a mite an' Marion looked down at the fella.

"Well?" he said.

"What yew want them boys for?" the fella asked, pantin' some an' hangin' onto his arm agin.

"They kilt one woman an' got another one cut to pieces in the Blue Island Saloon down by Saint Joe," Marion said.

"The way I heer'd it," the fella said, "them two was just whores."

Marion slapped him then, right on that busted up ear a his. The fella hollerd an' fell back, tears runnin' down his face.

"Go ahead on," Marion said, an' Homer tightened the loop an' started off.

The fella come to yellin' for him to stop. Marion walked over to where he was.

The feller laid there pantin' a minute afore he spoke up, that rope diggin' into his arms.

"I doan know Jim an' Jack," he said. "But I know who they are. A young feller name a Swede told me he was on the trail with 'em when they come to the Blue Island that night, an' said that Jim cut one whore up some, an' Jack throwed one inta a lookin' glass. Then they lit out. Swede was still settin' downstairs when it happened. He left with 'em an' said they was laughin' about what they done. He spooked an' cut trail to git away from 'em before laws showed up. Claimed he wadden around when they tangled with that posse."

"Where would they be right now?" Marion asked.

"They woulda run north," the feller said, "but I doan know to where."

"How can I find Swede?"

"I think he had kin up by Clearmount, but I doan know for sure."

"What's he look like?"

"He's near as tall as you, got yaller hair, young, 'bout twenny. Rides a chestnut gelding."

"All right," Marion said. "I see you agin an' you ain't got empty hands an' a smile on yer face, bub, I'll finish what has been started today. You hear me?"

"Yessir."

"Then we'll kill everbody that's with ya. You hear that?"

"Yessir."

Marion looked at him. "You believe it?"

"Yessir, I do."

Marion looked at Homer. "Loose yer rope," he said.

Homer shook his loop out an' Marion lifted it off a the fella. Homer caught the rope up, Marion an' me got back in the saddle, an' the three of us rode off, leavin' him settin' there on the side a that hill. We hadn't gone very far when Homer spoke up.

"See ya gotcha a little mule, Rube," he said.

"My packhorse got hit by lightnin'," I said.

"Purty good mule is he?" Homer asked.

"Fair," I said. "Named him Arliss."

Homer studied on that for a minute. "Not Marion?" he said.

* * * * *

We kept on north for the rest a the day an' a little afore dusk we come on what Marion said was the Nodaway River an' pitched camp. Homer got a couple a cans outa a sack he had tied on his saddle an' brung 'em over.

"You boys got any bacon?" he asked.

I said we did.

"Well, fry some up," he said, "an' git out the pot. I got some beans an' pork here I picked offa a tradin' feller I run into when I was trailin' the two of you."

I got the pot out while he was prisin' on the top a them cans, an' he dumped 'em in. We let that stuff stew while the bacon got fried an' commenced to eat. I'd never had nothin' like that outa a can afore. It was right tasty. Beans with a little fat in 'em an' tomato an' sugar an' some kinda spices.

"This here is some good," I said.

"Brings back memories," Marion said. "Et this a time 'er two back in the war."

"Folks in the big cities eats a lot of it," Homer said. "I was pleased to git it. Been savin' it 'til I found ya."

"How'd you locate us?" I asked him.

"You boys leave a memory behind ya. I got information from some of the folks ya run across. Found a horse, or what was left of it, an' that tree that got hit. Trailed ya some from there. The feller at that little place was out plantin' corn. He tolt me which way ya went. I tracked ya after that rain. I know Marion's horse. That roan's got feet the size a wagon wheels. The mule tracks throwed me some, though, afore I put it together ya musta replaced yer packhorse. How's that little mule workin' out for ya."

"He's steady," I said. "Ain't ya, Arliss?"

That mule switched his tail.

"Dependable too, ain't ya?" I asked.

That mule switched his tail agin.

Homer grinned. "I'll be durned," he said. "Ain't that somethin'? Doan you hobble him of a night?"

"I tried two or three times," I said, "but he chews 'em off an' hangs around anyway. He's still here at sunup, ain't ya Arliss?"

That mule switched his tail.

"Besides," I said, "it's a lot easier for him to make mornin' coffee for us without them hobbles on."

Homer nodded. "Would be," he said.

* * * * *

We started off the next mornin' with frybread from the leftover bacon grease an' was on the trail a little after sunup. A couple a times we come on bunches a cattle roamin' an' one herd a thirty or forty horses. Around the middle of the day we hit railroad tracks an' followed 'em into Clearmont. Looked like they was movin' part a the town from around them tracks. Freight wagons an' teams a horses an' mules was hustlin' around, some places bein' torn down, others put up, whole sheds an' small buildings bein' drug around on skid drags by big ol' plow horses an' such. It was a purty busy place.

We found a likely lookin' spot to eat an' tied up an' went in. Marion an' me both shifted our badges so folks could see 'em. All of us ate chicken. I had mine with stewed apples. It was good havin' town food for a change. The fella that brung us our food was agreeable. When he come to git paid, Marion spoke up.

"You know a young man that might hang around this neck a the woods name a Swede?"

"We have a couple of Swedish families east a town a ways," the fella said.

"This feller would be near as tall as me. Twenny or younger, rides a chestnut horse."

"What's he done?" the fella asked.

"Nothin' that I know of," Marion said, "but he may know some boys that has. It's them I'm wantin' to ketch a hold of. I'm hopin' he can help."

"Sounds like to me it might be the Thorsen boy. Follow the right of way about six or seven miles, and their place is a little south. You can see the house. It's white and has a windmill out front. They keep goats."

"You know his first name?" Marion asked.

"I believe they call him Anger or something like that."

"Thank you kindly, sir," Marion said. "I trust you'll keep our conversation to yerself. No point in alarmin' the boy or his family or bringin' on any trouble for you."

"Absolutely," the man said.

"Good," Marion said. "We might see ya in the mornin' for breakfast."

* * * * *

We went on an' found a livery then, an' paid the fella there two bits extra to let us put our rolls on some a his straw. We was up afore daybreak an' gone by first light. We followed the railroad on a short lope for a spell to git some distance from town, then slowed down to save the horses. It warn't long afore we seen a white house with a barn an' a windmill about a half a mile away down a wagon path. It was a purty little place, nestled on a low rise almost agin a fair hill to the east side. They was some pens close up with big ol' beefy lookin' meat goats, an' a few skinny ones of the milkin' variety. Marion an' Homer rode up to the front, an' I kindly drifted over to the west side a ways where the land come out onto the flat. There was a bunch more goats out that way grazin' loose in the mornin' light, with a couple a dogs keepin' a steady eye on 'em. I was thinkin' how purty it was an' enjoyin' a passel a crows yellin' up on that east hillside, when I seen a rider on a chestnut horse head out from behind the place at a dead run, scatterin' them goats as he went. Willie seen him too, an' commenced to dancin' sideways. I give him his head an' hissed at him, an' that little buck durn near run out from under me settin' off on the chase.

There really ain't no reason a horse as small as Willie, who warn't quite even fifteen hands I guess, should a been able to run as fast as he could, but nobody never tolt him I reckon. Belly down an' stretched out, he gained on the chestnut right smart. We hadden gone a quarter of a mile afore Willie warn't mor'n thirty feet behind him. I eased him to the right a little an' come up beside the rider. I couldn't see no gun on him.

"Federal marshal," I yelled at him. "Rein yer horse!"

He glanced at me an' got down a little lower, like it was gonna help.

"Goddammit," I hollered, "stop it! Ya cain't outrun me!"

He ignored me an' went to whippin' that chestnut with the reins. I thought about ropin' him an' then remembered my skill with a rope. I pulled that little shotgun an' held it out where he could see it.

"If you doan stop," I yelled, "I will shoot yer horse! Rein him in right now!"

He still kept goin'. I got up close to him an' touched that twelve gauge shorty off in front a that chestnut's face. The horse didn't care for that too much, an' turned away from me right smart. The fella on him lost his seat then an' come off, hittin' the ground an' slidin' a little ways before he rolled over a time or two. I showed Willie the bit an' hustled back. The fella was on his hands an' knees, lookin' around like he just woke up. I dismounted, put the sole a my boot agin his shoulder, an' pushed him over on his side.

"What the hell is the matter with you?" I said. "Ya coulda ruint a perfectly good horse! Yer name Thorsen?"

"Yessir," he said, near cryin'. "I ain't done nothin'."

He was young. Couldn't a even been twenty-year-old. "What's yer first name?" I asked him.

"Agner," he said. "Agner Thorsen. I didn't hurt them girls. I didn't. Honest."

"You ride with some bad company, boy," I said. "You was with the Waxlers that night, warn't ya?"

"Yessir," he said, "I was. You gonna hang me?"

I durn near grinned then, but I held on. "What Waxlers was ya with?" I asked.

"Jim an' Jack," he said. "I didn't know they was gonna do nothin' like they did. I was downstairs when they done it. I just rode with 'em a day. I was out just lookin' down that way, an' met 'em when I was breakin' camp on my second day out, fixin' to come on home. They talked me into goin' down to that place. I don't never git to do nothin' much like that."

"You damn shore left with 'em after they did what they done. Why?"

"I got scared at all the screamin' and such. Everbody seen me come in with 'em. I thought I had to run!"

"Did you ever stop to think that those folks that seen you come in also seen you stay downstairs an' not have no part in that mess?"

"Not 'til I was already runnin'. I come straight home," he said. "I ain't been three miles off the place since."

"How old are ya?"

"I'm seventeen, Mister," he said. "Everybody says I'm big for my age."

"Them Waxlers say anything about where they was goin?" I asked.

"Somplace up in Iowa," he said. "Melinda or somethin'. They said I could come with 'em, but I headed on home. You gonna hang me, are ya?"

"Not today," I said. "You wait right here while I go over yonder an' ketch up your horse."

CHAPTER TEN

Mister and Missus Thorsen was some upset with their boy, an' some relieved he warn't gonna be drug off, kickin' an' screamin', to dangle from a rope or suffer behind cold gray walls the rest a his days. They was right nice an' insisted we stay for dinner. My Lord. Miz Thorsen brung us fried chicken with potaters mashed up with cream an' butter, some good an' salty green beans, some big ol' hot rolls about the size of a derby hat, sweet milk outa the springhouse, an' finished it off with apple cobbler that had raisins an' little bitty cherry kinda things in it. About the middle a the afternoon, when we was able to move an' mount up, Miz Thorsen sent us off with a sack a potaters, a chunk a smoke-cured ham, an' a little bag a brown sugar an' blueberry sweets. Homer allowed as how we oughta stop by there ever week an' let me run the boy down, just so we could stay an' eat. Me an' Marion thought it was a heckuva good idea.

* * * * *

We got in five or six miles afore we give up an' made camp. Warn't nobody terrible hungry. I hobbled the horses while the other two set up. It got a mite cool that night an' come a heavy dew. I was all right though, under the blanket an' my slicker. When I woke up, Marion had coffee on an' Homer was fixin' ham an' fried potaters. It was some of a treat to have a good breakfast like that on the trail an' not havta fix it myself. I thanked 'em for the courtesy, indicatin' it was well deserved. Age an' experience was brung up, an' I wound up havin' to break camp while the two a them supervised my ability.

We rode that day in eyesight of the Nodaway River. Long about the middle a the afternoon we come on a couple a fellas movin' about a hunnerd head a cattle south. We jawed with one of 'em an' asked if he knowed where a town name a Melinda might be. He said he'd never heer'd of Melinda but they was a town called Clarinda about twenty miles on. We thanked him an' made another eight or nine miles afore we quit. Homer had another can a them beans. I throwed it in the pot with some chunks a that ham Miz Thorson give us while he fried up some more a them potaters, an' we et right good.

Homer rolled hisself a smoke after supper an' leaned back on his saddle to take a puff.

"Clarinda has got to be the place," he said. "Cain't be no Melinda an' Clarinda in the same neck a the woods. Must not be a terrible important spot. I ain't never heard a neither one of 'em, an' I know about everthin' they is to know."

Marion tossed a little clod a dirt at him then, an' Homer set there smokin' an' chucklin'. I gotta admit that I felt some pleased to be in the company of such men, settin' around a little fire a white oak while 'yotes hollerd in the distance an' a ol' hoot owl spoke in that quiet way they got from over near the river. I kindly got wrapped up in them type a thoughts fer a spell until Arliss the mule brung me back when he grunted layin' down. I looked around an' seen Marion had give up the day an' Homer was fussin' with his blanket. He pulled it up over hisself an' tilted his hat down over his eyes.

"Nice ta be on the trail, ain't it, Rube," he said.

"Yessir," I said, "it truly is."

Homer grunted an' I swear, in no more than ten seconds, he started to snore. That hoot owl called' an' another one answered him from down river. I pulled my blanket up an' eased into it, watchin' sparks float up outa a crackle in the fire now an' then, thinkin' about how nice it was to be on the trail.

* * * * *

We come on a roadhouse early afternoon the next day, at least the sign said it was a roadhouse. Didn't look to me to be much more than a saloon with a second story. We went on past it an' about a mile later come on a town. It was a purty good size place, some bigger than Deer Run. They was a sign sayin' we had come to Clarinda, the Page County Seat. On the main street we seen two roomin' houses, a place that claimed to be a hotel, a placed called Cathcart General Store, Bridges Shoe Store, an' a couple a places ta eat. On down the way was a blacksmith shop an' past it was a livery. They was a bunch a other streets comin' offa the main one. We seen two churches an' two schoolhouses, a ladies shop, a doctor's office, an' I doan know what all.

Marion stopped at the livery an' we got off. A older fella with a arm that was kindly twisted an' didn't seem to work real good come out an' greeted us. He give us his terms an' directions to the Sheriff's Office, which was on down the way past the county courthouse, an' we give him our horses an' Arliss the mule. We struck off on foot, an' Marion pinned his badge back on the inside a his vest, an' give one to Homer. He stuck it in his pocket. I put mine back under my kerchief. We come up on the Sheriff's Office an' walked inside.

The fella in there was about fifty with a full beard an' eyes under heavy brows. He was about my height, but thicker. He wore a ol' white shirt with black suspenders, an' had a Schofield forty-four in a cross draw. His hands was heavy. He got up an' looked at the three of us.

"Hello, boys," he said, "and a good afternoon to you. Kyler Tibbs. I'm the town law and the Page County Sheriff. You men are gonna have to check them firearms. Nobody in town carries guns but me an' my deputies."

Marion smiled at him. "At least nobody that you know of," he said.

The sheriff bristled a little bit at that. "Beg pardon?" he said.

"I believe that's a good policy," Marion went on. "Give him yer guns, boys."

Homer an' me laid our guns on his desk. He took note a that little scattergun some, an' looked at me when he seen the Schofield.

"Don't get a lot of these," he said.

"Most folks doan know quality," I told him.

He smiled a little at that, an' looked at Marion. "Now yours," he said.

"Believe I'll keep mine," Marion said, flippin' his vest over so the sheriff could see his badge. "Name's Marion Daniels. I'm a U.S. Marshal." He stuck out his hand an' the sheriff took it.

"Marion Daniels," he said. "I'm not unfamiliar with that name. You are a man of reputation, sir."

"These here fellers is marshals, too," Marion went on, an' innerduced us.

"What brings you boys to Clarinda," the sheriff asked.

"We're lookin' for a couple a fellers name of Jack an' Jim Waxler," Marion said.

"Waxler?" the sheriff said. "That is a infamous name in this part of the world."

"I doan doubt that one bit," Marion said. "These fellers are responsible for the killin' a one woman an' the mutilation of another one down near Saint Joe a month or two back."

"There paper on 'em?" the sheriff asked.

"There will be after I ketch 'em," Marion said. "You know where they are?"

"The Waxler bunch usta have a spread about halfway between here an' Council Bluffs. They came up this way ten or twelve years ago after they left the river down near where the Nodaway runs into the Missouri. I hear they had a business there involving theft an' probably murder of river travelers."

Marion nodded. "That's purty much the way I heer'd it. The ol' man come into that area afore the war, I believe."

"That was before my time here," the sheriff said. "I ain't never heard anythin' about the old man's death. Clovis, I believe his name is. He may still be alive. Out of my county, though. Could be unwise for you gentlemen to ride up there an' announce that those boys are under arrest."

Homer spoke up. "We thought we'd let ol' Rube, here, take care a that for us while we hang around an' visit the barber an' such."

Sheriff Tibbs smiled. "Son," he said, "you may need another Schofield."

"An' a couple dozen pistoleers," I said.

"I thought," Marion said, "that I'd let these two walk around and see what they kin see fer a day or two, and find out what the talk is. I'll hang this badge where folks can git a peek at it so none a your deputies git messages about a armed and dangerous stranger on the loose."

"All right with me," the sheriff said. "I'll alert my deputies that you're in town, Marshal. I won't say nothin' about these other two. You want them kept secret, then that's the way it is."

"Thank ya, Sheriff," Marion said. "There a barber shop an' a bath house around?"

"Two," the sheriff said, an' give us directions. Marion struck off for one, me an' Homer headed back to the livery for a change a clothes an' a visit to the other. Walkin' back, I noticed I missed the weight a my gunbelt.

CHAPTER ELEVEN

After we had our baths an' such, me an' Homer found this little roomin' house that was good for four-bits a night an' got our rolls an' possibles from down at the livery. Homer went back to the sheriff's office to leave word for Marion as to where we was an' collect our guns an' belts to put in the room. I took a little walk.

I come on that shoe store an' went inside. I'd never seen no place like it. They was more shoes in one spot than I had ever seen afore in my whole life. I plumb enjoyed lookin' at all them shoes, an' I found several diffrn't pairs that I thought Harmony woulda been proud to have, but I didn't know how big her feet was. I did git me a new pair a Preacher's Boots, as my old ones had been wore out for a spell. Miss Harmony had been remindin' me about it some now an' then.

I had her on my mind when I went in a ladies shop down the street a little ways. They was fixin' to close, but the lady there was right patient with me, an' friendly too. I found a necklace that I admired. It was a tiny silver chain with links so small I wondered how a fella could ever have forged 'em. Hangin' on it was a little silver bird with his wings stuck out like he was flyin'. It caught my fancy an' I paid her near six dollars for it. She wrapped it up real good for me, an' stuck it in a little box so it wouldn't git hurt none out on the trail. She allowed as how she thought my wife would take to it right off, an' smiled a lot. I doan believe I ever met a nicer lady than she was. I went back to the room then an' found Homer waitin' on me. I showed him that little bird an' he grinned at me some while I stashed it away in a saddle bag.

We went out an' walked around a little then an' come up on this café that didn't look too fancy. They was several cowboys on hand so we went in. I had two big ol' porkchops with boiled potaters an' greens. Them chops had been baked I reckon, instead a fried, 'cause they was terrible tender an' good. For desert I had what they called egg custard. I'd never et it afore. I liked it quite a bit an' reminded myself to ask Harmony about it when I got home an' see if she knowed how to make it.

Homer said we might go out to that road house we passed on the way into town, so we each emptied out one side a our saddle bags an' stuck our guns an' belts in there. Then we went back to the livery an' saddled up. Willie was a little nervous, 'cause a the town I reckon, but once we got movin' he settled in. When we got to the place, they was quite a few horses an' a couple a wagons tied out front. We seen two fellas come out an' they was packin', so we tied up, put on our hardware, an' went inside.

The place was some bigger'n the Houston House, with oil lamp chandeliers hangin' everwhere. They was a long bar down one side an' a mess a tables an' chairs out on the floor. A stairway went up the other side to several rooms an' a narrow walkway. They was a couple a girls in shiny lookin' dresses leanin' on the rail up there, lookin' down on the crowd. An' they was a crowd. Cowboy types an' workers, fellas in dirty clothes an' others in cutaway coats an' vests. Some was settin' an' jawin', some was playin' cards an' such. There was a fella in the corner pickin' on a banjo, an' two or three girls in dresses that looked to me to be some fancy was walkin' around an' talkin' to fellas. They was a lot a people in there, an' a lotta noise too. I noticed Homer smilin' at me.

"What are you grinnin' about?" I asked him.

"Welcome to civilization, Rube," he said. "Just follow my lead."

He went over to the bar then, an' I went with him to a space between some other boys. Homer looked at the fella next to him an' spoke up.

"Howdy," he said. "Name's Homer. Yer next one's on me."

"Much obliged," the fella said. "I'm Dodge. Right nice of ya."

The bartender come up an' Homer asked for a beer. His new friend ordered a rye. Homer tossed a dollar on the bar, an' the bartender turned to me.

"How 'bout you, young fella?" he asked.

I asked for a beer an' put down two-bits. He left an' come back purty soon with the two beers an' a shot. I doan have no taste for beer at all, but Homer got one, so I did too. Plus, if we was gonna be in there very long, I could stretch that beer out a ways. Hard liquor woulda done me in purty quick. I had just took a sip when this lady come up beside me. She was nice lookin' an' friendly like, an' she smelled terrible good.

"Hi there," she said. "I'm Nola. Buy me a drink, cowboy?"

Homer spoke up. "If'n he won't, I will," he said.

"Yes M'am," I told her. "I'll buy you one. Right proud to."

She nodded at the bartender, an' he made a little mark on a piece a paper with a pencil an' set a shot glass in front of her. She tossed that shot down right quick an' looked at me.

"I haven't seen you in here before," she said.

"No M'am," I said. "I ain't never been here. I'm just passin' through."

"What's your name, honey?" she said.

"Ruben," I said, an' felt my face heat up a little.

"You're a nice lookin' young man, Ruben," she said. "I bet the girls just line up to go a walk with you."

My face got hot then. I jumped in. "Yes, M'am," I said. "They's a dozen or two waitin' outside for me right now. I come in here to git outa the crowd."

She tossed back her head an' laughed, an' it was kinda like birds singin' or somethin'.

"Ruben," she said, "you are a sweetie. Would you buy me another drink?"

"Yes, I would, Miss Nola," I said. That bartender made another mark with his pencil an' set down a glass. She drank it an' patted me on the shoulder.

"It's been nice to meet you, Ruben," she said. "I'll see you a little later."

I watched her walk off an' Homer spoke up.

"C'mon, boy," he said, an' headed for a little table over by where some fellas was playin' cards.

The bartender looked at me. "That's two dollars, son," he said. "One for each a Nola's drinks."

I paid him an' went over an' set with Homer.

"You an' Nola seemed to git along well," he said.

"You said to do what you done," I said. "You offered to buy her a drink."

"I did," Homer said. "That's the expected thing to do in these places."

"Her drinks cost me a dollar each," I said. "That's terrible high, ain't it?"

"She gets a commission on them drinks folks buy for her," Homer said. "The more she drinks, the more she makes."

"She shore must be able to hold her liquor," I said, "if everbody just buys her drinks all the time."

Homer grinned at me. "She ain't drinkin' liquor, boy," he said. "It was prob'ly just tea or somethin'. Pure profit for the saloon."

That hit me a little bit. "That's why she was bein' so nice to me an' all?" I said.

Homer grinned. "What," he said, "you thought it was yer sparklin' personality?"

"Well, hell, Homer," I said, "is she a whore?"

"No, Rube," he said, "she ain't no whore. She's a saloon gal, son. Makin' a livin' like everbody else. She can earn three or four dollars a day doin' this. That's a damn site more than if she was doin' washin' an' ironin' or somethin' like that."

"She was kindly nice," I said.

"Shore she was," he said. "She's prob'ly a good gal, easy to talk to an' such. Got a talent for it an' has found a way to pay her bills an' feed herself doin' it. What's wrong with that?"

"Not a thing, I reckon."

"You buy that little bird necklace from a woman at that store?" he asked.

"I did," I said.

"Was she nice to ya?"

"Right nice," I said.

So," he went on, "they was a nice woman that treated ya good an' was friendly, an' you spent some money. That about it?"

"Yessir."

"Like I told ya, boy," Homer said, "welcome to civilization."

* * * * *

We set there for a spell, watchin' folks an' such, when these two cowboys come in. They was some drunk I reckon, an' loud. Miss Nola warn't far from the door when they come through. The first one stumbled into her an' then pushed her into the second one. The second one wrapped his arm around her from behind an' kindly held onto her. She didn't care for it an' squirmed some. I stood up an' took a couple a steps in that direction an' that fella reached down an' grabbed her backside. I was comin' up behind him when she spun around an' slapped his face. He drawed back to smack her an' I caught holt a his arm inside his elbow an' just flipped him over my hip an' down onto the floor. He hit some hard. I pulled his pistol, drug him outside, an' dropped him by the hitch rail.

I turned around an' there was Homer with the other one, arm up behind his back an' walkin' on his tippy toes.

"You boys go along now," he said. "You come back in this place tonight an' you'll still be bleedin' tomorra. The bartender'll have yer guns when ya sober up."

They cussed at us some, but they rode off.

When we went back inside, some a them fellas cheered an' such. The bartender brung us two shots that was on the house. Miss Nola come over an' set down beside me. She thanked us an' said how much she appreciated the way we stood up for her an' such.

"The name Waxler mean anythin' to you, M'am?" Homer asked.

Her eyes flashed some. "You with that bunch?" she said.

"No, M'am, we ain't," Homer said. "We're lookin' for two of 'em though. Jack an' Jim. We want 'em fer killin' a lady down toward Saint Joe, an' cuttin' another one up purty bad. You know 'em."

"I know them," she said, "and I heard about those two girls. From what I hear, you might locate those two up around Council Bluffs. Let me ask around."

"Yes, M'am," Homer said. "That'd be good of ya. One of us'll stop by tomorrow evenin' an' see if ya found out anything."

She smiled then. "Send Ruben," she said. "I like the way he blushes."

CHAPTER TWELVE

Me an' Homer went back to the roomin' house an' cashed in for the night, but I couldn't hardly git no sleep. I guess it come from bein' on the trail for so long. I felt kindly boxed in an' shut up there in that little room. An' the cot I had was some soft an' saggy like, an' bounced on them springs. I listened to Homer snore for a spell, then opened all the windas an' tossed my roll on the floor. It was hard, but it didn't move none an' I finally drifted off.

The next mornin' we went to breakfast at the same little cafe an' walked around town some, lookin' at the sights. Early afternoon we seen Marion's roan tied up at the sheriff's office an' went over that way. Marion said all he come up with was them Waxler boys had run north, but he heard they might be in Council Bluffs or Omaha. Homer tolt him that I'd made a new friend out at the roadhouse an' she wanted me to come by that evenin' so she could see me blush' an' might have a little more for us to go on. Marion an' Sheriff Tibbs found some humor in that an' Homer allowed as how he'd seen the whole thing an' was some disgusted at the way a newly married fella like me, with as nice a wife as Miss Harmony was, would throw hisself at a saloon gal the way I done. I knowed they wasn't no use in tryin' to stick up for myself in the face a them three ol' cobs, so I just left out an' went down to the livery to take Willie out fer a spell. We'd stalled the horses. Bein' on the ride as much as he had, he'd need a little exercise or his hocks could git some swole up.

The fella at the livery had already fed 'em. I got Willie an' crosstied him while I went over him an' checked him out. I brushed him down an' picked his feet an' such, then saddled up an' took out. As soon as I was outside a town I set him on a high lope for a ways an' got his breath up. Then we waded out in the river an' I let him drink an' kept him there for a spell to cool his feet an' knees an' hocks. I doan know how a fella could have wanted a better mount than that little buckskin. No matter how his mind was set, Willie always paid attention to the bit an' never give me no trouble. I was gentle with him an' used a short-shank snaffle, not wantin' him to git no hard mouth.

We stayed out for quite a spell, lookin' at the country an' such. On the way back we come on a couple a fellas with a team a mules an' a freight wagon off the road, with two wheels down in the mud. I got a rope on the front axel an' took a dally around the saddle horn, an' Willie dug in. It took some strainin' but, between him an' them mules, we got the wagon out. Just as we did, I felt my saddle slip backwards offa Willie's withers a little. I got off to git my rope back an' noticed the breast collar had come apart some. It was just one a them made out strands a cotton an' wool rope. When I got back in town, I found a drygoods store an' got a new one. It was cut from mulehide an' lined in wool fleece, some nicer than the old one. Willie deserved it, I reckon.

* * * * *

It was gittin' on toward evenin' when I got back an' I seen Homer's gray tied up in front a that café. I found him just gittin' into a beefsteak an' set. I had some ham an' beans with cornbread an' blackstrap, an' we struck off back out to that roadhouse. The place was real busy, it bein' a Friday an' all, an' we took a small table just inside the door a little ways. Miss Nola was there, along with four or five other girls. I watched her for a spell, an' she musta drunk ten or twelve shots a that tea or whatever it was, while talkin' to several different fellas for a minute or two. I was suckin' on a beer, slow like, when she seen us. She went up to the bar then, an' come over with shots for Homer an' me, an' set with us.

"Thank ya, M'am," Homer said. "You all right this evenin'?"

"Why, I am just fine," Miss Nola said, smilin' at us. "And I have learned a little something that might be of help to you. North of Council Bluffs a little ways is a place called Cresent. The Mormons was thick there years ago before they all mostly went west. Now it isn't much more than a wide spot in the road. There's a saloon up that way to catch travelers before they get into the bluffs called the Wagon Trail, or the Wagon Line, or something like that. I hear that the Waxler bunch doesn't come into Council Bluffs much anymore, with the railroads and such making the area so much more populated. It's not the raw place it once was. My information says they stay east and north of there now. Mostly the brothers hang out in Chautauqua or Crescent. There is still a fair amount of wagon traffic through that area, even some westbound into the high plains, though not nearly as many as before the place got all those railroads."

Homer took his shot then, an' stood up. I drank mine an' did likewise. "Thank ya kindly, M'am," he said. "You've been a big help to us an' we appreciate it."

She looked at me. "Ruben," she said, "I thought we were friends, and yet you haven't said a word to me. Did I do something wrong?"

That kindly got me, her sayin' what she did. "Why, no, Miss Nola," I said, reachin' in my pocket. "I doan know how a lady as purty as you could hardly ever do nothin' wrong. I'd appreciate it if you'd take this here gold piece for all yer trouble."

She stepped right up in front of me then, terrible close, an' took that gold piece outa my hand an' stuck it down inside the front of her dress. She looked up at me an' smiled.

"You are a sweet young man, Ruben," she said. "If I was ten years younger, I'd do my best to cause a scandal with you."

She kissed me on the cheek then, an' I felt my face come all over hot.

"There it is," she said, an' walked away laughin'.

"C'mon, boy," Homer said, an' I foller'd him outside.

* * * * *

We was collectin' our horses when two riders come up an' went inside. It was them two fellas we tangled with the night before. I took out my ol' Barlow pocketknife an' went over an' cut both their cinches about halfway through. Homer stood there, grinnin'.

"Who'd a thought a sweet young man like you could be so et up with revenge," he said.

* * * * *

We stocked up on supplies, loaded Arliss the mule, an' struck out for Council Bluffs the next mornin'. We hit it purty hard an' made the trip in two days, but the horses was some wore down from it. Truth be told, we was too. It didn't seem to make no difference to Arliss. We come inta town a little before evenin' the second day. It was a big an' busy place. There was folks everwhere. The streets was full a people, an' horses, an' wagons. Half the town was railroads it seemed like. Five or six different lines come through the place. Marion walked around like he sorta knowed where he was goin', so me an' Homer just trailed along.

We put the horses an' Arliss the mule in a livery an' struck out walkin'. Marion took us to the Emigrant House Hotel. Just as we was goin' in, this fella was comin' out an' seen Marion.

"By God," he said. "The things ya run across when you ain't got a axe handle."

Marion smiled a little. "Howdy, Ben," he said. "You ain't in jail?"

The fella grinned. "Broke out a hour ago," he said. "The gal that brought my breakfast hid a file in my eggs. Took me all day to git through them bars."

"Boys," Marion said, "unless he's changed his name for illegal purposes, this here is Ben Marks. Don't never play no cards with him. He's a artist with a deck an' ya cain't beat him. He won't let ya."

Ben nodded at us. "Boys," he said, an' turned back to Marion. "You still upholdin' the law are ya Daniels?" he asked.

"Cain't find no other thing suited to my talents," Marion said.

Ben nodded. "Who ya after?"

"Jack an' Jim Waxler. Know 'em?"

"Know the names," Marks said. "They doan come around as much as they did a few years ago. Mostly stay with that wild bunch north an' east a here. This about them whores down in Saint Joe?"

"It is," Marion said.

"Bad business," Marks said. "Hope you git 'em. I hope that bunch don't git you first. I ain't never been too friendly with the law, but from what I knowed a you, you was always straight."

"Any a the other boys around?" Marion asked.

"Naw," Marks said. "The law got kinda rowdy around here after the James boys an' the Younger bunch got to robbin' trains. Pinkertons was thick as fleas for a while. Canada Bill Jones lit a shuck back in seventy-nine I guess it was. 'Bout a year later John Bull an' Frank Tarbeaux took off. I'm about the only one left. Last year a train car full a dynamite blew up over in the rail yards, right during a memorial service for President Garfield, an' the stockyards flooded out that spring. Place just ain't what it usta be. Durn railroad has took it over mostly. Even they are havin' trouble. Too many lines, too much competition. I'm gonna stick it out though. Down the road a piece, when things git settled a little, I figure I'll go into politics. I'm a liar an' a gambler. I should fit right in."

Marion laughed then. "Ben," he said, "a feller cain't hit nothin' unless he's got a bead on it. The law in this town honest?"

"Some is an' some ain't," Marks said. "Just like anyplace."

"Who can I trust?"

"There's a county law named Chet Hawkins. Got a office over by the Drover's Hotel on Tenth Street. He's always seemed square to me. The fact that I don't like him might be in his favor."

"Ben Marks," Marion said, "it's been long enough since we tangled that I can honestly say it's been good to see you."

"There were a lot of 'em a damn site worse that you were, Marshal," Marks said, an' they shook hands. Marks nodded at me an' Homer. "Boys," he said, an' walked away.

The Emigrant House had a laundry an' a bakery. We registered an' got a nice size room with three cots, dropped our dirty clothes off at the laundry, then stopped by the bakery an' got some cinnamon rolls an' a apple pie to eat in our room. I doan know about Marion or Homer, but I slept hard that night.

CHAPTER THIRTEEN

The next mornin' the three of us, badges hid, went out an' found a place just down the street to git breakfast. After we got settled an' the little gal brung us our ham an' eggs, Marion got on with it.

"You boys can view the sights today if you care to," he said. "I gotta make some calls and see some people."

"What are you up to?" Homer asked him. "An' how much trouble is it gonna mean for me?"

Marion smiled. "I'm tryin' to avoid trouble. First I'm gonna go over to the headquarters of the Union Pacific and talk with them boys. If I cain't git what I want, I'll try the Illinois Central, then the Wabash, then the Burlington and Quincy if I have to. Once I git that squared away, I'll go see this sheriff Chet Hawkins and lie to him."

Homer took notice. "Lie to him?" he said.

Marion nodded. "Ben Marks cain't be took for his word," he said. "I asked him what lawman I could trust so I'd find out the biggest crook in the bunch around here. Ben ain't gonna do me no favors. We've locked horns a time or two over the years and he's come up short. If he thinks he can screw me, he's lookin' for the lard. The hog with that fat is Hawkins. Anything I tell Hawkins'll get right back to Ben. He'll figger out a way to use it to his advantage and git the best a me. That there just ain't gonna happen, boys."

"What are you gonna tell him?" I asked.

"I'm gonna tell him that we're gonna hole up in this neck a the woods for a week or two while the five other marshals I got comin' git here. And that then, because we got solid information, as to them Waxler's whereabouts, we're gonna head over to Carson an' arrest those boys and anybody that's with 'em, and take the whole shitaree back to Saint Joe for trial."

"Carson?" Homer said. "Where the hell's Carson?"

"Due west a here a piece. Little burg. Just got a plat a couple a years ago. Wouldn't surprise me if they sent a mess a fellers down that way to ambush the law that's comin' just to show who's boss around here. Meantime, I'm gonna talk to a couple a fellers I know and find out if them brothers is most likely in Chautauqua or Crescent. We git a line on 'em and we'll go git 'em and head back this way."

"What's the railroad got to do with that?" I asked.

"If I can arrange a sneaky way to do it, we'll git back here and take us, them, and the horses back to Saint Joe in a freight car, git out on a sidin', and come in on horseback from the east. With luck, we'll have them boys in the hoosegow afore the rest a the bunch even knows they're gone."

Homer looked at him. "That's yer plan, is it?" he asked.

"It is."

"Sounds purty good to me," Homer said. "Reckon it'll work?"

"Might," Marion said. "Might not."

Homer nodded. "Maybe the three of us oughta just pool our money, go up into Nebraska someplace, an' start raisin' horses for the army or somethin'," he said.

"Sounds purty good to me," Marion said. "Reckon it'll work?"

Homer smiled. "Might," he said. "Might not."

* * * * *

We walked the town that day, me an' Homer, from the business district to the square, through alleys an' down streets lined with houses, to what was left of the stockyards an' plum down to the railyards. The placed changed quite a bit down by the yards, goin' from houses to shanties an' proper women to whores. Twice we stopped in saloons, although one was called a tavern, to git a drink or a beer, an' at a couple a restaurants, too. One of 'em served some thin sliced roasted beef that was terrible good. We stopped at a place that sold saddles an' such an' I got new pair a spurs. Not that the ones I had was wore out or nothin', they wasn't, but Willie had got so good at doin' what I wanted, I didn't want to take the chance a puttin' that at risk. My spurs had fair sized rowels on 'em that was some sharp, too. The new ones had smaller rowels that was blunt on the edges an' fixed in position so they didn't spin. Truth be tolt, I didn't need no spurs on Willie at all, so I used the easiest ones I could find. I coulda just done without, but it warn't seemly.

We come across this one place that was kindly a notions an' foofarah store that had some pipes in the winda an' went in 'cause Homer needed to git hisself some tobacco. We looked around some at all the different stuff in there, includin' razors an' soap mugs an' brushes, an' cuff links, an' string ties, an' concho belts of the Mexican style, even several kinds a lotions to put on yer face after ya shaved, an' none of 'em Bay Rum. Just a mess a things to admire. Then Homer asked this feller that worked there for some chawin' tobacco, an' this old boy come up with ten or twelve different kinds, most of 'em Homer had never heard of, an' even three or four types a snuff all the way across the waters from England.

He got hisself some twists a chaw an' then said as how he needed some rollin' tobacco an' papers. That fella smiled an' told him he didn't. Homer looked at him across that counter sorta curious like.

"I believe I do," he said.

The fella grinned to take any sting outa his words. "And I'm tellin' you that you don't," he said.

Homer reset his hat afore he spoke up. "I ain't payin' the price for no hand rolled tailor-mades when I can shore twist em' up myself," he said.

That feller reached under the counter an' brung up a little cardboard box. He opened it up an' handed it to Homer. Inside they was twenty or thirty cigarettes, all lined up just as purty as you please, ever one of 'em lookin' just like ever other one.

"Would you look at that," Homer said, inspectin' the box real close. "Now that there is some fine rollin'. The ol' boy that made these here is a master. How much?"

"Ten cents a box," the fella said.

Homer's eyebrows went up a mite. "What's wrong with 'em?" he asked.

"Nothin'," the fella said. "A machine made 'em. A man by the name a Bonsack out in Virginia come up with a machine that can make thousands an' thousands of 'em a day. Got a bunch a them machines runnin' around the clock. I tell you, friend, it won't be long before won't hardly nobody'll be rollin' their own. It's the comin' thing."

"Well, I'll be durned," Homer said. "Don't that knock the 'possum off the fence."

The feller handed Homer a match. "Try one," he said.

Homer struck that match an' lit up. He stood there for a spell, puffin' away, then looked at the fella. "Gimme four bags a rollin' tobacco, four packs a papers, a box a them waxed matches, an' a half dozen boxes a these machine-made smokes," he said. "By God, these here things is progress."

I had never seen Homer Poteet to appear prideful about nothin', but walkin' back to the hotel smokin' them new cigarettes, he was almost struttin'.

We hadden been back in our room but a half a hour when Marion come in, carryin' some more a them fine cinnamon rolls.

"Got us a treat for later, boys," he said. "Tomorrow we take off for Crescent. Them Waxlers was over that way with some other fellers a couple days ago. They's a whore there they's fond of. One of 'em rides a big ol' black with one white foot, an' the other'n sets a paint. Shouldn't be too hard to locate if they're still around."

Homer picked up one a them little boxes he'd bought.

"Lookie here what I got," he said.

CHAPTER FOURTEEN

We was up at daybreak the next mornin' 'an off to the livery, munchin' on the last a them cinnamon rolls as we went. When we got our long guns from up in the house where he'd kept 'em for us, we asked the old man to keep Arliss the mule caught up 'cause we might have to git him in a hurry. We saddled up, an' I give Willie a chunk a roll I'd saved for him. He seemed to like that cinnamon quite a bit, even if it did make him sneeze when he smelt of it.

We avoided trails an' took to unbroken land. In about four hours we come up a little rise in post oaks an' cedar an' stopped. Down the other side the slope was purty bare. In a wide draw at the bottom of it they was a small town. Stayin' in the trees, we circled the one side of it from about a quarter mile away. A purty worn trail an' wagon path come through the place an' headed off back toward Council Bluffs. Settin' off from the north end a town a little bit was a buildin' some bigger than a normal house. It had been whitewashed at one time, had a hitchin' rail out front with only two horses, an' a big ol' cabin tent attached to the south side.

"Liquor an' gamblin' in the buildin'," Homer said. "Whores in the tent I speck. Doan see no paint. Doan see no black with a white foot neither."

Homer's eyesight was uncommon. I reckon that's why he could shoot that Sharps a his so good. At the distance I could tell a rider from his horse, Homer could give ya his eye color an' how long it had been since he shaved.

We pulled back off the ridge an' got down. I loosed Willie's cinch a bit so he could stand easy, an' tied him to a little post oak. Marion an'

Homer done the same. It had been a little cloudy on the ride, but the sky commenced to clear up an' the winds, which had been some fresh outa the west, laid quite a bit.

Homer looked at Marion. "You got a plan for this too, or we just gonner set fire to the place an' shoot everbody as they come runnin' out?"

"Little drastic, shootin' everbody in the place, doncha think?" Marion said.

"Some," Homer agreed, "but effective."

"Thought we'd send ol' Ruben down there if a bunch comes in," Marion said. "If he can keep his mind offa them gals, he can size it up an' give a signal. If it's still light, knowin' yer skill with a handgun like I do, you can set up here an' cover us with the Sharps. If it's dark, we'll both go in. You can back me an' Ruben up with my coach gun. Somethin' about a shotgun at close range that make a lot a fellers thoughtful."

"What we gonna do with 'em if we git 'em?" Homer asked.

"I got manacles in my bag," Marion said. "We'll chain 'em to their saddle horns an' impress on 'em that if they run, all we gotta do is shoot the horse."

"What about the horses?" Homer went on. "We doan want a mess a fellers on our ass. Shoot the horses at the rail?"

"Lord," Marion said, "I hate to do that."

"Take the headstalls," I said.

Homer looked at me an' blinked. "What'd you say?" he asked.

"Take the headstalls," I repeated. "They ain't gonna chase us without no way to steer their horses. How many a these boys you think got a horse good enough to guide with their knees?"

Marion looked at Homer an' grinned. "Mouths a babes," he said.

* * * * *

We laid up on that hill most of the afternoon, watchin' the place. Two fellas come out an' left on the only two horses we could see about a hour after we got there. Everthin' was quiet except for a little footwork from down in the town until about a hour afore dusk. Then come in eight riders, runnin' their horses an' actin' like fools. They went inside an' we could hear yellin' an' such clear up where we hid.

"Paint an' a black with a offside rear white sock," Homer said.

"All right, Ruben," Marion said, "you go on down there. Leave yer scattergun in a saddlebag. Go on in, have a drink or two, an' keep a eye on things. When it looks right, come outside an' give a signal, put that scattergun back on yer belt, an' go back in an' set back outa the road. Me an' Homer'll be on our way."

"Here, Rube," Homer said, handin' me a box a them cigarettes an' some matches. "Stick these in with that shotgun. If it's full dark when you come out, stand where we can see ya an' light a cigarette. Strike three different matches. That's the signal."

I checked the load in my Schofield an' the scattergun, put it and the smokes an' matches in a saddlebag, made sure my Yellaboy had a full magazine, tightened up Willie's cinch, an' swung up. "See ya," I said, an' struck off through the trees to the north a ways, so I'd ride in from a different direction than from where Marion an' Homer actually was. To tell the truth, my mouth was purty dry.

* * * * *

When I got offa Willie at the front a the saloon they was a smack sound come outa the tent.

A woman's voice kindly cried out. "Don't, Jack, yer a-hurtin' me!" Then come a man's voice, laughin'. "You hear that Jim?" it said. "She thinks that hurts. Shit. I didn't feel nothin'. Did you?" A couple a men laughed then, an' I went in the saloon so I didn't have to hear no more of it. Had it been up to me, I speck I woulda tore into that tent an' messed everthin' up. I reckon that's why it warn't up to me.

I got a beer at the bar an' took it to a front corner a the room an' set. They was three fellas at a table in the rear a the room, an' three more standin' a little ways from 'em at the bar. Everbody there looked me over some, but nobody come my way. I kept my eyes from 'em an' sipped the beer. After a while two fellas, some drunk by the look of 'em come in, laughin' an' such. Neither one of 'em was thirty yet I reckoned. They was both about my height, an' the one in the gray hat was thicker than the one in the brown hat. Gray hat looked at his pards.

"You boys is gonner havta wait a spell," he said. "We wore her down some, didn't we Jim?"

"We shore as hell did," brown hat said, poundin' on the bar with his fist. "Gimme a goddam shot!" he hollerd, "an' be goddam quick about it!"

They all went to laughin' then, an' raisin' hell. I got up an' eased outside. I went over to Willie an' got my scattergun outa the bag an' strapped it on, then I took out the cigarettes an' matches. I moved to Willie's off side so Marion an' Homer could see me from up on the hill an' lit a match. I let it go out, lit another one an' let it go out, then struck another one, an' lit a cigarette.

I ain't no smoker. I tried it when I was younger with some a my daddy's makin's an', Lord, I got so sick I thought I was plumb done for. I took a little pull on that cigarette an' durn near blowed out my eardrums tryin' not to cough. When that settled down, I took another pull an' started back into the place, but come over so dizzy like, I had to stay where I was an' lean on Willie some. My eyesight got kindly red around the edges, an' my head felt full. It didn't last too long. Purty soon I come back to myself, put that little box in my shirt pocket an' headed off to go back inside. A big fella met me at the door.

"What the hell you doin' out chere aroun' are horses?" he growled.

"Settle down," I tolt him. "I warn't doin' nothin' around your horses. I was doin' somethin' around my horse. I was gittin' these." I held up that little box.

"What the shit is that?" he said.

"Machine rolled cigarettes," I said, an' opened the box so he could see.

He looked in that box an' softened some. "Them was rolled by a machine?" he asked.

"Come all the way from Virginia," I said. "Fella over there invented a way to roll millions of 'em." I handed him the box. "Help yerself. I got plenty. Keep 'em."

"No kiddin'?"

"Go ahead on," I said.

He sorta grinned at me then. "Thanks, mister," he said, an' went off toward the back.

I set down, real happy that Homer had give me more cigarettes than just one.

* * * * *

It warn't too long afore Marion Daniels, his badge showin', come through the door an' walked straight to the back a the room where them boys was all gathered. Homer Poteet was behind him, that coach gun held down beside his leg. He moved to the left an' close to the bar. I stood up an' walked toward the rear, stayin' on the right side a the room. The brothers was still with them fellas at the bar so there was five of 'em there an' three settin' at the table. Marion spoke up.

"Which ones, Ruben?" he asked, not lookin' in my direction.

"First two at the bar is Jack an' Jim," I said.

Marion never looked at nobody directly, but kindly kept his eyes in a gaze like, takin' in everthing, I reckon. He drew a revolver.

"Jack an' Jim Waxler," he said, "I am United States Marshal Marion Daniels. The two of you are under arrest for murder an' mutilation of two women in Saint Joseph, Missouri, on or about two to three months ago. Put yer hands over yer heads an' do not move."

That big fella that I give them cigarettes to was standin' at the back end of the bar. He went for his Colt. Marion shot him. Twice. His gun never even cleared leather.

"I got three more in this'un, boys," Marion said, "five in the other one, and two shotguns backin' me up. How many more a you wanna die here tonight?"

Nobody moved or said a word.

"Fine," Marion went on. "Guns and gunbelts on the floor where you stand or set, then in the middle a the room and flat down on your bellies. Anybody that misbehaves will be drug out by the heels."

In the face a what had just happened an' Marion's attitude, they give up an' done exactly what he said. I kept the room covered while him an' Homer took the brothers out an' manacled them to their saddle horns, then Homer come back in an' held 'em while I got his machine rolled smokes offa that dead fella, then picked up all the hardware, took it outside, an' tossed it under the porch along with two rifles I pulled outa scabbards on the horses. When I finished that, I took the headstalls offa the horses an' strung 'em on my saddle horn. I watched the room while Homer come out an' put Marion's coach gun back where it belonged. He got on the gray, brought Willie up to the front, an' took the reins a one of the brother's horses, while Marion kept the other.

Homer grinned at me. "You hurry along now, honey," he said, an' he an' Marion took out. I give 'em a minute or two to git gone, then me an' Willie was off, scatterin' them loose horses an' runnin' down the trail under the light of a three-quarter moon.

CHAPTER FIFTEEN

We went after it purty hard for the first four or five miles, gallopin' through the dark, them Waxler boys cussin' an' dammin' us durn near ever foot a the way. Finally Marion brought his roan to a stop an' turned on them fellas.

"Now you two crybabies listen to me, Goddammit," he said. "I'm sick ta death a yer bitchin' an' moanin' mouths. You ain't no place you don't deserve ta be. Considerin' what you done ta git where you are, you are damn lucky you ain't in the ground. So here's what's gonna happen. You are goin' to quit yer cussin' an' cryin' and shut the hell up, or yer teeth is gonna be stickin' out the backs a yer necks. The next one a you two sonsabitches that says one goddam word is gonna answer to me an' the barrel a my Colt. Now if'n either one a you don't wanna eat solid food for the rest a yer miserable days, go ahead on and say somethin' to me. I fuckin' dare you to!"

Both a them boys shut up. About that time, the big black with the white foot let outa a long heavy cough, dropped his head, an' begun to wheeze.

"Oh, hell," Homer said. "That damn horse is windbroke. Listen to him. One a these two dumb shits has been ridin' a windbroke horse. If we try to keep our pace up, he's gonna give out. That paint cain't carry both of 'em very far. We're gonna have to slow down. We need to rest that black for a while."

I got offa Willie, lifted down them headstalls, an' cut the reins offa one of 'em with my big knife, the one that Arliss give me with the coffin handle. Then I tied a rein to the end a both the reins on each of them Waxler horses, so Marion an' Homer would have longer lead lines to mess with.

"You reckon they're after us?" I asked.

"By now they are," Marion said. "They've had enough time to git mounts or tack from in town."

"Willie's purty fresh," I said. "Loan me yer coach gun an' rest that black some. I'll go back an' slow them fellas down."

Marion looked at me. "You sure about that, Ruben?" he asked me. "They'll be five."

"Gimme the damn gun," I said.

We swapped long guns, I hit the saddle, an' me an' Willie headed back the way we come.

* * * * *

It warn't hard to keep to the trail. The sky was clear an' there was plenty enough moon to see where we was goin'. Willie just kept on. He didn't slow, he didn't falter, he just stayed at a high lope an' et up the ground. I give it about two miles an' come on a big oak. I reined Willie in then an' moved next to the trunk a that tree in heavy moon shadow. Settin' there on that horse an' listenin' to him blow some, I thought about what Marion might do in such a situation. 'Course I knowed the answer. He'd take the reins in his teeth an' go right at them boys. I was some aware of the fact that I warn't no Marion Daniels, not by a damn site. He took steps quite a bit longer than me, an' I knowed it. So I turned my mind to what Ruben Beeler might do. I was thinkin' about that very thing when I heard 'em comin', an' not just the sounds of their horses, but them yellin' back an' forth at each other. Them fellas knowed they still had a ways to go afore they'd ketch up to any of us. The thought that we might be layin' for 'em somewhere never crossd their minds. They was the chasers an' we was the chased.

I held Willie tight up under that tree an' slid Marion's shotgun outa the scabbard. Purty soon they come by me, out on the path, goin' as fast as what the slowest horse among 'em had left. Willie started dancin' then, wantin' to go. I give 'em a little distance an' turned him loose.

We was maybe a hunnerd yards behind 'em when we hit the trail. They was foolish, ridin' in a tight cluster, two in front an' three behind, durn near nose to tail an' knee to knee, their concentration focused on what was in front a them an' givin' no thought at all to what might be comin' up behind. Between the noise a them jawin' at one another an' the hoofbeats a five horses, they couldn't hear me an' Willie gainin' on 'em. We was on a dead run an' closed up on 'em purty quick. At about thirty yards I got worried they might notice me, leveled that coach gun over Willie's ears, an' touched off the right barrel first, then the left one just as quick as I could. As soon as them shots went off, I kneed Willie to the left, dropped the coach gun, an' pulled that little twelve gauge a mine.

It's a damn good thing Willie an' me turned away, 'cause horses an' riders went ever direction. One horse fell purty much in front of us, an' I kept my seat when Willie just sailed right over him like he'd done it ever day a his life. All three riders in the rear an' that horse was down. The two in front had both gone to the right an' made the mistake a stayin' together. I set Willie after 'em an' he picked up on my intention right off, layin' his ears back an' givin' chase. One a them two horses couldn't keep up, an' commenced to slow a lot. I couldn't tell for sure, but he musta took a hit or two a that double-ought buck, makin' his rear end to kindly come out from under him, an' he fell, throwin' his rider hard an' rollin' on top of him. Willie kept after the one still runnin' without me havin' to do a thing. The rider turned to try a shot, lost a stirrup, an' nearly slipped outa the saddle. At about sixty feet I touched off one barrel a that little scattergun, an' he come off. His horse squealed an' turned away, runnin' to the left.

I pulled Willie up then, an' went back to where that other fella hit the dirt. He was layin' in a heap an' puffin' some, tryin' to reach his pistol where it lay a few feet from him an' havin' no luck at it. I stopped an' looked down at him, sprawled there on the ground.

"You shot?" I asked him.

"I doan know," he said, kindly wheezin'. "I cain't feel nothin' hardly at all."

"Can you move?"

"Not much," he said.

"I speck yer back is broke," I said.

"You gonna shoot me?" he asked.

"No need," I tolt him. "You ain't no threat to me now."

I got down offa Willie an' picked up his revolver an' stuck it in a saddle bag, then mounted up an' turned back up the trail. As we walked off, that fella commenced to cry.

I checked everbody else an' the two horses that was down, an' come away with seven handguns, one ol' Henry rifle, an' Marion's coach gun that was gonna need a good cleanin', me droppin' it the way I had to do. I put Willie in a short lope an' we took back to the trail.

I come up on Marion an' them purty soon an' dismounted, hangin' on to that Henry. Him an' Homer was settin' on the ground by the horses. Them Waxler boys was standin' up, manacled to their saddles the way they was, one of 'em bleedin' from the mouth. I reckon he didn't take Marion serious enough. The black had settled down quite a bit an' was only givin' a little cough now an' then.

"Heard shots," Homer said. "You all right, Rube?"

"Yessir," I said. "We ain't got no need to hurry."

"Whatcha got there?" he asked, lookin' at the rifle.

"Got a Henry," I said, "an' seven handguns in my saddle bag."

"That right?" Marion said.

I nodded. "I had to drop yer coach gun," I said. "I'll clean it for ya."

"You damn right you will," he said. "Any of 'em left?"

"Three dead, one dyin', an' one with a broke back," I said.

Marion nodded. "Three outa five ain't bad," he said.

"I was in a hurry," I tolt him. "If you'd care to git up off the ground, we can move on down the line."

Marion grinned at me then, an' slapped me on the leg. "Ol' Ruben," he said.

Them Waxler boys never said one word.

CHAPTER SIXTEEN

We didn't git back to Council Bluffs until some after sunup 'cause a the black an' his lung trouble. When we was still a couple miles outa town, Marion sent me on ahead to git our possibles an' Arliss the mule. I went on in an' collected Arliss an' put the pack saddle an' panniers on him, stickin' them pistols an' that Henry down inside an' coverin' everthin' with the tarp. The old fella come out an' I paid him an' give him a dollar boot. Willie went after the water trough so hard I had to pull him offa it a time or two so he wouldn't git too much too fast an' bloat or somethin'. Marion an' them come up soon after an' watered their horses, an' off we went, followin' Marion down to the train yards.

Willie was on high alert, passin' through them yards, steppin' over the rails an' crunchin' across that gravel an' cinders, them big ol' freight cars an' such shiftin' an' clankin' like they done now an' then. All the horses was kindly nervous. Arliss the mule didn't seem to notice. Once, when one a them engines that warn't too far away belched steam out from down by the wheels, Willie give me some trouble, crow hoppin' sideways an' thinkin' about runnin' off or buckin'. But he paid attention to the bit, an' held onto hisself.

We stopped by the yard office an' waited while Marion went inside. Purty soon he come out with a feller name a Finley, who was the Yardmaster. We all got down then, an' Marion shackled them Waxlers together, facin' each other, right hand to left hand an' left hand to right hand, like they was gittin' ready to play Ring Around the Rosie or dance with each other or somethin'. Off we went on foot, leadin' the horses an' Alriss the mule down through them tracks.

In about a quarter of a mile we come on this set a rails that was a little ways off from everthin' else. They was a boxcar settin' there with the doors open an' a big ol ramp up to 'em. We stopped an' Finley spoke up.

"That's yer car, boys," he said. "In about a hour a tender'll come by an' move ya on down a ways, an' they'll hook you up to the main train. Should git you fellers to a sidin' just north a Saint Joe about three this afternoon. There's some fair grass on the other side a the car. You got time to graze them horses a bit."

Marion signed a paper for him then, so the railroad could git payment from the Marshal Service. Homer took the Waxlers up into the boxcar, an' me an' Marion went on across the tracks an' out into this little stand a grass with the horses an' Arliss the mule so they could git a bite to eat. We was standin' there in the sunshine when I yawned.

"You all right, Ruben?" Marion asked me.

"I'm a little tired," I said.

"That ain't what I'm talkin' about, boy," Marion went on. "You tangled with a bad bunch a couple a times last night, an' killed some."

"I did," I said. "Backshot 'em, too."

"How you doin' with all that?" he asked.

"I been thinkin' about it some," I said. "Them boys didn't havta come after us like they done. It was a choice. I figger they woulda chose to have kilt us all if they coulda, but they couldn't. They coulda chose to spread out when comin', instead a bunchin' up like they done, but they didn't. They coulda chose to watch their backtrail, but they never done that neither. They was the kinda fellas that had probably gone most a their lives like they was just lookin' for somebody to deal harsh with 'em. They was low men an' killers. Now they been kilt or laid low. Seems kindly fair to me. I do sorta regret leavin' that one with the broke back just layin' out there like I done. I considered shootin' him, but I just couldn't do it, him helpless an' all like he was."

Marion smiled at me then, an' his eyes kindly twinkled. "Ta hell with him," he said.

* * * * *

The inside a that boxcar had a bunch a gates attached to the wall on each end past the doors. A fella could lead a horse back to the end a the car an' turn him sideways an' tie him to a ring set into the wall, then swing a gate that would come clear across the width a the car an' lock him into kindly a short an' narrow stall. Then bring in another horse next to the first one, tie him, an' swing another gate an' lock it in place, makin' another narrow little stall right next to the first one. In no time we had all five horses an' Arliss the mule penned up just as nice as ya please, although Marion's roan was some cramped. There was even a mess a straw at each end under them gates. It warn't long after we got them horses penned afore a engine showed up an' bumped us purty hard, then off we went for a ways an' stopped. Marion chained them Waxlers to one a them wall rings an' shut a stall door on 'em. About that time, we got another bump, an' off we went though the countryside, watchin out them big doors as everthin' kindly flew by at a terrible fast rate. I had never been in a train afore, an' never gone that fast afore neither, except at maybe a dead run on a good horse for just a little ways. It was some strange to just set there, rockin' back an' forth gentle like, an' seein' everthing zippin' by.

I liked it.

* * * * *

I was amazed at how soon we come to Saint Joe. No only did that train go fast, it didn't havta go around no thorn patches, or find a place to ford a stream. It could travel in a hour what a responsible fella on a good horse would take a whole day to do. In the yards at Saint Joe we stopped an' there was another bump, an' the train went on an' left us settin' there. Purty soon a fella stuck his head in the door.

"Be a few minutes, boys," he said, " an' we'll gitcha moved an' on yer way."

In a little bit we got bumped agin an' went backwards for a ways an' come up beside this ramp. There was a hinged extension on it that unfolded right up agin the bottom of the door. Me an' Homer flipped that over an' led the horses out. Marion come down then with them Waxlers, manacled 'em back to the saddle horns, an' we went into town.

* * * * *

Saint Joe was a really big place. It took us a spell just to git to the city jail. The marshal there tolt us he could keep them fellas overnight for us, but we'd havta git 'em out the next mornin' 'cause the saloon where they broke the law was in the county an' not the city. That irritated Marion some, but he let it go an' the three of us went out an' et, then got us a room at a house down the block a piece. Marion left me an' Homer then, an' struck off. It was near dark when he come back, mad as a wet hen.

"Goddamn guv'mint sonsabitches," he said. "If Jessie James had a tried to give hisself up here, instead a gittin' shot like he done, these stupid bastards would told him to come back an' try again' next week while they figgerd out who should take his man-killin' ass inta custody!"

"What's goin' on?" Homer asked.

"The goddamn city won't take them boys 'cause they claim the saloon is in the county. The county won't take 'em because they claim the saloon is in the city. The city judge I talked to said he couldn't make no decision on authority over the case 'cause that would be the bailiwick of a circuit judge 'cause I'm a goddamn U.S. Marshal, an' the circuit Judge doan git back this way for two weeks or better. Meantime, nobody seems to know what to do with them Waxlers, but tell me they cain't hold 'em for us."

Homer grinned at him. "That make ya mad, does it?" he asked.

"Hell no," Marion said. "I'm this goddam color 'cause I'm such a happy bastard!"

I couldn't help but laugh some then. Marion set down on his cot an' took his head in his hands for a minute.

"I'll git to a telegraph tomorra an' send a message over to Cameron. It ain't even in this county, but they got a jail. Maybe they'll show a little concern about this whole mess. I think the circuit Judge stops there before he comes over this way anyhow. If we have to wait on him, at least we won't have to wait as long. Meantime I'll see if we can't git some kinda federal warrant for these boys outa Jeff City 'cause they fled across state lines."

"Maybe we should just shoot 'em," Homer said.

Marion nodded. "Right after we shoot these politickin' shitheads that got us in this mess," he said.

CHAPTER SEVENTEEN

When I woke up the next mornin' Marion was already up an' dressed an' Homer was layin' in his bed, still sleepin'.

"Mornin', Ruben," Marion said to me. "I'm leavin' for the telegraph office to see if I cain't git some a this shit straightened out. You an' Homer go to the livery if ya will, an' see if we can git another horse an' lose that broke down black. Fetch yerselves, the horses an' our truck an' possibles over to the jailhouse, an' I'll met ya over that way as soon as I can. That fine with you?"

"Yessir," I said, my brain tryin' to ketch up to everthing.

"All right then," he said, an' went out the door.

The minute that door shut, Homer sat up, wide-awake.

"Hey, Rube," he said, reachin' for his pants.

"I thought you was sleepin'," I said.

"Playin' 'possum, boy," he said. "Marion ain't in a terrible good mood, ya know. I figgerd it might be better for all of us if he give you his instructions for the day than me. My mood ain't real good neither. He's some gentler with you that he is with most folks. I was up a hour ago an' took care a business. Then I laid back down an' waited for him to git up an' git gone. I'm a sneaky sumbitch ain't I?"

I grinned at him. "Yer sneaky alright, they ain't no doubt about that," I said. "As for the rest of it, I ain't no judge, not never knowin' yer mother an' all."

"Salt of the earth, Rube," he said, "but godawful handy with a willow switch."

* * * * *

We had sausage an' eggs at this little ol' place an' walked over to the livery. They was a fella in there workin' that warn't the same one we'd already done business with.

"Mornin' gents," he said. "You the boys with that Marshal that rides that big ol' roan?"

"Guilty as charged," Homer said.

"You know that black you left here has got some bad lungs doncha?"

"Yessir, we do," Homer said. "We'd care to replace that black. We got some murderers we're on the road with, an' we need a horse that can travel."

"Whatcha gonna do with the black?"

"We'll trade him in. He ain't worth nothin' to use, but a knacker might give a feller five dollars for him."

The fella thought for a minute afore he spoke up. "Gotta bay mare that might do well for ya," he said. "She was broke to saddle an' harness. Was a carriage horse, but she got to where she couldn't abide bein' strapped up next to another horse. Start bitin' an' pickin' a fight. She's all right around horses, but in harness she gits nasty. Well broke to saddle. We rent her out now an' then. I suppose I might sell her if the price was right."

Homer nodded. "I might buy her if the price was right. Bring her out."

* * * * *

We took that mare. She was a purty thing, a little delicate a leg for my taste, but with a deep chest, good feet an' knees, an' a nice way about her. Homer was some upset about how much he had to pay for her, but he had his receipt an' the marshal service was bound to pay him back if he didn't sell her.

Goin' over to the jailhouse we each had to lead a horse, which is not a real convenient thing to do as most ridin' horses ain't led around like that too much, plus there was Arliss the mule. I took a chance an' brung Arliss out like I was fixin' to lead him, but just tossed that rope over the pack. I'll be durned if he didn't foller along like that rope was tied to somethin'. Even when we come into traffic a other horses an' wagons an' such on busy streets, that little mule stayed right behind us, doin' his job like he was born to it. Homer was some amused by it an' commented that Arliss the mule was probably worth more than that bay he just bought.

We got to the jailhouse an' went inside. The feller in charge was little an' cocky, with a nose on him that kindly reminded me of a beak on a chicken.

"You them boys what brung in them two Waxler brothers?" he said, never botherin' to git up from behind his desk or offerin' to shake.

"We are," Homer said. "We're waitin' for our partner. When he shows up, we'll take 'em off yer hands."

"One of 'em has got a busted up mouth, ya know," that feller said. "He was bitchin' about it most a the night."

"Anybody git a doctor for him?" Homer asked.

"Why should we?" the jailer said. "He ain't our prisoner."

Homer smiled then. "Well," he said, "I doan know. I thought that maybe, since he was in your jail an' all, that you just might be responsible for him. Seems to me like if he's behind your bars, in your buildin', under the care a your people, that'd be sorta the Christian thing to do. Was I wrong?"

"An' another thing," the little rooster said, "they gotta be gone from here by noon. If'n they ain't, I got orders to release 'em. So yer pard better damn well be on time."

"I see," Homer said. "Yer tellin' me that, because a the time a day, you'd let two low-life criminal woman killers go free? Just turn 'em out in the street because of a clock?"

The little feller puffed up some. "Them's my orders," he said.

Homer looked at me. "You want this 'un?" he asked.

"Yessir, I do," I said, an' walked over an' set down on the side a the jailer's desk an' looked down at him.

"Sir," I said, keepin' my voice low an' my manner respectful, "two nights ago these fellas was in custody. Five other fellas took it upon theyselves to attempt to release these two an' let 'em go free. At heavy personal risk, I killed four of 'em an' crippled another one with a broke back. He's prob'ly dead by now, too. Five heavy armed an' capable men had to die by my hand, because they tried to do what yer tellin' me you are gonna do at noon today. Now friend, how do you think that makes me feel?"

He couldn't look at me, an' kept his eyes on his desk. "I dunno," he said.

"It makes me feel purty sad," I tolt him. "That's how it makes me feel. To think that I took five men's lives just so you could turn the reasons for all that killin' loose, wears on me. Whether you got orders or not, I don't believe you should do that. If you turn them boys loose, I'm gonna have to arrest 'em agin. After I arrest 'em agin, I believe I'll have to take action toward you. Federal action from a federal marshal. I'd hate to do that. Wouldn't you hate to do that, sir, if you was in my place?"

"Yessir," he said, still not lookin' up.

"Then they ain't no need for anybody to do anying they'd hate to do. Already been enough trouble an' several men kilt over this. We'll git them fellas outa here as soon as possible. Hopefully before noon. But if not, I expect 'em to be right here, in custody, when we are ready to take 'em. That all right with you?"

He looked at me then, an' was kindly pale. "That's fine," he said.

"Ain't that nice," I said. "Me an' Marshal Poteet here are gonna go for a stroll. We'll be back afore noon. It'd be good if, by the time we git back, a doctor had been here to tend to that fella's busted up mouth. Can I count on you to take care of that, friend?"

"Yessir. I'll git a doc."

"I appreciate it," I said an' walked out the door.

Homer caught up with me outside an' slapped the brim a my hat right smart.

"Ain't you a mess?" he said.

* * * * *

Marion showed up a little after eleven, just as the doctor was leavin'. We got things took care of an' was gone by a quarter 'til twelve.

CHAPTER EIGHTEEN

We was still in town when I rode up beside Marion an' asked him where we was goin'.

"Cameron," he said. "I usta know the town marshal there. A feller by the name of Henry Culver. He got hisself kilt two or three year ago by them Kidder Boys an' a couple a their bunch. Was a purty good feller. I doan know who's the law over there now. I just sent a telegraph to the office an' got one back sayin' to come on over. We could use their jailhouse 'til we git this straightened out."

"How far is it?" I asked him.

"Far enough," Marion said. "Long as the horses hold up, we ain't stoppin'. We might make it by nightfall. I got another telegraph off to Jeff City an' put 'em onto gittin' me a federal warrant for these two. By rights, we should be able to git one, them runnin' up into Iowa like they done. Plus, I asked for charges on resistin' arrest, armed misconduct an' such, an' any other federal or state warrants they could come up with. I went by the Blue Island Saloon an' talked to that gal that got cut up. When I told her it wodden cost her nothin' an' that I could git her expenses for travel an' such, she agreed to testify. When she found out them boys was in custody, she admitted to knowin' exactly who they was, an' one a her friends confessed she'd seen 'em there that night an' said she stand up an' testify, too. The gal that got cut up is movin' to her sister's place in Clinton. She told me how to git aholt of her."

"So what do we do now?" I asked him.

"We git these boys behind bars afore somebody tries to take 'em away from us," he said.

"You think they will?"

"I think they would," Marion said, "if we was close to 'em, but we got a fair head start. That bunch may not even know that we got 'em yet, much less where we're goin' with 'em."

"So we're all right then," I said.

Marion nodded. "For a little while, but this ain't gonna be no big secret very long. You know how word travels. We got the brothers under arrest and, between you an' me, we kilt a few of the herd. We're fine now, Ruben, but you can damn shore bet there's some ol' boys out there that ain't terrible happy about the situation. I ain't fixin' to sell my guns or nothin'."

The brother with the busted teeth, Jim, spoke up. "Yer all dead," he said. "You just ain't been et by the buzzards yet."

Marion smiled an' turned in his saddle. "Busted nose would go right smart with them missin' teeth," he said.

Jim had nothin' to say to that.

* * * * *

We come into town a little after dark an' went to a place that warn't like no jailhouse I'd ever heard of. It was kindly a hotel like. A deputy come out an' greeted us an' we tucked Jack an' Jim away for the night, but the cell was actually a hotel room. It warn't fancy or nothin' like that, an' it was locked up tight, but that's what it was. Sherrif Knox showed up. He had some age on him an' was a short fella an' broad, with big ol' shoulders, near no neck, an' arms that helt the material a his shirt right snug. He looked to me like he could just pick Arliss the mule up an' walk right on away with him. He wore a Colt, an' when he come in he had a big ol' double barrel, Long Tom ten gauge.

He shook hands with Marion an' Homer, an' turned to me an' smiled. "Looks like you are the young'un a the group," he said. "Them other two make you do all the dirty work?"

"Yessir," I said. "It's terrible the way they treat me."

"Youth has it's price, son," he said, an' stuck out his hand. I took it. It was like grabbin' a chunk a wood.

"I'm Ruben Beeler, Sheriff Knox," I said. "Good to meet you."

"Call me Stump, Ruben," he said. "I doan hold much with titles. Title doan make the man. You fellers got them two rascals shut up?"

"Yessir," I said.

"Have ya et?"

"Nossir," I tolt him.

"Neither have I," he went on. "Let's go over to the Victory an' git a bite. Supper's on the sheriff's office."

* * * * *

We didn't talk much durin' the meal, which was some chicken that took considerable effort to git chewed up so a fella could swaller it. After we et, we walked back to the hotel an' set out on the porch. A deputy had took our horses an' Arliss the mule to a livery while we was gone. A nice light rain started up then, an' Stump come up with a bottle a whiskey. He passed it down the line a time or two, an' eased back in his rocker.

"How much time we got, ya reckon?" he said.

"If that bunch is clear up in Iowa," Marion said, "we got a few days. Could have a lot less, but they ain't gonna use no train. They'll come on horseback."

"They in Ioway, are they?" Stump asked.

"I ain't rightly sure," Marion said. "Them brothers an' their bunch was, but I heer'd that the main herd hung out up in Nodaway County or thereabouts. They could be here in a couple days if they wanted to go at it that hard."

Stump pulled on his mustache. "Mebbe we need a scout," he said.

Marion nodded. "That ain't the worst idea I ever heard," he said.

Everbody just set for a spell then, listenin' to the rain an' watchin' a Junebug git too close to the top of a oil lamp's globe ever so often. Purty soon, Stump spoke up.

"Can Ruben do it?" he said.

Marion smiled. "When we took Jack an' Jim," he said, "I had ta shoot one a them boys that was with 'em. As we was on the trail we had a horse come over bad, so ol' Ruben here went back an' took down our pursuers. They was five of 'em."

Stump nodded. "That's notable," he said.

"Yessir it is," Homer said. "He's got a purty good horse, too. That little buck is steady."

"Well," Stump said, "I reckon he outa strike off day after tomorrow then."

Marion an' Homer nodded.

"Wait a minute," I said. "Ain't I got no say in this?"

"Not much," Homer said.

Sheriff Stump spoke up then. "Like I mentioned before, Ruben," he said, "youth has its price."

* * * * *

After breakfast the next mornin', I found out where the livery was an' went over there to look in on Willie an' Arliss the mule. Our horses was all in stalls an' on fresh beddin'. I was checkin' Willie over when this fella on a peg leg come out.

"I grained all of 'em this mornin'," he said. "I'll do it again' this evenin'. They's all in good shape, considerin' how much you boys been travelin'. That little buck is a nice feller. Right agreeable. A day's rest an' he'll be good as new. You ain't ridin' off 'til in the mornin' are ya?"

I was some surprised at how much he knowed. "Nossir," I said, "not 'til tomorrow."

"I'll trim him up real good this afternoon," the fella said, "and git some new shoes on him. His feet are sound. I looked him over real close."

"I appreciate all yer trouble," I tolt him.

He waved a hand at me. "Nothin' to it," he said. "Stump says yer a good man an' a tough marshal. That's enough for me. After I shoe that buck, I'll stand him in the creek out yonder. It's spring fed an' nice an' cool. You won't have nothin' to worry about. Yer possibles is locked up in the shed, safe an' sound."

He limped off then, goin' about his business.

* * * * *

I didn't figger I'd be on the trail too long, an' I'd havta travel light. Arliss the mule couldn't go with me. If'n I had to hurry, his short legs wouldn't be near able to keep up with Willie, an' I wouldn't wanna just ride off an' leave him. I'd growed some fond a that little mule.

I went to a general store an' found they had some cans a that beans an' pork. I got a half a dozen of 'em an' a fair bit a jerky, an' some canned peaches, too. I'd havta keep cold camps, not wantin' the night sight of a fire or the smell a woodsmoke to let on where I was. They had some peppermint sticks that I bought, an' some maple sugar candy that, by the smell of it, had cinnamon in it. I got a few a them too, knowin' how Willie seem to kindly enjoy cinnamon an' all.

After I done all that, I went back to the sheriff's office an' cleaned the Schofield an' my Yellaboy. I was workin' on the little scattergun when this young fella come in. He was wearin' a badge.

"Howdy," he said, holdin' out a hand. "Names Dally. Yer Ruben, ain't ya?"

I shook with him. "That's me," I said. "Proud to know ya."

"Thank ya, Marshal," he said, "but it's me that's proud to know you. I heard whatcha done when them fellas come after ya. That was somethin', that was."

"It was somethin'," I said. "No doubt about that."

"Lord!" he said, lookin' at that little shotgun. "Ain't that fearsome? You shoot them boys with that?"

"One of 'em," I said.

"I bet that knocked the shit out of him," he said. "Mercy!"

I didn't say nothin' then, just give the scattergun a final wipe, loaded it, an' slipped it back in the holster.

"You wear that mankiller on yer belt?" he asked me.

"Sometimes," I said.

"Shotgun on one side an', what's that? A Schofield?"

"It is," I said.

"An' a Schofield on the other," he went on. "By God, that is a battery, that is. What kind a rifle ya carry?"

"A Yellaboy," I said. "You mind a question?"

"Nossir, Marshal," he said, "go ahead."

"You ever shoot a man, Dally?" I asked him.

"Not yet," he said.

"There ain't no pride in it, son," I said. "Ain't no joy in it neither. There's just blood an' guts, an' tears, an' life, the same damn life that's in you an' me, leakin' outa a person an' bein' wasted on some foolish purpose that ain't never worth what it costs. I ain't no hero, Dally, not by a damn site I ain't. I'm a killer is what I am. Nothin' but a killer, an' that is a hard thing. Ain't but a short step between bein' a killer an' becomin' a murderer. It seems to me that a murderer ain't nothin' more than a killer that's got so proud of it, or so used to it, that he let it git away from him. They ain't but one Angel a Death, Dally, an' that poor sonofabitch is to be pitied by those a us he ain't come for yet."

He stood there lookin' at me for a minute, then swallerd.

"I'm sorry, Marshal," he said.

"Not yet you ain't," I tolt him. "I just hope you ain't never as sorry as I am."

He left then, an' Sheriff Stump come walkin' up from outa the back. He smiled at me.

"I heard whatcha told Dally," he said. "How old are you, Ruben?"

"I ain't yet twenty-one," I said.

"Marshal," he said, "you coulda fooled me."

CHAPTER NINETEEN

I set out the next mornin' under cloudy skies an' a warm west wind, with full saddle bags an' a big bedroll. Willie was carryin' his feet some high, the way a horse'll do now an' then when wearin' fresh shoes they ain't used to. I headed north stayin' away from worn trails to avoid actual runnin' up on nobody. It made the goin' some harder, bein' in unbroke country like I was, but Wille was as game as ever an' usually picked the best way through without me sayin' a word about it. We had to detour a time or two 'cause a that bob-wire fencin' that was beginnin' to crop up now an' then. Free range was gonna be a thing a the past afore long, I reckoned. I warn't no cowboy so it didn't make a big difference to me, but I could shore understand why a lot of the hands didn't have much use for it, it gittin' in the way like it done. In the afternoon we come on a calf that had got stuck in some of it, gittin a loose strand around one a his legs an' caught up. His momma, a brindle longhorn, was stickin' close to him an' took some exception to me fussin' with him like I done, tossin' her head an' comin' at me on short charges. He was gouged up a little in that leg, but not too bad. I was on the off side of the wire an' got him loose after a bit a fussin' an' she was right glad when he come scamperin' away from me an' up to her.

I made camp that night by a little wet-weather crick that had some water in it. I et a cold can a them beans an' pork after havin' a helluva time gittin' it open. It started spittin' a light drizzle. I put on my slicker, stretched out, an' pulled that ground cloth up over me, layin' it on my hat to keep it off my face, an' slept real good. The next mornin' it was clear an' bright, an' things warn't terrible wet. I reckon that drizzle was all they was an' it never did come to a real rain. The wind had shifted to the north-northwest an' was right smart. I took a chance an' made a fire an' had bacon an' frybread for breakfast, figurin' what smoke they was would blow away an' spread out real quick. I do like a hot breakfast on the trail.

Long about midday we was in a little valley east of a purty good-sized run a hills, when Willie tossed his head an' snorted some. I went up on one a them hills near most a the way, then tied Willie off on a post oak, grabbed the Yellaboy, an' went on up, crouchin' down an' stayin' low at the top. Down in the bottoms on the other side an' north a ways I seen two riders. They was spread out on each side of the trail quite a bit, movin' at a walkin' pace. I figgerd right then, them bein' so far apart an' all, they was outriders for somebody else. I took off my hat an' laid low. About the time they come abreast a me, another bunch appeared to the north. They was far enough away I had to wait a spell for 'em to git close enough to git a good look. Turned out it was a buckboard wagon with one feller drivin' the team an' another one settin' up in the bed in a big ol' padded chair.

They was ten or twelve other fellers ridin' with that wagon. Time it got even with where I was, two more outriders showed up, comin' along close to a half-mile behind. It was unusual to see folks travelin' in such a manner, an' I reckoned that this was probably the bunch everbody was so concerned about. I got down off that hill then an' turned back south with Willie at a high lope. I sorta missed little ol' Arliss the mule bein' with us, but I was glad we'd left him back at the livery. He woulda never been able to keep pace.

* * * * *

Willie an' me kept after it 'til it got too dark for him to see, an' made a cold camp. We was both some wore out. I give him a couple a them maple-cinnamon candies I'd brung with us an' didn't bother to hobble him. He was easy as tired as I was an' would stay close. While I stretched out under my slicker, I heard him grunt when he laid down. When I woke up the next morin' it was just comin' light. Willie was standin' over me, head down. I took another one a them candies outa my pocket an' give it to him. He backed off then an' stood there munchin' on it. That horse was a hog for them things.

We had a fair lead on that bunch. After I got organized an' ready, we went up a hill an' down onto the trail on the other side. I give Willie his head an' asked for a little hurry. He hit his stride in a short lope an' off we went, me eatin' jerky in the saddle. He kept that pace up until a ways into the afternoon, an' we come back into town. I dropped him off at the livery, sweatin' an' blowin'. The fella there said he'd cool Willie out an' brush him down for me. I thanked him an' hustled down to the sheriff's office. Marion, Homer, an' Stump was settin' outside when I come up. Homer grinned at me.

"You did remember to take a horse on your little trip didn't ya?" he said.

"His name's Willie," I said.

"Son, ya look like ya done the whole thing on foot," Homer said. "Are ya all right?"

"We hurried," I tolt him. "There's a bunch of 'em comin', but I doan think they'll git close afore late tomorrow. A dozen or so fellas an' one settin' in a big chair in the back of a buckboard wagon."

"That'd be Clovis, I speck," Stump said. "I'm kindly surprised he's still above water. He's gotta be seventy or better. You say he's got a dozen with him?"

"Mor'n that, countin' the outriders," I said. "They was four a them."

"Ruben," Marion said, "ya look plumb wore out. Why doan you git over to the barber shop an' git a bath an' a shave, then meet us at the Victory an' we'll see if they got anythin' worth eatin'."

I did. Their pork chops was some better than the chicken. After we et, I went down to the livery to check on Willie. He was lookin' fine an' eatin' a nice mash. Even though it warn't full dark, I went to bed then an' slept until a hour or so after daybreak the next mornin'. I gotta admit, I was some stiff an' sore when I woke up.

* * * * *

Stump put two a his three deputies on duty the next day. The one name a Dally was stationed to the north outside a town a ways, but nobody showed up. The third deputy was set out after dark as nighthawk. The followin' mornin' we was sure that bunch'd git to town, but' things was quiet. We was settin outside the office on the porch near suppertime, when a rider come down the street on a classy lookin' big ol' rangy sorrel with a white blaze and four white socks. He was a thin fella wearin' a black hat with a flat brim, a buckskin vest, an' carryin' two Colts in crossdraws. He brung that big sorrel to a stop at the rail in front of us an' spoke up.

"Marshal Marion Daniels," he said, his voice low an' whispery. "Arkansas Bill Cole," Marion said. "How the hell are you?"

CHAPTER TWENTY

It was kindly like time just stopped for a minute or two, like they was nothin' else but Bill Cole an' Marion Daniels lookin' at each other, neither one of 'em worried, neither one a 'em scared, neither one of 'em in no kinda hurry. The air got thick it seemed, an' none of us moved a inch.

"Neither one of us got this far 'cause we was stupid, Marion," Bill said, keepin' both his hands on the saddle horn.

"Might not be a winner," Marion said, settin' real still.

"Might not," Bill agreed.

"Might bury both of us," Marion said.

"Might," Bill said.

They looked at each other for a minute.

"That was a mess over in Deer Run," Bill went on. "I never intended for things to go that way. Pig Wiggins done a terrible thing. Shame yer boy Ruben there didn't kill him the first time they tangled. Bigger shame he come with me in the first place. I regret it. I do."

"You think yer regret fixes anything?" Marion asked him.

"Nope," Bill said. "You can fix somethin' that's broke. Ya cain't fix nothin' that's shattered. Things got shattered that day."

"What brings you here, Arkansas Bill Cole?"

Bill might have smiled then, it was hard to tell. "Heer'd about this mess when I was over in Saint Joe," he said. "Know about Clovis Waxler an' his bunch. In the ol' days, they killed a lot a folks up on the Missouri an' the Nodaway. Some of 'em was families with women an' children. I doan hold with that. I figger he's as bad as he ever was. Even if he ain't, it's a unpaid debt. Thought I might be able to help."

"What makes you think we need help?" Marion asked.

"What makes you think you don't?" Bill said.

Marion nodded. "How much?" he asked.

"Just a badge," Bill said.

"Piece a tin ain't a lot to pay for Arkansas Bill Cole's gun hand," Marion said.

"They was a time when it was enough," Bill said. "I ain't forgot them days."

Marion looked at him for a spell. "I reckon I ain't neither," he said. "We'll be here when ya git done at the livery. It's back the way ya come in."

The air thinned up then an' everthing settled. I never saw no change in Marion or Bill, but I shore felt it. Homer did too. After Bill Cole turned that sorrel away an' went off, Homer looked at me an' winked.

"By God, boys," he said, liftin' his twist outa a pocket, "this here is what ya might call strange bedfellers."

Everbody was quiet 'til Homer cut off a chaw an' set it in his cheek. Then Stump spoke up.

"Arkansas Bill Cole," he said. "I know the name. Pistoleer ain't he?"

"Is now," Marion said. "Used to be a U.S. Marshal. We had some bad business with a feller that was with him over in Deer Run a ways back. Ol' boy name a Pig Wiggins. Kilt a deputy an' the woman that was with him. Ruben had to shoot him."

Stump didn't say nothin', just nodded.

"Bill is one of the two best hands with a gun I ever seen or heer'd of," Homer said. "The other one is settin' on the porch with us."

Stump nodded agin. "You gonna take him to use, Marshal?" he asked.

Marion studied on it for a minute afore he spoke up. "Reckon so," he said. "If Bill gits the badge, he'll live up to it. Any a your boys worth much?"

Stump shook his head. "Untried," he said. "They're drunk wrasslers an' rounder thumpers. They ain't never been in nothin' like this could git to be. Hell, neither have I, boys. I won't run on ya, but I ain't no slinger. A shootist like Arkansas Bill Cole could be right handy."

Marion nodded. "Always was," he said.

* * * * *

Nobody talked much when we et. It was comin' dark when we got back to settin' on the porch. Bill Cole rolled a cigarette an' spoke up.

"Never seen no jail in a hotel before," he said.

"We're trend setters here in Cameron," Stump said. "Thinkin' about puttin' a stable in the schoolhouse."

Everbody kindly chuckled at that, even Bill. "How many comin'?" he asked.

"Mor'n a dozen I reckon," I said. "Mebbe fifteen or sixteen. I never got too close."

"You seen 'em?"

"Yessir," I said. "I come on 'em near two days north a here. They've had time to show up."

"The ol' man with 'em?" Bill asked.

"They was a fella ridin' in a big ol' chair up in the back of a buckboard."

Bill nodded. "Old bones," he said. "You boys all stayin' here of a night?"

"Are," Marion said. "Prob'ly shouldn't."

"Need to thin out."

Homer spoke up. "Marion, why don't you squat at the livery tonight," he said. "Rube, you git yerself over toward the Victory in that roomin' house. Me an' the Sharps'll find a perch down the street a ways. How 'bout you, Bill?"

"I'm good where I set," Bill said.

"Well," Homer went on, "I'm done." He stepped in the office an' come out with that big ol' Sharps an' struck off down the street.

Marion looked at Bill. "I'm fresh outa badges," he said.

"Nothin' but tin anyways," Bill said. "I kin do without. Badge doan make the man, nohow."

"Nossir, it don't," Marion said, "but the man can shore make the badge. Good to have ya, Bill."

Marion stood up an' headed off toward the livery. I took up my yellaboy an' follerd along.

* * * * *

I checked on Willie an' Arliss the mule while I was there, an' they was both good. I was fixin' to leave as Marion spread out his roll.

"Bill just gonna set out in front a the jail all night?" I asked him.

"I reckon," he said.

"When we had supper," I went on, "he didn't hardly eat mor'n a bite or two."

"Never does," Marion said.

"What's wrong with him?" I asked.

Marion smiled. "Mebbe nothin'," he said. "Mebbe there's somethin' wrong with the rest of us. He's been this way as long as I knowed him. Don't hardly sleep, don't hardly eat, just keeps goin'. Bill is like a razor, boy. A razor ain't got but one purpose. Ya git it out when ya need it. The rest a the time ya leave it alone so ya doan cut yerself."

"Seems kindly queersome to me," I said.

"It's Arkansas Bill Cole, Ruben," Marion said. "That's what it is."

* * * * *

I studied on it some, walkin' to the roomin' house. It seemed to me like Bill was mor'n human an' less than human at the same time. I knowed Marion would rather not mess with him. If a fella could put Marion Daniels on the balk, he was somethin' terrible good to have on yer side. An' just somthin' terrible, too.

* * * * *

My little room was fine, an' the bed warn't too bouncy, but I never did really sleep, I guess. I dozed some, off an' on, but was glad to see the sun comin' up. I put on my boots an' went out back to the convenience. Then I cleaned up in the washstand, put on my gunbelt with that twelve gauge, grabbed the Yellaboy, stepped outside, an' looked down toward the office. Bill Cole was still settin' right where we left him. I seen Marion walkin' my way an' pointed to the Victory. He nodded an' I went in an' set. He come in an' joined me at the table.

"Ruben," he said. "Git any sleep did ya?"

"Like a baby," I said. "I even wet the bed."

He grinned some at that, an' we ordered ham an' eggs. We was about halfway through 'em when Homer come in, draggin' that big ol' Sharps. Folks in the place was lookin' at us some.

"Where'd you spend the night?" Marion asked him.

"Saloon down the way has a flat roof. I'm goin' back after I eat. Good cover, good range, good field a fire. Thought I'd set up there with the Sharps an' play God, in case them fellers wanna take a run at us today. I doubt they will, though. They doan know enough yet."

"They got somebody in town lookin' things over I bet," Marion said.

Homer nodded. "Be fools not to," he said. "If the ol' man is still in charge, might not be a bad thing. He's purty much had shit his own way for a spell. Ain't overly used to nobody with ability standin' up to him. Could be in for a surprise."

"Could be," Marion said.

Homer looked at me. "Jump in here any time, Rube," he said. "Yer part a all this, ya know. You got a opinion on something?"

"I already took down five a them boys," I said. "I'm just waitin' for you ol' fellas to ketch up."

Homer grinned at Marion. "Humble ain't he?" he said.

"Rare in one so young," Marion said, an' slapped me on the shoulder.

* * * * *

Me an' Marion finished our breakfasts an' hung around 'til Homer was done. The three of us stepped outside then. There warn't hardly nobody on the street at all. Word had spread, I reckon. 'Bout that time the deputy name a Dally come tearin' up on a little line back dun an' slid to a stop in front a Stump's office. He was outa the saddle in headin' inside afore the horse collected hisself.

"Shame the Pony Express went outa business," Homer said, an' we walked over that way. Stump met us on the porch.

"Wagon an' three outriders comin' in," Stump said.

"I'm gone," Homer said, an' struck off down toward the saloon.

"Keep yer boys inside, if ya will," Marion said.

"They is yer prisoners," Stump said. "We'll back ya up."

"Thank ya. That winda in the cell that faces the front a the place open?"

"It is," Stump said.

Marion nodded an' walked out onto the porch. I follerd along. He looked over at Bill Cole, still settin' in the chair like he done all night, I guess. The only thing I could see that had changed was a badge on the front a his vest. Marion noticed it, too.

"Bill," he said, "I see ya found some tin."

"Never give it back," Bill said. "Been carryin' it all this time in case I might git needful of it."

Marion smiled. "Looks good on ya," he said.

"Sets off my eyes," Bill replied, brimin' his hat a mite. "Got fellers comin' for a parlay, I guess."

Marion nodded. "You got it?" he asked.

"Have," Bill said.

Marion turned to me. "Ruben," he said, "I'll do the talkin'. You see me lift my hat, you shoot the team with that little twelve gauge. That'll upset everbody's applecart. Got it?"

"Yessir."

"Good. Take the left side a the porch."

I went over an' stood leanin' up' a post with my left side facin' the street. That way I was a skinnier target for anybody that come up. 'Cause the shotgun was already pointed in the general direction a where that buckboard would be as it set in the holster, it would take less time for me to aim. Bill got up, moved about ten feet to his right, an' set down agin. Warn't mor'n a minute or two 'til a buckboard come down the street with a old fella settin' up in the bed in a big ol' chair. There was two fellas ridin' behind the wagon, an' one on the left side. He caught my attention.

He had on a skinny brim hat with a pinched crown an' was some heavy set. His mouth was mostly covered up with a long black mustache that hung down over his lips, an' he was wearin' two navy conversions in a double crossdraw rig an' had a coach gun layin' over his saddle between him an' the horn. It was hard to tell, but it looked to me like he was smilin'.

The fella drivin' the buckboard pulled the team up to the rail an' waited while them other two got off an' tied their horses to the rear a the wagon. Then they swung down kindly a ladder-like affair on the end a that buckboard, an' the ol boy in the chair got up an' walked back to where they stood, usin' a cane in each hand. They helped him git down that ladder, then they spread out some. He worked his way around the wagon an' up to about twenty feet from us, then leaned on them canes purty heavy an' looked us over. It took awhile for all that to happen. The whole time, that fella with the mustache just set an' smiled. The ol' fella looked at Marion.

"You got my boys locked up here," he said.

"Anything is possible," Marion said. "Who are you?"

"You know damn good an' well who I am," the ol' man said.

"I ain't never seen ya afore," Marion said. "What's yer name?"

"I am Clovis Waxler, goddammit!"

"We got a couple a fellers name a Waxler here in a cell," Marion said. "They any a your kin?"

"Yer about a smartass sonofabitch, ain't ya?" Clovis said. "I wanna talk to my boys!"

"Go ahead," Marion said. "They're right through that winda yonder. They can hear you."

"In private, goddammit!"

"Nope," Marion said.

"No?" Waxler yelled. "What the hell you mean, no? I got a right to talk to my boys in private!"

"You ain't got right number one with me, mister," Marion said. "You talk to them shitheads on my terms or you doan talk to 'em at all. You ain't in Nodaway County today."

One of the boys yelled out the window then. "That bastard knocked out my teeth, Daddy!"

"The older they git," Marion said, "the harder it is to teach 'em manners. Reckon you failed 'em when they was children."

"You kilt six a my men, you sonofabitch!" Waxler yelled.

"I killed one a your men," Marion said. "This young feller over here killed the other five. It can stop there. Up to you."

Waxler took a minute to collect himself. "Maybe you don't understand," he said. "I'm gonna git my boys. There ain't no doubt about that."

"Your boys killed one woman an' ruined another one. They'll be goin to trial if they live."

"Them was just whores!" Waxler shouted. "You ain't keepin' my boys for a pair a no gawdammed whores! I'll have them an' kill ever one a you bastards afore this is over."

Things got quiet, an' I heard Bill Cole speak up.

"Why wait?" he said.

Then come a shot, an' the feller with the mustache pitched sideways offa his horse, a pistol slippin' outa his grasp. Right behind that shot come two more, real quick, an' Clovis Waxler fell. Marion an' me both had guns to hand an' none a the rest a them fellas moved. About that time Waxler started cussin'. I looked at him then. He warn't hit at all, but one his canes was splintered an' broke. Arkansas Bill Cole had shot that cane a his right out from under him. Just like that.

Marion looked at them two fellas standin' there. "Git him an' the pistolero in your wagon, boys, an' git out. When he settles down, tell him that if I see him again outside a courtroom, I'll kill him. He don't git his way no more, an' if'n he wants to take this to the grave, I'll damn shore be glad to oblige him."

It took them boys a while to git the ol' man carried up into that wagon, an' he never stopped cussin' the whole time. Once he got loaded they didn't delay, but left town right smart. We watched 'em go, an' Marion turned to Bill Cole.

"Well, you ain't lost a step, have ya?" he said.

Cole smiled. "Warn't nothin' you couldn't a done," he said.

"Doan know if I woulda tried it," Marion said.

"I prob'ly wouldn't a tried it neither," Bill said, "if I warn't in a hurry. That's why it took two shots."

"What are you in a rush about?" Marion asked him.

Bill stood up. "Goddammit, Marion," he said, "I've had ta piss for a fuckin' hour. I didn't think you was ever gonna shut up."

He walked off the porch then an' left us, laughin'.

CHAPTER TWENTY-ONE

After Bill went off, them deputies come outa the office an' commenced to makin' a fuss. Marion stood it for a minute or two, then started off toward the Victory. I fell in with him.

We had just set, an' ordered pie an' coffee when Homer come in, packin' that Sharps a his, an' took a seat.

"That was some shootin'," he said.

"I doan understand how come that fella, with three of us standin' there like we was, an' more inside, woulda gone for his gun like he done," I said. "It doan make no sense to me."

"Bill flinched him," Marion said.

I didn't know what he meant an' I told him so.

"Arkansas Bill Cole is a ol' bull, boy," Marion said. "That feller come up here an' didn't show no respect to him, settin' there on that horse cocky like he was, smilin' an' all. A man like Bill Cole, skillful as he is, doan cotton to that kinda behavior from somebody. He knowed them other three warn't slingers or nothin'. Pistoleers doan drive no wagon for a cripple or lift one up an' down from a buckboard neither. You coulda done for them boys right smart. Plus, the dead feller was scared. That's why he was smilin'. That's also why he had the coach gun across his saddle. Stupid. Tryin' to balance that shotgun like he done was just a distraction. Folks like Bill don't let theyselves git distracted. All Bill had to do was take in a short breath, or just jerk a arm a tiny little bit, or maybe just lift his chin a mite, an' that fool, bein' short on confidence like he was, would try for his gun. Make no mistake, Ruben. Bill started it an' Bill finished it. It warn't nothin' but murder, boy. Legal murder. Arkansas Bill Cole is harder than hickory."

"How come he shot that cane out from under that ol' fella?"

"'Cause he couldn't shoot Waxler hisself. That ol' man was no threat to him, but he had ta do somethin', so he put him down the only way he could."

"An' because he was just showin' off," Homer said. "Ol' man Waxler ain't used to nobody standin' up to him. He's had it purty much his way for quite a spell. He come in here makin' threats an' shit, an' Bill shoots his slinger an' knocks the ol' boy flat down in the dirt. Got the best of him. That there is whatcha call a unusual development. Waxler is gonna have to study on that some. An' word a what happened will spread through his bunch like wildfire. With three shots, Arkansas Bill Cole has created what is knowed as unease among the opposition."

"That was some shootin'," I said.

Marion nodded. "It was," he agreed.

"Could you a done it?" I asked him.

Marion smiled at me then. "Didn't have to," he said.

* * * * *

We finished up an' went on back to the office. Stump was settin' at his desk when we come in.

"Mayor was here," he said.

"Scared shitless, I reckon," Homer said.

Stump nodded. "Purty much," he said. "Doan want no bullets flyin' around his town, doan want his citizens put in no danger, doan want no innocent bystanders gittin' shot to shit."

"Don't want to lose no votes in the next election," Marion said.

"That's the big one," Stump said.

"I reckon," Marion went on, "he'd like us to take our prisoners an' move on down the trail."

"He mentioned that," Stump said. "I told him that this wadden about them boys no more. Not really. That Waxler probably had a hard-on for the whole town by now, an' that if you left it'd just be easier for him an' his bunch to make more trouble. He don't see it that way."

"He wouldn't," Marion said.

"So," Stump said, "I am officially expressin' to you the mayor's desire that you take your prisoners and vacate the City of Cameron. Unofficially, I'm remindin' you that, you bein' federal an' all, you can tell the mayor to shove it up his ass an' all this'll be over afore a herd a lawyers has time to figger out who has what authority."

Marion smiled. "Where's yer telegraph?" he asked.

"In the Overland office. On down south a the livery where you got your stock about a block."

Marion nodded an' struck off. Me an' Homer went out onto the porch then an' settin' there, in his usual spot, was Arkansas Bill Cole.

"I ain't big on runnin' from nobody," he said.

Homer grinned. "Hell, Bill," he said, "this is yer fault anyways. If you hadden a missed Waxler an' just shot that cane like ya done, all this would be over."

Bill nodded. "Must be gittin' old," he said. "Losin' my eyesight."

"I doan know myself," Homer said, "but they say that with advancin' age, the eyes is the second thing on a man that quits workin'."

"More than that," Bill said.

* * * * *

It was early afternoon when Marion come back. He was not happy. He set down right smart like an' stared out inta the street for a spell, then shook his head.

"Goddam politics an' goddam politicians," he grumbled. "They ain't got nothin' figgerd out yet on the jurisdiction mess for Saint Joe. Circuit judge won't git offa his ass an' make no decision or we could just make a run for it over there. Nossir. They did git a federal warrant on these boys for runnin' across state lines to evade apprehension by a federal officer, or some kinda shit like that. They're gonna talk it over an' send me a telegraph in the mornin' an' let me know what they want us ta do. Damn nice that a pack a ol' boys, settin' on their asses in a office somewhere's, gits ta decide how we gotta take care a this mess, ain't it?"

"We got a little time," Homer said. "That bunch ain't likely to come tearin' in here too quick all fulla try. They got to think it over. Hell, Marion, they cain't be terrible far outa town anyways. Look how early they come in today. Why doan me an' Rube go for a little ride this evenin' an' locate them fellers. Make a cold camp, git up nice an' early in the mornin', an' discourage their asses a little bit."

"All right with me," I said.

Marion stood up. "I'm hungry," he said, an' struck off toward the Victory.

Homer looked at me. "I could eat," he said.

I got up an' we stepped down off the porch. Arkansas Bill Cole didn't move.

"You comin', Bill?" I asked him.

He give his head a little shake. "Better not," he said.

That evenin', me an' Homer walked down to the livery an' collected our horses. I was shakin' out the saddle blanket when he spoke up.

"You any good with that Yallerboy?" he asked.

"Fair," I said. "We gonna be shootin' folks?"

Homer shook his head. "Ain't my intent," he said. "We got to slow them boys down, Rube. Much as I hate to do it, we're gonna have ta shoot a few horses."

"Lord," I said, "I wish we wouldn't."

"So do I, boy," Homer said, "but we cain't just dry-gulch a bunch a fellers. They come at us fixin' to kill us, that is a different matter. That's self-defense. I ain't fixin' to walk inta their camp and start yellin' come an' git me, or nothin' like that. You can if ya want to, but I'd advise agin it."

"Reckon not," I said.

"Can ya hit a horse at a hunnerd yards?"

"Reckon so," I said.

"Can ya miss one?"

"Reckon so," I said.

"All right," Homer said, tossin' his saddle up on that gray with the bad ear. "Let's go find 'em."

* * * * *

Warn't hard to do. A little after dark we smelt their smoke an' stayed down wind an' follerd it up a rise that looked down over the camp from less than a quarter mile. They was two camps, actually, an' two fires.

"Lookee thar," Homer said. "Got another bunch with 'em now. Looks to be close to thirty of 'em total. We must be some nasty sonsabitches for 'em to need that many hands to git us. Come first light, we'll deal with 'em."

* * * * *

We pulled back about a mile to the east then, an' made a cold camp. We was settin' in the dark under a half moon, eatin' on some jerky an' biscuits, when Homer spoke up.

"We'll set up a little afore dawn," he said. "On the east side a the camp is a low hill about three hunnerd yards out. I'll be up there. You'll be down on a little rise down in front of it just over a hunnerd yards out. They was drinkin' quite a bit. Outa be purty thick-headed come mornin'. Won't expect us to come after 'em. Their ridin' stock is all on a picket line."

"How can you know all that?" I asked him. "I looked that place over just like you did, an' all I could see was them two fires an' some shadows an' shit."

"I always been able to," he said. "It kindly amazes me that other folks cain't see everthing like I do. I'll take the first shot in the mornin'. The sun'll be comin' up behind me when we start an' will be right in their eyes. Once you hear that big 45-90 go off, git ta shootin' along the picket line down around them horse's feet. Shoot yer ten, reload, an' shoot ten, reload an' shoot ten more. If they ain't nobody on horseback comin' your way by then, try some more rounds if ya feel like it, but doan push yer luck. I'll have hit two or three of the horses by the time yer done with the first loads. Between the blood-scent in the air, them fellers all runnin' around, an' you kickin' up dirt an' dust by them horses, they'll spook, tear out the picket line, break the rope, an' run off. Time comes, you git on that buck a an' ride right toward me. Won't be nobody able ta git a bead on ya, lookin' into the sun. I'll just keep shootin' inta the camp 'til you git to me, then we'll head for town. Them boys'll be only half awake an' scared shitless, with their mounts scattered out down the way. I really doan think nobody'll chase us. I didn't see no horses under saddle, an' with all the confusion an' blood scent in the air, they'll play hell ketchin' aholt a any mounts anyway. We oughta be able to put most of 'em afoot by the time we're finished. I know ya hate the thought a horses gittin' shot. Better them than you. We got it to do, Rube. We need to git it done."

He was right, an' I knowed it. I thought on it for a spell, but I couldn't say nothin' to him. Homer was already in his roll an' snorin'.

* * * * *

It went purty much the way Homer thought it would. Only a couple a fellas was even up when we started in on 'em. It was a mess. Men runnin' ever which way, horses screamin' an' buckin' an' tearin' off an' draggin' pieces a broke picket line. I shot thirty rounds afore I quit an' struck off up that hill toward Homer. I don't believe I hit nothin' livin'. If I did, I didn't intend to. Two riders managed to come after me. As I topped the hill, Homer shot one of 'em offa his horse, an' the other one give up. Them ol' boys musta thought the wrath a God had descended on 'em. I never seen such confusion. I doan know how many horses got kilt, but Homer wouldn't a shot no more than he had to, I reckon. What we done would give them fellers somethin' to think about afore they tangled with us, but hell, they was a whole mess of them boys. I didn't know how we could ever stand agin 'em.

CHAPTER TWENTY-TWO

We kept up a smart pace back to town, checkin' our backtrail regular, but nobody come our way. When we got to Stump's office, some lady from the Victory was just bringin' in the breakfasts for Jack an' Jim. Homer sent her back to git two more, an' he an' me et the one's she brung. Marion warn't there. Stump said he was down at the telegraph office. We finished eatin' an' went out on the porch to where Bill Cole was settin', just like he always done.

"Did they kill ya?" he asked.

"Not yet," Homer said, takin' a seat beside him, that big 'ol Sharps layin' across his lap.

Bill nodded. "You kill them?"

"One of 'em," Homer said. "Ol' Rube here was runnin' from him at the time."

"The hell he was," Bill said.

"It was pitiful," Homer went on. "Rube yellin' fer me to save him, tears runnin' down his face, whippin' that little buck for all he was worth. Right sad."

I was fixin' to defend myself when this feller come walkin' up. He was short an' had never missed many meals. He had on a vest an' a cutaway coat, a string tie an' a derby hat. He climbed the steps to the porch an' stood there.

"Which one of you men is in charge here?" he said, kindly like he was accusin' us a somethin'.

Right off, I didn't like him none. I knowed Bill Cole well enough by then to recognize it when he was smilin'. He hooked a thumb my way.

"He is," he said.

The feller turned to me an' kindly puffed up some. "I'm the Cameron city mayor," he said, "June Peabody. And you are?"

"United States Marshal Ruben Beeler," I told him. He didn't offer a hand, an' I didn't neither.

"When are you leaving?" he asked.

"I just et," I said. "Thought I'd let my breakfast settle a mite afore I run off."

He give a little jerk then. "I want those two men out of my town," he said.

"I'll sign 'em over to ya, Mayor," I said. "Once they're in your custody, you can do what you want with 'em."

"My custody?" he yelled. "Young man, I will file a complaint with the Marshal's Service on you. I don't like your attitude!"

"Mister Mayor," I said, "our intention is to git them fellers outa here just as soon as we can, but if yer fixin' to file a complaint, maybe we should stick around until it gits settled. I'd hate to run off with somethin' that important hangin' over me."

About that time Stump walked out on the porch. "Mornin' Mayor," he said.

Peabody drew a bead on him. "And just what are you doing about all this?" he said.

"I got a deputy stationed a mile or two outa town," he said. "He'll let us know if them fellers are comin' back in."

The mayor was gittin' purty red in the face. "I mean those prisoners, Goddammit!"

"Well, why don't I just go in there an' shoot 'em, June?" Stump said. "Just walk back in there an' kill both of 'em an' throw their bodies out in the street. Christamighty!"

The mayor shook his finger at Stump then. "I'll have your badge for this, Stump!" he hollered.

"You ain't man enough to carry a badge!" Stump roared, an' took a step toward him. The mayor backed up a ways.

Things got real quiet then, an' Arkansas Bill Cole spoke up.

"I got a question for ya, Mister Mayor Peabody," he said.

"What is it?" the mayor said.

"How do ya git it to fit?" Bill asked.

"What?" the mayor said.

"How do ya git it to fit?" Bill repeated.

The mayor's face come over puzzled some. "How do I get what to fit?" he asked.

"Yer fat ass," Bill said. "How do ya git it to fit under the bed, ya chickenshit little pud."

The mayor made five or six noises then that I didn't understand as words, an' stomped off down the street.

"Right sensitive, ain't he?" Homer said.

It warn't terrible long afore Marion come back. He was lookin' some grim. He come up on the porch an' set kindly hard in a chair, an' stared out in the street for a spell.

"Well, boys," he said, "it could be worse I guess. I got orders to bring them brothers to Jeff City."

"That's a fair piece," Homer said. "A couple a hunnerd miles draggin' them shitheads with us. Hell, Marion, that bunch won't have no trouble ketchin' us. Cain't move too fast, haulin' prisoners."

"I know it," Marion said. "But we got a out, if'n I take it. They've issued warrants on each of them boys for murder an' aggravated battery, wanted dead or alive. That bunch after us is wantin' to git them brothers back. If the brothers wasn't a issue an' they kept after us, that'd mean they was fixin' to kill us. Somebody fixin' to kill us ain't subject to no mercy, the way I see it."

Bill Cole stood up. "Couple a hours afore dark?" he said.

"I speck," Marion said. "Maybe some earlier. I want to make real sure they know we've moved on."

Bill walked off, stiff legged like, around the corner of the porch. Marion looked at me.

"Git us some chuck an' such for the trip, Ruben," he said, "an' pack that mule up. I'll go to the livery an' take care a the stock."

"All right," I said.

"I'll talk to the sheriff," Homer said, "an' git these assholes ready to travel. Cole comin' with us?"

"I reckon," Marion said. "Tend to your hardware right smart, boys. I speck we'll be needin' it afore this here is all over."

* * * * *

I went to the Victory an' asked them to bake us up a bunch a biscuits, then down to the general store an' stocked up on bacon an' beans, jerky, coffee, some a them canned peaches an' such, an' left it there until I could git back with Arliss the mule. At the drygoods place I picked up another ground cloth, a good-size coil a rope to make a couple a lead lines with, an' a box a shells for my Yellaboy. They didn't have nothin' near big enough for Homer's Sharps, but I figgerd he had that purty much took care of anyways. By the time I got done, it was near the middle a the afternoon.

I went down to the livery an' saddled Willie, then took him an' Arliss the mule to pick up everthin' I'd got. By the time I had things packed up an' went back to the stable, Homer an' Marion was there, tendin' to the horses an' possibles. We rode down to the sheriff's office an' collected them brothers. Marion manacled both of 'em to their saddle horns. Knowin' Marion like they done, an' what he was capable of, neither one of 'em said much. Just as we was fixin' to leave, Arkansas Bill Cole come up on that big ol' sorrel a his, settin' kindly off center in the saddle. Stump tolt us to be careful, an' off we went, stayin' to the trail an' headin' out for Excelsior Springs, around forty miles away.

* * * * *

We hit it purty hard an' as fast as the slowest horse, Homer's gray, would let us. Arliss the mule couldn't keep up, so I tied his lead rope up short an' turned him loose.

"Yer gonner lose all our truck," Homer said to me.

Marion grinned at him. "You seem a little short on confidence in Arliss," he said.

"By God," Homer said, "if'n you're lookin' for a feller with confidence in a sawed-off little mule, ya better scratch someplace besides around this ol' boy!"

We rode off then, leavin' Arliss the mule an' his short trot in our dust, an' went at it heavy for around ten miles. We stopped at a little crick to water the horses some an' let 'em blow, an' purty soon, off in the distance, we could see ol' Arliss, headin' our way, shufflin' along in that trot a his.

"I'll be damned," Homer said.

"That mule will still be comin' when that pore ol' gray a is wheezin' on his knees," I said.

Homer didn't say nothin'. He just reined that gray around right sharp an' struck off at a high lope.

Marion plumb chuckled then. "Takes a durn fool to race a mule," he said.

He handed me one a the brother's lead ropes an' we took off at a trot, Bill's sorrel fussin' some, wantin' to run after the gray.

About a hour afore dark we come on another little crick an' stopped beside it close to a big ol' oak. By the time we got them brothers took care of, the horses unsaddled and hobbled, an' a fire built an' burnin' good', Arliss the mule trotted in, not goin' one bit faster nor slower than when we left on the ride. I got the panniers an' the packsaddle offa him, an' he wandered off a little ways to roll, then farted a couple a times and went to the crick for a drink.

"You gonna hobble him?" Homer asked.

"Hey, Arliss!" I said. "Should I hobble ya?"

Arliss switched his tail at me, an' commenced to eatin' grass.

"That means 'no' in mule," I said.

Homer snorted. "Takes one jackass to unnerstand another one, I reckon," he replied.

* * * * *

It was after dark when them beans an' bacon was ready. Everbody et it an' some a them biscuits from the Victory except Bill. He had a half a biscuit maybe, then went over an' leaned up agin that tree. After supper, Marion took them brothers over beside where a big ol' limb had fell from that oak, an' manacled them to each other, their arms around that limb an' between branches to where they couldn't git off of it.

One a them boys took exception. "How the hell you expect us to sleep a huggin' on this thing?" he said.

"Ain't my problem," Marion said, "an' that's all the bitchin' you git. Keep it up an' I'll knock out yer back teeth."

I looked over at Homer an' saw him grinnin'. "Marion Daniels is a rough ol' cob," he said. "Lord God, I do admire his style."

The next mornin', Marion hung them two brothers.

* * * * *

While I was fryin' up some of the bacon, Marion spoke to Homer fer a minute, then the two of 'em went over an' loosed them brothers from each other, an' tied they hands behind 'em with piggin' strings. Marion took them lead ropes, tied a slip-knot in the end a each one of 'em, an' tossed 'em over a limb about ten feet offa the ground. He tied the other ends to that big ol' downed branch so them loops was around eight up in the air. Then Homer brung the brother's horses up with just their headstalls on 'em. The brother that had his teeth knocked out an' me both figured out what was goin' on at about the same time. He commenced to bawlin' and yellin' that Marion couldn't do it. That he an' Jim deserved a fair trial. When that didn't work, he started up about how Jim done it all, an' that he was innocent an' such.

Arkansas Bill Cole come up then, settin' on that big sorrel, an' moved the first horse under a loop. Marion and Homer lifted Jack up onto his horse, with Jack kickin' an' screechin'. I gotta admit I felt some sorry for him when he pissed hisself, but when that rope went around his neck, he settled down quite a bit, with just tears runnin' down his face.

Jim went easier, not fightin' at all, but kindly acceptin' what was gonna happen. They put him on his horse an' Bill put a loop around his neck with no trouble. Jack started in agin, cryin' about how unfair it was an' such. That's when Jim spoke up.

"Shut up yer damn bawlin'!" he said. "If you hadden a had that new buck knife a your'n with ya, none a this wouldn't a happened, ya goddammed coward. You cut that whore up for no reason more than ya just could. Now yer gonna pay for it an' so am I. Quit yer damn bellyachin' an' act like a man. Ya done pissed yer pants for chrissakes!"

Jack kept on blubberin', quiet like, an' Marion asked 'em if they had any last words.

"The devil can take me," Jim said, "an Jack too. Maybe that'll shut the damn crybaby up. Go ahead on. I'm sick a this shit anyways."

Arkansas Bill Cole set off then, leadin' them two horses out from under the brothers. That branch sagged some, but not enough so their feet could hit the ground.

* * * * *

I'd seen a fella that had been hung once, but I had never seen nobody git hung afore, an' I had to turn away from it, the way they was twistin' an' jerkin' an' gaggin' an' such. I didn't really know exactly what I was doin' I doan think, 'cause I found myself back by the fire, turnin' that bacon just afore it got burnt on one side. Purty soon, Homer come over an' picked out a couple a pieces an' sopped a biscuit in some of the grease. He set down an' looked at me.

"You all right, boy?" he asked.

"I ain't sure," I said. "I mean, I have kilt some fellas an' such, but it warn't nothin' like that. Them boys didn't stand much of a chance."

"Neither did them girls, Rube," Homer said. "The boys didn't have to kill an' maim them women like they done, but they did. Their pards was comin' to kill us after we caught 'em. Their daddy has showed up with a little army, an' is prob'ly on our trail right now. They was dead or alive warrants issued on both them brothers. Now, legal like, they're dead. Their daddy'll find the bodies soon enough. It can stop there. If'n it doan, then we got a better chance a gittin' through all this without them two skunks a hangin' on our necks. You wanna feel bad for somethin', Rube, you feel bad for them two girls, special the one that's young, alive, an' cut an' scarred to hell for the rest a her life. She's the one deserves the sorrow. Neither one a these pieces a shit."

* * * * *

I didn't have no appetite, but Marion come over an' et then, an' Bill Cole took half a biscuit an' a bite a bacon. At Marion's request, I dropped the saddles that had belonged to the brothers on the ground below where they was hangin' an' cut the twenty or so feet a that loop a rope that was left into ten foot pieces to use as leads on the two extra horses. Marion figgerd we oughta take 'em with us in case one a our'n come up lame or somethin'.

It warn't long afore we was on the way', leavin' Arliss the mule behind, takin' back to the trail to Excelsior Springs, mostly because nobody had mentioned anywhere else we might go.

CHAPTER TWENTY-THREE

Ridin' on I was some depressed, I reckon. I mean, I knowed them boys had done a terrible thing to them two women back in Saint Joe an' all, an' that might not have been all they done in their lives neither. They may a had hearts as black as coal. Prob'ly did. It bothered me some when I shot that fella that was with the Duncan bunch, an' a lot more when Homer finished him off, but not as much when I kilt Pig Wiggins back in Deer Run after he gunned down Clarence an' poor Miss Margie, nor when I come at them fellas that was chasin' us when we took them Waxler Brothers outa that saloon. Any a those times I did what I had ta do agin folks that was loose an' just as able to do for me as I was able to do for them. It was what ya might call a honest encounter. As awful an' wasteful as it was, they was a kind a fairness in it, I reckon. A fightin' chance, ya might say.

Jim an' Jack Waxler was helpless. They was tied up an' strung up, danglin' from them loops with spit an' snot runnin' down their faces, chokin' an' floppin' until the life was wrung out of 'em as they bounced at the end a two ropes, foulin' theyselves while they strangled to death. I turned away, but I couldn't keep it outa my ears. I couldn't keep it outa my mind neither an' the more I thought about it, the worse it got. Even though I hadn't et no breakfast, I leaned offa Willie some an' throwed up. I come over right weak then an' had to stop. I slid off the saddle an' kindly fell to the ground, retchin' an' hangin' on to the reins so Willie wouldn't run off after them other horses.

I was settin' there, dizzy like an' tryin' to git my breath, when Marion rode up. He got offa that roan a his an' set right down on the ground across from me. I was shakin' some when I looked at him.

"Godawful terrible thing ain't it, Ruben?" he said to me.

"Yessir," I said. "It is."

Him settin' there an' me speakin' them few words brung me back to myself some. I took my hat off an' wiped my brow with my shirtsleeve. I was sweatin' quite a bit.

"Seems to me," I said, "like we just kindly murdered them fellas without givin' 'em no chance at all."

Marion smiled a little. "We didn't give 'em no chance," he said. "Yer right there. But we kilt 'em, boy. We didn't murder 'em. We didn't do a damn thing to them brothers they didn't ask for."

"I speck so," I said, "but I hate it, Marion. I hate it right down to the ground."

"I know ya do, Ruben," he said, "an' I'm proud of ya for it."

That comment hit me sorta sideways. "Proud of me?" I said.

Marion nodded. "Yessir," he said. "Them boys was bought an' paid for the minute that dead or alive warrant was issued. Their daddy, as low a man as has ever drawed breath, has got a small army on our ass that'll kill us if they can. My life is a damn site more valuable to me than the life of a woman killer. So is yours, an' Homer's, an' even that rascal Bill Cole's. Them brother's was slowin' us down. Now they ain't. Clovis Waxler damn sure was countin' on the fact that us draggin' them sons a his would put us in reach. He also knowed that what happened might happen. He didn't care. His need not to be stood agin is more important to him that the lives a his own boys. His cane saved his life at the office the other day. That won't work the next time we run across his ass. I'll shoot the ol' bastard myself, if'n I git the chance."

We set quiet for a spell then, afore Marion spoke up agin.

"Doin' better?" he asked me.

"Yessir," I said.

"Can ya ride, boy?"

"I believe I can," I told him, an' used Willie's stirrup to help myself git stood up. It took some effort for me to git a leg over the saddle, but I done it. I gathered the reins an' looked at Marion.

"You said you was proud a me," I said.

Marion nodded. "I am," he said.

"What for?" I asked him.

"Ruben," he said, "hangin' them fellers run you off and made you sick. If they'd a hung you, they woulda stood there and laughed while you choked to death, dancin' your life away on the end of a rope. That's why I'm proud of ya. That is also why I'm glad to give their lives to maybe save yours." He smiled at me then. "And to save mine," he went on. "I ain't stupid."

We come in sight a Excelsior Springs in the early afternoon, an' stopped outside a town a ways by a runoff creek to rest a spell an' give the horses a break. Just as we was fixin' to leave, here come Arliss the mule trottin' up to git hisself a drink. Homer shook his head.

"I gotta say," he said, "that ol' Arliss is the damndest mule I ever seen. It's a shame he's such a little feller or he could keep up better. Maybe we oughta lighten his load. If that bunch behind us ketches up to him, they'll have him an' all our truck."

We took the panniers an' packsaddle offa Arliss the mule and switched 'em over to the paint, him bein' bigger an' stouter than the bay we got to replace the black with lung trouble. Arliss rolled around on the ground for a spell, then got up an' shook hisself, stretchin' his neck out as far as he could an' yawnin'. Homer stood there, grinnin' at him. Then he walked over to that mule an' commenced to scratchin' on his back. Arliss kindly drawed hisself up, puttin' his rear feet an' front feet close together an' humpin' his back under that scratchin'. Purty soon he was kindly gruntin' from it.

Bill Cole spoke up. "You two wanna be left alone for a spell?" he said.

Homer quit scratchin' then an' looked over at Bill.

"Well hell, Arkansas Bill Cole," he said. "Yer back ever itch?"

"I ain't sayin'," Bill said. "I doan know you that well."

* * * * *

We made it around Excelsior Springs an' near halfway to Richmond afore we give up for the day. Takin' the load offa Arliss the mule made a difference. He showed up afore I even got a fire goin. We still had some a them biscuits left, but I went ahead on with frybread an' bacon, leavin' them for the mornin'. After we et, Bill Cole tightened up the cinch on that long legged sorrel a his an' left camp, headin' to the northeast. Knowin' he'd be out there between us an' them was settlin'. I slept purty good.

When I woke up around daybreak, Bill was back an' had a fire built, coffee ready, an' bacon fryin'.

"Mornin', Rube," he said to me.

"Hello, Bill," I said. "Don't you never sleep at all?"

"Don't hardly need to," he said.

"Do ya ever eat a whole meal?" I asked him, then thought I mighta said too much.

Bill shook his head. "Not for quite a spell, I ain't," he said.

"I don't know how ya do it," I said. "Don't seem right."

Bill Cole looked me straight in the face. "Boy," he said, "you may be the only person on the globe that thinks he's got the right to show any concern about me an' my habits."

"I'm sorry if'n I spoke outa turn," I said. "It ain't none a my business."

Right then, he flat smiled a regular human smile at me. "Yer right," he said, "it ain't none a yer business. But it is a comfort that ya give a damn, Ruben. It shorely is."

I didn't know what to say to him about that, so I kindly nodded at him an' went off to take care a my mornin' business. Arliss the mule tagged along.

CHAPTER TWENTY-FOUR

We covered a fair bit a ground over the next two days, considerin' we had to spare the horses. We got around Richmond an' Lexington, an' Higginsville, avoidin' towns purty much, tryin' to keep movin' on the sly, an' camped on the east side a Sweet Springs for the best part of a day to let us an' the horses rest up an' such. All the horses was wore down some, even Willie, but Homer's gray was sufferin' more than any of 'em. Homer threw his saddle on the bay we was leadin' an' struck off late mornin'. When he come back in the middle a the afternoon, he was leadin' that bay an' settin' on a stout dun mare that was right likely.

She warn't terrible big, not much more than Willie, but she was smart-headed an' short-backed, set up real square, kindly like a bulldog. Maybe seven or eight year old, she was fresh shod an' slick, with just a little snip a white on one side a her nose. She had quick eyes, never missin' much goin' on around her, an' I liked her right off. Homer got her hobbled an' set with us.

"That mare ain't awful bad, is she?" I said to him.

"She'll do 'til I kin git a good 'un," Homer said. "My gray is wore out. Hell, Rube, I've had him for better'n ten year an' he was a ways from young when I got him. Age ketches up to all of us I reckon. I know some folks over by Gasconade where I can just turn him out an' let him live on."

"How's the dun?" I asked.

Homer smiled. "She's got the damndest trot I ever set," he said. "That gray has done well for me, an' I ain't sayin' nothin' against him, but his trot is right awful. Jar yer teeth plumb outa yer head. This mare shuffles. Most a the bounce is a side to side shift like. She doan waste no energy on it, an' goes near as fast as a short lope. Shame ol' Willie is cut. A colt or a filly outa them two would be a horse an' a half."

We were lookin' at her when Arliss the mule grazed over by where she was standin'. She didn't like that much an' squalled, takin' a swipe at him an' nippin' Arliss on the withers. Arliss spun around right quick an' kicked her in the shoulder with both rear feet. The two of 'em just stood there for a minute, thinkin' things over I reckon, then that mare moved sidways a step from him an' Arliss ignored her an' went back to the grass.

Homer chuckled. "Arliss the mule," he said.

* * * * *

When I woke up the next mornin', Marion was gittin' a fire goin', Arkansas Bill Cole was cleanin' a pistol, an' Homer an' that dun mare was gone. I looked at Marion.

"Checkin' our backtrail," he said. "He'll ketch up to us."

* * * * *

We didn't hurry as much that day as we had been. We was makin' camp close to dusk a little ways north a Sedalia when Homer come in. That mare had gone considerable farther that day then we had, an' she didn't seem much wore down from it. Homer dropped the saddle an' I hobbled her for him. He flopped by the fire an' looked at me.

"We got any a them peaches?" he asked.

I got him a can and worried half the top off so he could git at 'em. He et a couple, drank some a the juice, an' belched.

"They're back there, boys," he said. "A dozen an' a half of 'em, mebbe two dozen. The ol' man an' his buckboard is gone, though. Ol' bones like his cain't get caught up in no chase. This bunch is a little more than just hands, I speck. I couldn't tell for absolute sure, but I believe that Charlie Redhorse is with 'em. If it is Charlie, Youngblood is prob'ly in the herd someplace."

"Ain't that nice," Marion said.

"Who's Charlie Redhorse?" I asked.

"He's a breed," Marion said. "Half nigger an' half Cheyenne. Tracker. Damn good one, too. He's on our backtrail, we won't lose him. He worked for the guvmint years ago when they run the Sioux outa Nebraska. Youngblood is his sidekick. White feller. His name ain't even Youngblood, I reckon. They say he got that nickname from how he liked killin' injun kids when them camps would git raided. Chopped 'em up with a 'hawk. Last I heard they was out in the territories, but that was eight or ten year ago. I guess maybe they ain't no more. Them is the kinda boys ol' man Waxler would know. Hell, they mighta even been with him up on the Nodaway back in them days. I'd guess they is both in their fifties by now."

"I run across 'em a few years back in west Texas," Bill Cole said. "They was drinkin' in this little roadhouse. I stopped in for some whiskey. I'd heard of 'em but didn't know what they looked like. They left an' the bartender there that I knowed asked me if'n I was after 'em. I told him no an' he was some relieved. I'd got shot a little before that an' wadden at my best, so I took out. I guess they didn't know who I was neither or they'd probably run me down if they could. They ain't no true pistoleers I suppose, but they'll cut yer throat in bed or shoot ya when ya go to shit."

Things got quiet for a spell, then Homer spoke up.

"Boys," he said, "we got to split up."

* * * * *

Them words kept runnin' through my head after everbody turned in. I hadn't never thought that the four a us would separate, an' it scared me some. In the company a them men, I just never worried much about everthin' workin' out good for everbody. Together, Marion, Homer, an' Bill Cole was just about unbeatable I reckoned, an' I was proud to be in the company a fellas like they was. Somethin' that could come along an' give 'em reason to go off separate ways seemed to me to be fearsome. I worried about it most a the night, I guess, not restin' real good, them thoughts in my head like they was. I 'spose I did go to sleep, 'cause I woke up durin' the false dawn, an' noticed the three of 'em settin' around a small fire, eatin' bacon an' the last a our biscuits. I set up, an' seen the horses was all saddled. I crawled outa my roll an' walked off a ways for a minute, then set with 'em an' got some coffee.

"You awake, Ruben?" Marion asked me.

"Purty much," I said.

"All right," he said. "Me an' Homer is gonna take the packhorse an' the paint an' head for Jeff City. You an' Bill will take Homer's gray an' Arliss an' make tracks south a ways, then cut over toward Linn an' head for Deer Run. There's heavy trails down that way an' they won't be able to track ya. None a them boys probably know who ya are, so they shouldn't git after ya once you git past Linn. We git over close to Jeff City, the same'll be good fer us. These ol' boys ain't got no real personal stake in this, an' the ol' man ain't with 'em to keep 'em steady on business. They prob'ly'll just give it up after a spell and head off. Right now, they got us outnumbered about six or seven to one, an' they is still serious. Ain't no point in any a us gittin' kilt. You doan wanna git kilt, do ya Ruben?"

"Rather not," I said.

"That's good," Marion said. "You git yer business done an' git a bite. I'll pack yer roll up for ya and sack up some chuck and such, then we light a shuck. Git back to that wife and that baby that'll be here afore long. We've done what we needed to do and they ain't no 'cause to chase this hog no farther. You unnerstan'?"

"Yessir, I do."

"All right then," Marion said.

* * * * *

I didn't eat much, everthin' tastin' kindly like wood an' all. Purty soon, I went off a way to take care a business, an' when I come back, Marion an' Homer was to horse. Marion looked down at me.

"See ya on down the trail one a these days, Ruben," he said. "Yer as good a pard as a feller could want, and I'm proud to have rid with ya."

"Thank ya, Marshal," I said.

"Arkansas Bill Cole," Marion went on. "Good to have you back after all these years."

"Marion Daniels," Bill said.

Homer spoke up then. "Take care a that mule," he said, an' the two of 'em reined off and loped away.

"You go on, boy," Bill said. "I'm gonna have a look-see at our back trail. I'll ketch up to ya this afternoon. Just head due south. I'll find ya."

I swung up on Willie then, an' headed out. I looked back once to make sure Arliss the mule was follerin' along. That was when I seen Bill Cole take three tries gittin' his leg over that big ol' sorrel a his.

* * * * *

I kept us at a short lope most a the day, knowin Bill's horse wouldn't have much trouble ketchin' us. Late afternoon he done just that. I stopped Willie an' waited for him when I seen him comin'.

"Dozen or so of 'em 'bout ten miles behind us," he said, "usin' their horses too hard. We keep a fair pace an' they won't ketch us. We're mounted better than they are. We settle in about dark an' leave afore daybreak, an' we'll be all right."

We went on then. About a hour afore dark we was ridin' through some rocky scrub when Bill's sorrel give a squeal an' shied sideways real sudden like. Bill kept his seat an' held him, then drawed his pistol an' shot twice into the ground. He was gittin' down when I got to him.

"Damn it to hell," he said. "Goddamn copperhead. Hit him in the left front. That's some bad luck."

I got down offa Willie an' looked at the sorrel. A feller coulda easy missed the bite. It was just above the left sock, two little spots a blood. Didn't look like nothin' at all, 'til it commenced to swell. I tied the sorrel to a scrub oak an' walked over to where Bill was settin', hunched over like, on a rock.

"He gonna die from it?" I asked.

"No," Bill said. "He'll be all right in a day or two, special if we could cool him in a creek. Purty soon, though, he'll be bad off in that leg. He can walk, but not with nobody on him, an' not terrible fast."

"We can walk all night," I said.

Bill shook his head. "They'll ketch us, Rube," he said.

"Turn him loose an' git on the gray," I said.

"That ain't good neither," Bill said. "We do that an' they'll find him an' know one a us is on a wore out horse. They been trackin' us. They know the horse we been leadin' ain't got much left. They'll ride us down, boy, if'n they gotta kill their horses to do it. I figgered somthin' like this would happen when I joined up with this outfit. That's why I done it, I reckon."

I didn't unnerstand, an' I tolt him so.

"It's my time, Ruben," he said. "It's why I found Marion' an' took up the badge once more. I ain't much proud a my life 'cept when I was a marshal. I wanted it to go out that way."

"Go out that way?" I said. "What the hell are you talkin' about?"

"I got a growth on my liver," Bill said. "I found out about it a while back over in Kansas City. I'm dyin' from it, Ruben. It's why I cain't hardly eat an' why I sleep settin' up if I can sleep at all. I'm a gone beaver, but I doan wanna go out layin' in no bed suckin' on laudanum with folks lookin' at me. I have lived by the gun, boy. I'll die by it. Only fair."

"I doan know what to say to ya, Bill," I tolt him. "I hate to hear ya tell of it. I know that much."

He smiled at me. "Rube," he said, "you git the saddle offa my horse an' put it on that gray for me, please. Then you take that sorrel an' go ahead on. Walk him easy all night so that poison doan settle in one spot too long an' he'll come out of it. Git yerself back home to yer family, an' good for ya."

I done it. There warn't nothin' else I could do. I doan believe I ever lifted a heavier saddle than when I tossed his up on that gray. I looked in my bags for a box a extra shells for him an' run across that silver Colt Marion took from them fellers that tried to kill us. I carried it an' that box a bullets over to where Bill set an' give 'em to him. He thanked me an' I asked him if he wanted my Yellaboy.

"Wouldn't know what to do with it," he said. "I ain't no sharpshooter. I'm a pistoleer."

"Ya might be able to keep 'em off from ya some with a rifle," I told him.

Bill shook his head. "I want 'em close, boy. I wanna see they eyes."

"Bill," I said, "I doan cotton to runnin' off an' just leave ya like this. I feel like yer my friend."

"An' yer mine, Ruben. The only one I got an', by God, yer enough, son. Ya truly are, an' I am glad to have ya. Git on that purty little buck a your'n now, an' go ahead on."

"I hate ta do it, Bill," I said. "I shorely do hate to."

"That speaks right well of ya, boy," Bill said. "Now I need for ya to go on along. It's the best thing you can do for me, Ruben. It's the only thing you can do for me."

I shook hands with him then for the first time, an' done what he said. I hated to do it, but I did. My friend, Arkansas Bill Cole, asked me to.

CHAPTER TWENTY-FIVE

Me an' Willie walked all that night, leadin' the sorrel with Arliss the mule comin' along behind. The sorrel had some kindly hard time of it, limpin' terrible an' I felt sorry for him the way that leg was treatin' him an' all, but he was game an' didn't hardly fight the lead much. Still it was a terrible long night.

I reckon I musta dozed in the saddle some, 'cause I went back in my mind to other times with Marion an' Homer an' Arkansas Bill Cole an' it was like I was there agin with 'em when trouble was all around an' a fella didn't have time to be scairt. It was more than just pictures in my mind, or some type a dreamin' I think. I believe that if it hadn't a been for Willie's steady walk under me, sorta keepin' me settled into where I really was, I coulda got lost in it or somethin'. I'd pull back from it now an' then an' think a buildin' my little house behind Arliss' gunsmithin' shop, or my daddy an' me workin' together, or the first time I seen Miss Harmony, or studyin' on what our baby might be like. I'll tell ya the truth. I warn't used to them kinda sights runnin' around in my mind like that, an' I was plumb relieved when dawn come an' kindly pushed 'em outa my head.

We come on a crick a little after daybreak an' I led that Sorrel out inta it to let the horses drink an' cool his leg. When I checked him over, I was kindly surprised to see the swellin' was goin' down quite a bit. I'd seen a dog git face bit by a copperhead once, an' he swole up so bad he couldn't see an' finally come to not bein' able to git his breath an' died from it. I guess that sorrel bein' so much bigger an' all is what let him keep goin'.

We kept after it all day, me eatin' jerky in the saddle an' them horses gittin' what they could as we walked. By the middle a the afternoon, I was trottin' that sorrel some, an' he done good with it. I stopped for a early camp an' rode from the trail a ways so as not to bring attention on us. It was a cold camp, but it didn't make no difference. Me an' the stock was all purty tired an' glad for a rest. I didn't need to hobble nobody an' I fell asleep some afore dark, wakin' up only once to run a 'possum off that was fussin' around my possibles. I got up' at false dawn an' built a little fire an' fixed myself some bacon an' frybread. While I was gittin' out the chuck, I come across a few a them little maple cinnamon candy pieces. I give a couple to Willie an' he went right after 'em. That sorrel favored 'em too. Arliss the mule didn't think much a the one I tried to give him an' turned away, so I et it.

We trotted an' short loped most a that mornin', an' made better time that we had been. By noon the swellin' was plumb gone outa the sorrel's leg an' I was glad for it. We come across some other folks on the trail. A couple a cowboys found some humor in Arliss the mule taggin' along behind us without no lead, an' we come on three or four wagons an' buckboards with workin' men an' a family or two. I kept my marshal's badge hid from 'em, not wantin' to git caught up in nobody else's troubles an' in a hurry to git out from under some a my own. We was less than twenny miles from Deer Run when we camped that night, an' I was restless to git there. I knowed that Willie coulda kept on, but I didn't wanna risk the sorrel, him doin' better an' all. I fixed bacon an' beans, an' thought about Harmony's sourdough bread with honey an' cinnamon, an' then just thought about Harmony. It had been a spell since I'd seen her an' I favored the thought a gittin' home.

About a hour after I broke camp the next mornin', I come on another crick an' stopped for a spell to let the horses drink. It was a little cloudy, the sun peakin' through now an' then, an' fair windy, too. A few a them white-face cattle that I'd heard about was scattered out across the way an' it was right purty seein' them cloud shadows chasin' each other across that green with five or six a them red cows with white faces, shinin' when the sun hit 'em. A cow had a young calf with her, an' his little face was as white as white could git, I guress. They was some different than the stock I was used to an' I admired the sight of 'em.

We hadden gone another three or four miles afore Willie started fussin' at me some. If we was walkin', he'd wanna trot. If we was trottin' he'd wanna lope. I kept him checked in an' he didn't like it much. The sorrel seemed game, so I let that little buck git after it some an' off we went. I purty much let Willie have his way for a mile or so to git some a the feathers outa his feet, an' that big ol' long legged sorrel a Bill's kept up with no trouble at all. I durn near had to rein Willie into a circle to git him to settle, him finally realizin' how close to home we was, an' wantin' to race the sorrel. I looked behind us an' there, a half mile back, come Arliss the mule, trottin' right along.

Deer Run come in sight about the middle of the afternoon, an' I turned Willie loose. I give a yell an' fanned him with my hat, just for the joy in it, an' he took out like somebody was shootin' at him, goin' for all he was worth. I kept a close eye on the sorrel, but he warn't havin' no trouble at all, stayin' right with us, once movin' up beside Willie just to show him he could. Willie give it everthin' he had, but I got to say that sorrel was hell for fast. I'd never run across any horse that could keep up with Willie, but that big red sonofagun not only kept up, but with no rider on him, he was just playin' while he done it.

When we passed the house I reined Willie in an' he come to a stop in front a the forge. I swung down offa him an' looked around just when Harmony come out a the livery. She seen me an' come a runnin', her arms throwed out in front of her an' grinnin'. I met her halfway, an' there we was, huggin' on each other an' kissin' one another on the face an' such. She was laughin' an' cryin' at the same time, an' I reckon I was too. It was kindly embarrassin', but we kept on with it 'cause neither one a us could stop for a spell. When we settled down some, I noticed she was quite a bit thicker than she was when I left.

"You puttin' on weight, girl?" I asked her.

She smiled up at me. "I'm not a girl anymore, Ruben Beeler," she said.

"Sure ya are," I tolt her. "You'll always be my girl. Yer the harmony an' the melody of my life."

I hung onto her then while she cried some more. Purty soon she settled an' pulled away, wipin' at her face with her apron.

"Where have you been?" she asked me.

"Plumb to Alaska an' back," I said. "I feel like I been gone a year."

"Two years," she said, noticin' the sorrel. "Who's this?"

"He was once Arkansas Bill Cole's horse," I told her. "He was snake bit an' couldn't git around much, so Bill give him to me an' took Homer's gray to go off an' git hisself kilt. He saved my life, I reckon."

"Homer was with you?" she asked.

"Yes M'am."

"And Arkansas Bill Cole saved your life," she said.

"I speck he did," I said. "He needed to die an' he sent me on so I wouldn't."

"Arkansas Bill Cole?" Harmony said, her eyebrows all raised up.

"It's the truth," I said. "He was my friend an' I was his." Tears come into my eyes then an' I couldn't keep 'em back.

Harmony put her hand to my face, an' smiled up at me. "You look tired, Ruben," she said.

"I'm near wore plumb out," I said.

"And you're thin, too," she went on. "You've lost weight."

I smiled at her an' patted her side. "I guess you found it, though," I said.

She stepped on my toe then an' turned around, headin' for the barn. "Bring the horses, Mister Beeler," she said.

She watched while I brushed Willie down, turned him an' the sorrel out, an' put up my saddle and tack. I hung my roll over a rail to let it air out an' strung my saddlebags up beside it. We hugged each other' some, an' she stepped back an' studied on me.

"I baked bread this morning," Harmony said. "We have some butter in the springhouse I churned yesterday and some sweet milk. Let's fatten you up a little and let you rest."

She took my hand an' started for the house. Just as she walked us outside, Arliss the mule turned the corner down by the road an' come trottin' up the lane toward us.

"There he is," I said. "Ol' Arliss."

Harmony looked around. "Arliss?" she said.

"Arliss the mule," I told her. "He's my pal."

"That's your mule?" Harmony asked.

"He shore thinks he is," I tolt her. "Cain't argue with Arliss the mule."

She grinned at me. "Well," she said, "let's put him up."

"Ain't no need in that," I said. "He ain't goin' nowhere. Arliss the mule is my pard. He'll just hang around with the chickens an' such."

Harmony looked at me, close like. "You have some stories, don't you," she said.

"I do," I said.

She took my hand. "Let's go to the kitchen, Ruben," she said. "You can talk with your mouth full."

CHAPTER TWENTY-SIX

Out on the trail a fella can eat good enough to keep goin' on an' such, if he ain't in a real big hurry, or if he's with a drive or somethin' that's got a chuck wagon an' a cook. If he's tryin' to make fair tracks an' is by hisself, bacon, beans, an' frybread can git awful tiresome an' it gits easy to kindly neglect yer diet an' git run down like. Harmony give me some a her sourdough bread an' that fresh butter, an' I was shore thankful for it. Then she brung out a jar a blackberry jam an' some pieces a yesterday's cornbread, an' I reckon I et more settin' there an' tellin' her about where I'd been, what I'd seen, an' what I'd done, than how much I'd et in the last three days. When I couldn't hold no more an' stood up, I thought I'd left my stomach in the durn chair. She herded me off to our bedroom then an' tossed a ol' quilt over the bed 'cause I was kindly dusty, an' put me down. I didn't wake up until the next mornin'. When I did, I was some glad I'd kept my boots on 'cause I was purty much on a dead run to the convenience. When I come in the back door, her daddy, Verlon, was waitin' on me. Durned if'n he didn't give me a little short hug. It was kindly strange, but I was glad for it. We had ham an' eggs an' biscuits for breakfast, an' I don't believe I ever enjoyed anythin' better than them fresh eggs.

After breakfast, I throwed some clean clothes in a sack an' headed off down to the barbershop for a shave an' a haircut an' a bath in one a them big ol' tubs. Lionel Davis was glad to see me when I come in. They warn't nobody waitin' so he started in on me right off. He wanted to know where I'd been an' what I'd done, so I told him a little of it while he worked on me, knowin' that half the town would have the story by suppertime. Barbers an' bartenders can shore spread the word. After he got done with me, I set in one a them big ol' tubs a his for near a hour, lettin' that hot water just soak in an' outa me as much as I could. When I got up to rinse off in that shower stall a his, I was near weak from bein' down in that water so long. Then I went back out front an' Lionel wouldn't take no payment from me for anythin', so I thanked him an' headed on down to Arliss Hyatt's gunsmithin' shop.

When I walked in, Arliss was settin' at his workbench with a ol' Colt scattered out in about a hundred pieces. Arliss jumped up like he was bee-stung an' took holt a my elbows.

"You ain't dead?" he said.

"I am," I told him. "This here is my ghost an' I have come to haunt yer tired ol' ass."

"Looks to me like you got a fresh shave an' a haircut," Arliss said. "I didn't know you haints went in for that kinda groomin'."

"There's a lot you don't know, pard," I said.

Arliss grinned at me then. "I guess you're fixin' to enlighten me, aint ya?"

"I believe I will," I said.

"Lemme have that Schofield a your'n while ya do, and I'll go over it for ya," Arliss said. "Guns suffer some out on the trail."

It took a couple a hours to git the story tolt, I reckon. In the middle of it my deputy, Emory Nail come in. Him an' Hank Burford had done well while I was gone, with no big trouble or nothin', an' I was glad to hear of it. By the time I was done jawin' with Arliss, he'd tore my revolver plumb to pieces, fussed with it, an' put it all back together, better than new, an' I headed to the livery to see Harmony. I never did tell Arilss the gunsmith about Arliss the mule. I figgered he'd find out about it soon enough.

* * * * *

On the way to the livery I stopped by the telegraph office. I'd never sent no telegraph afore, an' the fella there, name a Jacobs, helped me through it. I sent a message off to Jeff City tellin' Marion Daniels how me an' Arkansas Bill Cole had parted company an' what had most likely happened to Bill. I wanted him to know.

* * * * *

I hung around home for the rest a the day, an' Harmony pounded beefsteak an' potaters down my neck for supper 'til I thought I'd bust. I felt fair rested the next mornin' an' headed down to the livery takin' a biscuit with me for Arliss the mule. When I went out the back door, he was munchin' on some grass down toward the springhouse. When he seen me, he come walkin' over an' stood three or four feet away, lookin' at me. I give him that biscuit then, an' he took to it right smart, rollin' it around in his mouth an' chewin'. When he finished, he stretched his neck out an' rolled his lips back, the way a mule'll do sometimes, an' it tickled me quite a bit.

When I got to the livery, Harmony was in there brushin' down that big ol' sorrel that Arkansas Bill Cole give me. The sun was shinin' in through the gaps in the boards, puttin' stripes a light on her an' that horse, an' the dust in the air kindly sparkled with it. The sight of it was somethin' like a fella might see in a dream or a vision, an' it took a holt of me for a spell. I just stood there lookin' at how purty she was, talkin' to that sorrel real quiet while she run that brush over him. In a while she noticed me lookin' at her an' stopped, grinnin' at me.

"And just what are you doing?" Harmony asked me.

"Watchin' a good lookin' woman workin' on a good lookin' horse while I celebrate my life," I told her.

Tears hit her eyes then, an' she come over to me an' put her arms around my neck an' looked up at me.

"Ruben Beeler," she said, "I am so glad you have come home."

We stood there, holdin' on to each other an' kindly swayin' back an' forth together like they warn't nobody else in the world but us. Purty soon that horse nickered an' broke the spell. Harmony turned an' looked at him.

"He fast?" she asked me.

"He can run with Willie," I said, "an' then some. Long in the wind, too. I doan know how old he is. I never checked his teeth."

"He's seven or eight," Harmony said. "I can't find a blemish on him except for a little scar on his left hock. Barbed-wire probably. What are you going to do with him?"

"I doan know," I said. "I thought I might sell him. He's worth a dollar or two."

"He is," Harmony agreed.

"Or," I went on, "I could give ol' Willie up an' keep him. He's a helluva of a horse."

"You could do that," she said.

"'Course," I said, "I could just give him away, if'n I knowed somebody deservin' of such a fine animal."

"That would be nice," Harmony said. "Anyone come to mind?"

"Miss Harmony, M'am," I said, "would you be good enough to show me a kindness an' take this poor ol' broke-down plug off my hands afore he just drops down where he stands?"

"I'll think about it," she said, an' went back to brushin' on him.

I headed off up to the house for another biscuit or two. Arliss the mule trailed me to the door.

* * * * *

Three or four days later I was settin' in the office, knockin' some a the dust offa that little scattergun, when Jacobs come in from the telegraph office with a message for me. I read the durn thing two or three times, gittin' past all them stops an' such. What it boiled down to was that a fella had found eight human bodies layin' out over south a Tipton a ways. They was mostly stripped a all their goods an' boots an' guns, an' they waren't no horses hangin' around. The 'yotes an' such had been after 'em so there was no hope a tellin' who they was. Marion figgered that Bill Cole had done for seven of 'em afore they took him down, an' maybe wounded some more. He wanted me to know.

* * * * *

I went home an' throwed a saddle on that big sorrel then, an' took him for a ride while I thought about Arkansas Bill Cole. He was my friend, ya know.

CHAPTER TWENTY-SEVEN

As time went by, it wore on me less that Bill went off an' got hisself kilt to save me, mostly because I finally come to understand that he done it to save hisself, too. It become sort of a comfort to me, I reckon. Since we'd got rid a Arberry Yont an' them Bluevests a his, Deer Run had come to prosper some. In just the past year we'd got us a new church an' another roomin' house, Arliss had opened his gunsmithin' business up into sellin' more new guns than he had been, an' tradin' in things like second-hand jewelry an' pocket watches an' such. Miz Clary had even took to the café business in a little place up the street from Arliss that just served simple breakfasts and small dinners, an' warn't even open at suppertime. First off, she'd just rented the space for the Fourth of July celebration to make a little money. I was still out on the trail when all that happened an' didn't even know I'd missed nothin' 'til I got back. That little place done so much business, she hung onto it an' went at it permanent. A lot a people said her idea would never work in the long run, but it went over good. It was right handy to just step in an' git some biscuits an' gravy for a dime of a mornin', or stop by in the middle a the day for cornbred an' beans or something quick like that, an' be on yer way in fifteen minutes. Some folks got to callin' it fast food, an' I guess it was.

* * * * *

As the summer went on, I done some work at the house, puttin' in new cabinets in the kitchen, settin' up a outside cookhouse for hot weather an' such, even addin' a new porch on the east side so a fella could set out of a evenin' without gittin' the sun in his eyes. Hank an' Emory purty much took care of the law work, Hank bein' on duty durin' the daytime an' Emory of a night. I took a shift from late afternoon 'til near midnight so they'd be two of us on hand durin' the time when somethin' was more likely to happen, but nothin' serious hardly never come up. We had a knifin' at the Houston House between a couple a fellas playin' cards one time, the occasional fistfight or fool raisin' hell, an' Missus Kinney went after her husband with a skillet one night an' got in several heavy licks. She durn near kilt him, but said he deserved it. The women at the Methodist Church all stood behind her. Since he didn't die, they warn't much we could do. We still had the whores an' drunks an' such but, all in all, things was purty much quiet, Deer Run gittin' some civilized like it was. The railroad was even talkin' about runnin' a spur line out our way.

Harmony an' me settled back in together real nice I thought, but I was some concerned about her an' the baby, her gittin' bigger all the time like she done, an' yet not slowin' down much at all. I spoke to her about it once an' she purty much tolt me to go ahead on an' mind my own business. She said it a lot nicer than that, but I didn't have no trouble takin' her meanin'. She was a strong woman an' could back me up with not much more than a look. Verlon, her daddy, took some pleasure outa watchin' her deal with me, I think. Him an' me got close, too. I'd help out in the forge when I could an' we figgered on addin' onto the stable a little, to make room for two more stalls. As Deer Run grew, the need for rentin' horses an' such grew too. I reckon it was late September when we tore out a storeroom to git after them stalls an' come across that old Henry.

It was a 1860 model Henry trapper rifle with the short barrel on a brass frame, in 44/40. Verlon was surprised to see it, not even knowin' it was back there hid away like it was an' up inside a greasy ol' wrappin' a burlap.

"Look at that, Rube," he said to me when we unwrapped it an' seen what it was. "I've been here for fifteen years an' I had no idea that gun was stuck back here in this corner. Ya figure it's good for anything?"

I looked it over. "I ain't no gunsmith or nothin'," I said, "but it doan look terrible bad. I'll take it down to Arliss an' see what he thinks."

I carried that ol' Henry into town when I went on duty an' dropped by Arliss' shop. He studied on it for a spell, then turned to his tools an' went to work, tellin' me to come back in the mornin'. I knowed they wasn't no use in askin' him nothin'. When that ol' man commenced to workin' on somethin' that he was interested in, he plumb shut everthin' else out.

* * * * *

Knowin' Arliss like I done, I knowed he'd spend as long as he had to on that Henry, even if it took all night. The next mornin' I struck off to town, went by Miz Clary's little diner an' got two plates a biscuits an' gravy, cut down the alley, an' come in the back a Arliss' shop. I could hear him talkin' to somebody up front an' it caught my ear. The feller he was talkin' to had a voice with a accent to it that warn't like anythin' I was used to. I looked up through the curtain an' took a peek at him.

He was a little taller than me, an' bigger, bein' heavy through the arms an' shoulders. He was wearin' a black high-crown hat over dark hair that was kindly kinky an' braided down both sides a his head to the top of his shoulders. His shirt was buckskin, worn to real dark under the arms an' around his neck, kindly like some a them skinners wore when they followed the buffler hunters. His pants looked military to me, an' his boots was knee high with long dog-ears. He was packin' a Colt army conversion and a big ol' knife with a stag handle set up high in a crossdraw scabbard. His face was sorta edgy lookin', didn't have no beard on it, an' was darker than a Mexican. I didn't like him much. When I seen what he was showin' Arliss, I didn't like him none at all.

"Twenny dollars!" he said. "That's no money. I want fifty."

"Ain't worth fifty to me," Arliss said. "Too fancy. I might have to hold on to that Colt for years just to git my money back. I could go twenty-five. No more."

"Now you listen to me, ya ol' stob," the fella said. "I want fifty for it, an' fifty is what I'm gonna git!"

My mouth went kindly dry. Quick like, I opened the back door an' shut it hard. "Mornin' Arliss," I said, loud like, "I brung breakfast. How's that Henry?" I went through the curtain then an' up to the counter. "'Scuse me," I went on, "I didn't know ya had business."

Arliss caught my eye. "Feller here wantin' to sell me a fancy Colt that I can't afford," he said. "You might like it."

The gun was layin' on the counter by the workbench where Arliss had the Henry all cleaned up. I looked at the fella.

"You mind?" I asked.

"Go ahead on," he said. He smelt like a wet dog.

I picked up that Colt an' looked it over. It was all silver lookin' an' engraved heavy with pearl handles an' a gold plated trigger an' hammer. I rotated the cylinder, shuffled the action a time or two, an' took a sight on a lantern on the wall. The fella shifted stance a little an' took his balance.

"Right nice," I told him. "Purty, too. What do ya want for it?"

"I'll have fifty," he said.

"Purty steep," I said. "Ya know, I seen one looked a lot like this'un a while back. Fella by the name a Arkansas Bill Cole had it. I know that 'cause I give it to him the day afore some dirty bastards kilt him. He took a mess of 'em with him, though. I reckon yer one a them body-robbin' sonsabitches that didn't have the guts to face him down, ain't ya, Charlie?"

He went for his gun then, but there was a roar, an' he twisted sideways as I pulled my Schofield. Another roar come, an' he fell back agin the wall an' slid down to the floor, oozin' blood from his chest in two spots. He tightened up, jerky like, for a minute then relaxed an' sighed. Arliss stepped out from behind the counter with that Henry in his hands.

"I fixed the rifle," he said.

CHAPTER TWENTY-EIGHT

"You know that feller?" Arliss asked me.

"No," I said.

"Breed ain't he?" Arliss said.

I nodded. "I don't know him," I said, "but I know who he is. Charlie Redhorse."

"I'll be damned," Arliss said. "I heer'd a him. He's a rascal, he is."

"There's probably paper on him," I said. "If'n there is, you just made yerself some money."

"An' I jest thought I was doin' you a good deed," Arliss said. "I believe he usta run with a feller name a Youngblood. Child killer by reputation. Reckon he's around?"

"I got no idea," I said, takin' my eyes offa Charlie Redhorse for the first time since he fell.

"Wouldn't be a bad idea to behave like he was around, I reckon," Arliss went on. "Could be gunnin' for you, you bein' in the company a Arkansas Bill Cole an' all."

"I doan know how he'd even know who I was," I said. "Coulda just been a accident Charlie even showed up here. That's the case, Youngblood might be lookin' for you when word gits out you done for his pard."

Arliss grinned an' shook his head. "Might be lookin' fer both of us," he said. "You 'spose we oughta go hide under the shed fer a spell?"

About that time the door swung open an' Hank Buford come in, pistol drawn. He sized things up quick an' holstered it.

"As I live an' breathe," he said, "Charlie Redhorse, dead on the floor. Which one a you boys done fer him?"

"Arliss got him when he was drawin' on me," I said.

"Well hell, Arliss," Hank said, "you got yerself a bad'un there. Charlie was just a step up from ol' Scratch hisself. Mercy. He'll be dancin' with the demons in hell tonight."

"You knowed him, did ya, Hank?" I asked.

"I come across him ten or twelve year ago when I was jest a pup chasin' cattle for a feller in the Breaks. Seen him in a whorehouse. Didn't have no truck with him, but another feller tolt me who he was. He's was a shore enough bad'un. That there is the pure-dee straight of it. Had a ol' boy name a Youngblood runnin' with him. I heer'd Youngblood got a kick outa killin' injun kids durin' the mess up in Nebraska an' Ioway with them Sioux. Liked to chop 'em up with one a them injun 'hawks."

"Would you know Youngblood?" I asked him.

"Been a spell since I see'd him," Hank said, "but I might. Want me to look around?"

"I'd appreciate it," I told him.

"You betcha," Hank said. "I'll work late until we git this mess sorted out. That Youngblood is one sneaky sumbitch, I bet. Paid his way to the hot place a bunch a times."

"Thank ya, Hank," I said. "Would you mind gittin' aholt of the undertaker an' have him come carry this man off?"

"Mind?" Hank said. "Jesus, Rube, there ain't hardly nothin' I'd rather do than that. This ol' world is a damn site better off than it was afore Arliss touched off that Henry. The onliest thang wrong with Charlie Redhorse bein' dead is the facts that he wadden dead sooner an' that he ain't more deader than he is. See you boys later."

After Hank left, Arliss grinned at me. "Buford is a rare one, ain't he?" he said.

* * * * *

Me an' Arliss et them cold biscuits an' gravy while we waited for the hearse. After it had come an' gone I went down to the office an' put on that little scattergun in a crossdraw an' walked to the telegraph office. Jacobs sent a message off for me to Marion in Jeff City, tellin' him that Arliss had kilt Charlie Redhorse so Arliss could git any reward comin' to him, an' so Marion would know that he was dead. I didn't know if Marion was even in Jeff City or not, but I figgered them fellas over there could pass the word on if they knowed where he was. I also mentioned that Charlie was tryin' to sell that shiny Colt that I had passed on to Bill Cole. I figgered it might ease his mind some. It did mine, a little.

* * * * *

I went on home then, an' told Harmony what was goin' on, an' that I was gonna be tied up with my job more than usual for a while. She said that was all right an' she had some confidence in me an' my deputies. I went out an' collected Willie up then, an' threw a saddle on him. I usually left him at the livery, but I figgered that I'd keep him with me for a spell in case I'd have need of a horse real quick. I rode him down to Arliss' place an' tied him out back, loosin' the cinch some so he could git his breath without workin' for it while he just stood there. Alriss come out the back while I was fussin' with him.

"You givin' me my horse back?" he asked me.

"You losin' yer mind?" I said. "I had a helluva a sorrel that you coulda had, but I give him to Harmony. She's better lookin' than you are."

"I'm workin' on that purty Colt," Arliss said. "Have it ready for ya tomorrow."

I was some took. "Me?" I said.

"Yes, you," Arliss said. "I figger with what you told me about Arkansas Bill Cole, it might be fittin' if that gun come to you. You got some kinda problem with that?"

A lump kindly come up in my throat then. "Nossir," I said, "I ain't got no problem with that at all."

* * * * *

I tried to git Arliss to stay in Miz Clary's roomin' house that night, but he wouldn't do it. So I set with him 'til he went off to bed. I stayed out back, just hangin' around until after midnight, then got aholt a Emory an' made sure he'd keep an eye on Arliss' place in case somebody come sneakin' around. I tightened up Willie's cinch then, an' headed for home.

It had come over a little windy with a few long clouds chasin' one another across a half moon. I took a detour on the way home, ridin' out toward that little spring an' pool outside a town where me an' Harmony went when we was courtin'. It was purty out there anytime, but of a night it was some particular. Me an' Wllie stood out there for a spell, admirin' the feel of it an' there come a echo a thunder outa the west. I give him a drink outa that little pool an' we headed back, me not havin' my roll an' slicker an' all.

By the time we got back, them clouds had thickened up quite a bit an' it didn't take much of a nose to smell rain. The moon bein' gone like it was, everthin' was pitch black. I got offa Willie outside the livery an' led him inside, then felt my way over to a lantern an' lit the wick. There was a storm comin'. I could feel it in the air an' Willie was worried with it, shufflin' around while I loosened the cinch an' such. I couldn't git him to hold still, which was unusual, him bein' so dependable an' all. I finally had to speak to him about it, but it didn't do no good. When I finally did git the saddle offa him, it didn't help. He was tossin' his head an' rollin' his eyes. He durn near knocked the lantern offa the peg. I pulled the blanket off an' let it drop, then caught him by the reins an' pulled him up short, nose to nose with me, fixin' to have a chat with him about his behavior. As I looked at him, I seen his look shift to my left, an' I knowed somethin' was bad wrong. Without hardly thinkin' about it at all, I dropped the reins, throwed myself to my right, an' touched off that scattergun as soon as it cleared leather, aimin' at nothin' as I fell.

I never did even see him really, just kindly felt a shadow on my left side as I throwed myself away from it. My shot hit him in the upper thighs an' took the use a his legs from him. The momentum a his rush at me carried him past me when he went down, an' I was on him, pushin' that shotgun' his throat. He didn't even have no gun drawed or nothin'. Just one a them Injun axes called a tomahawk layin' beside him. He had a Colt on his belt an' I took it from him an' stood up, movin' the lantern so as to see him better. He laid there, quiet like in spite a the pain he musta been in, an' watched me.

"You'd be Youngblood, I reckon," I said.

"I am," he said, his voice not quite right, because a the pain I guess.

"That hawk layin' there the one you used on them children up in the Sioux Nation?" I asked him.

"An' others," he said, grinnin' at me.

"Not no more," I tolt him.

I put the muzzle a that little twelve-gauge agin his chest an' touched off the other barrel.

CHAPTER TWENTY-NINE

The sound a my second shot hadn't hardly died off when Verlon come through the door in his long-handles, a double twelve-gauge in his hands.

"You all right, Rube?" he hollered.

"Yessir," I said, feelin' my knees gittin' kindly weak. "I ain't hurt none."

Not more than a dozen steps behind him was Harmony in her nightdress, packin' a ol' Colt Navy, yellin' my name as she come through the door.

I had to holler at her that I was fine twice afore she detoured toward me an' quit hollarin'. She caught aholt of me like I was made a glass, askin' me over an' over again' if'n I was hurt. Finally I just hugged her an' she commenced to settle some. Lightnin' hit somewhere purty close then, an' that big ol' slap a thunder made her jerk an' she collected herself quite a bit an' stepped back from me.

By that time her daddy had lit another lantern an' brightened the space up some. He stood there lookin' down at the body.

"You know him, Rube?" he asked me.

"Yessir," I said. "I know who he is. His name is Youngblood. His pard, a fella name a Charlie Redhorse, was the one that tried me earlier today that Arliss done for. Youngblood was waitin' for me here in the stable when I come in, I reckon. Willie tipped me off to him, or he'd a chopped me with that hawk layin' there for certain. I was mighty lucky."

"Lord God," Verlon said, comin' over next to me. "Two outlaws in the same day."

The gunshot that went off then made me an' Verlon damn near shit ourselves. I jerked around to see Harmony standin' over the body with that ol' Colt still pointed down at Youngblood.

"Sonofabitch," she said.

* * * * *

I went on an' turned Willie out, tryin' to keep movin' an' git some strength back in my knees. Emory Nail showed up on horseback in just another minute, an' Verlon went outside to slow him down. It had started to rain right brisk, an' Emory come inside leadin' his horse. He talked to us for a bit, then got his slicker outa his roll an' put it on afore headin' back to git the undertaker an' his hearse. By the time everthin' got settled up an' the body took away, it was dawn, but not much a one, the sky bein' so covered up in heavy clouds. They seem to weigh on a fella like they was made a wool.

Harmony had coffee goin' up at the house, so I tossed a ol' saddle blanket over my back an' trotted up that way. When I come in the kitchen, she poured me a cup an' added some a that thick yella cream the ol' Gurnsey give. I set down at the table an' took a sip. She took a chair across on the other side an' studied on me. It always put me off my ease some when she looked at me like that. I waited an' didn't say nothin'. Purty soon she put a elbow on the table an' leaned in.

"I nearly didn't have a husband twice yesterday," she said.

"I was lucky," I said.

"No, you weren't," Harmony said. "You were fortunate. Fortunate to be in the company of Arliss Hyatt, and fortunate to have a horse that knew more than you did. If you think you lead a charmed life, Ruben Beeler, you are sadly mistaken and I will become a widow. I can recover from that because I have family, I am still young, I am still pretty, and I have good judgment. You, however, will not recover if I become a widow. The thought of that is distasteful to me. I love you and I am used to you. I would find it upsetting to go on without you."

"Thank you," I said.

"Everyday," Harmony went on, "it is in my mind to continue to earn your love and respect. I do that by being a good wife and, when it is time, I will also be a good mother. This is a partnership and I consistently labor to hold up my end of it and do my part as faithfully as I can. I know sometimes I fall a little short of the standards I have set for myself. But not often."

"Harmony," I said, "I ain't got one complaint. Not one."

"Of course you don't," Harmony said. "You're happy out on the trail with nothing but a blanket and a buckskin. Life here at home is a luxury to you, and I'm glad for that. I have never, not for one moment, thought you did not love me for who I am and appreciate me for what I do. I get a great deal of satisfaction from that, Ruben. And a great deal of satisfaction from you as well."

"But..." I said.

Harmony smiled. "But," she said, "and I will attempt to put this in a manner you can appreciate, if you get yourself killed by some low-life evil bastard, I will curse your name and the fact that your are absolutely irreplaceable for the rest of my days. I will never forgive you for that, Ruben. Not for one minute and not if I have three more husbands, ten more children, and live for two hundred years. I am fully prepared to tolerate any number of shortcomings on your part, but not that. Never that. Do you understand me?"

My chest felt kindly heavy an' it took a minute afore I could talk. "I reckon I do," I said.

"I reckon you better," Harmony replied, an' poured some fresh coffee in my cup.

I drank on it for a spell afore I spoke up agin. "Well, Miss Harmony," I said, "what kinda shortcomin's are we talkin' about here?"

"Among them are these two," she said. "Use the boot scraper before you come in the house and either grow a beard or shave at least every other day."

To tell the truth, them things seemed like trifles to me, but I figgered I'd pushed my luck enough. "I can do that," I said.

Harmony shook her head. "I don't want can," she said. "I want will."

I swallowed the last a my coffee. "All right," I said. "I will then."

"Thank you," Harmony said, standin' up. "Eggs and bacon for breakfast?"

"Don't go to no trouble," I said. "I'll git somethin' at Clary's Café. I got to go to the telegraph office an' swing by an' see Arliss. I'll be back afore long an' take a nap if I don't git kilt."

* * * * *

I walked back to the stable then an' got my slicker outa my roll an' put it on. The rain eased a little on my walk into town. I noticed my heels was strikin' the ground some harder than usual, an' I tried to settle down. I'd figgered on gittin' me an' Arliss some biscuits an' gravy, but afore I went to do that, I stopped by the barber shop for a shave. I got a new cake a soap for my mug back at the house, too. Truth is, anytime I ever tried to grow a beard, my face looked like clumps a weeds growin' on a sandbar. Shavin' wouldn't be so bad. I had my daddy's good straight razor.

* * * * *

Arliss was settin' up at the bench when I come in with them plates a biscuits an' gravy. He looked at me.

"You figure we'll git to eat this hot today?" he asked.

"We will if'n you don't shoot nobody," I said.

"I heer'd you shotgunned Youngblood last night, boy."

"I did," I told him. "He was layin' for me in the stable when I went home. Willie tipped me off he was comin' or he'd a had me with a Injun 'hawk. It was a terrible close thing, Arliss. Harmony is some mad at me over it."

"I wouldn't doubt that," he said.

"She come at me like it was my fault. Tolt me she would never forgive me if I got kilt."

"It is yer fault, Rube. Yer the one that took up the law an' all. If ya hadden a done that, Youngblood wouldn't a been on yer trail. Charlie Redhorse neither. Who the hell you fixin' to blame besides you?"

"Well dammit, Arliss," I said, "I got a job to do an' a promise to keep. You know that better'n almost anybody. You takin' her part?"

"I ain't takin' nobody's part," he said. "You was a lawman when Harmony married ya, boy. She's got nobody to blame for that but her. You remember when you found me out on the trail after them Duncan boys had damn near kilt me, doncha?"

"A 'course I do," I said.

"It seem reasonable to you to figger me gittin' shot up like that was their fault?" he asked.

"Yessir, it was," I said.

"I didn't have to be there," he said. "I coulda been anywhere's else in this ol' world, but I wasn't. I was there. That's my fault."

"Aw hell, Arliss," I said. "That there ain't right."

"I blame my momma an' daddy," he went on. "If the two a them had never got together, none a this woulda ever happened. Why, you wouldn't a come across me, never met Marion, never come here to be the town law, never met miss Harmony...look at all the grief my folks started."

"What's the matter with you, Arliss?" I said. "That's just foolishness."

He grinned at me. "It is, ain't it?" he said. "The two biggest reason for folks to git foolish is love an' fear. When ya put them two together, things can git plumb silly. That gal loves you, Ruben, an' she fearful for ya. Them two things ganged up on her an' she took it out on you. That ain't a bad thing at all. Now you know how she feels, an' you can take that inta account when you deal with her. I speck that, by now, she's takin' it out on herself anyways. That there is a helluva young woman, Rube, an' probably the best thing that'll ever happen to you. I was in yer place, I'd listen to what she says, try an' understand what she's sufferin' through, an' then work on bein' a comfort to her."

"She come in that livery behind her daddy packin' a ol' Colt Navy," I said.

"She didn't," Arliss grinned.

"She shore did. While Verlon an' me was talkin', dammed if she didn't put another shot through Youngblood an' called him a sonofabitch."

"The hell she did!" Arliss laughed. "Boy, a woman like that deserves somethin' special," he went on, reachin' under the counter an' comin' up with that shiny Colt I give to Arkansas Bill Cole. "You give her this an' take that ol' Navy off her hands. It's purty enough to be a pleasure to a woman, an' a damn site better than what she's got."

"That's a good idea, Arliss," I said.

"I'll tell ya somethin' else," he went on. "Our biscuits an' gravy is cold agin."

* * * * *

I went over to the telegraph office an' sent another one off to Marion, this time about Youngblood, an' went on to the house. Harmony was makin' dough to roll for noodles when I come in, after usin' the boot scraper. She smiled at me.

"Where you been?" she asked.

"Gittin' you a purty," I said, an' laid that Colt on the table. I figgerd I'd give her that bird necklace some other time.

She looked at that revolver for a minute then kindly batted her eyes in my direction.

"For me?" she said.

"The way you come stormin' into the livery last night," I said, "wavin' that big ol Navy around like you was fixin' to chop down a tree with it, I thought somethin' like this might suit you a little better."

She picked that Colt up, cleared the gate, rotated the cylinder, cocked it, eased the hammer back down, an' smiled at me.

"You shaved," she said.

CHAPTER THIRTY

From that day on for a spell, everwhere I went I had a shadow. If it warn't Hank Buford or Emory Nail, it was Arliss or Verlon. Seemed like folks thought there was a assassin lurkin' behind ever rock an' tree waitin' to git a clean shot at Ruben Beeler. It got right worrisome to me, bein' followed around like I was. After a few days I got a telegraph from Marion sayin' he got both a mine an' askin' me to tell Arliss his money for shootin' Charlie Redhorse should show up in a month or so to the tune a five hunnerd dollars. Arliss offered to pay me half for actin' as bait, but I doan think he meant it.

Another week or so went by an' I went in to work on a Saturday afternoon, stoppin' by Arliss' place like I usually done, on the way to the office. I was just openin' his door when I looked down the street an' here come Marion Daniels on that ugly roan a his. I waited while he rode up an' swung down, stretched out his back a mite, an' come up on the boardwalk beside me. I grinned at him.

"Marshal," I said.

He looked at me an' kindly grimaced. "They got Homer, Ruben," he said to me.

It felt like somebody had punched me in the chest or somethin', an' I fell back an' leaned agin the wall a Arliss place. "Homer's dead?" I asked.

"No, no. Take it easy, boy," Marion said. "Homer ain't dead. He's shot, but he ain't dead an' he ain't gonna die from it neither. Settle down."

"Well, Jesus Christ, Marion!" I said. "Ya coulda come at me with it some easier than that. Arliss'll wanna know about this, too." I opened the door an' went in the shop.

When Arliss seen me, he knowed somethin' was wrong. Marion comin' in behind me put a edge to it.

"What's happened?" he asked.

"Marion here has brung news that Homer is shot, but he ain't gonna die," I said.

"Happened around a week ago," Marion said. "Three fellers come at him while he was walkin' to his office after breakfast. He kilt one of 'em on the spot, an' another one of 'em died a day or so later. The third one got him in the right leg around the knee with a lever action shotgun. Tore him up purty fierce. The doc says he ain't gonna lose the leg he doan think, but his knee ain't gonna work no more neither. He'll be in a brace or somethin' to keep it stiff so he'll be able to walk on it. Homer says the pain is troublesome, but other than that, he feels all right."

"Lord above," Arliss said. "I hate to hear that. Does he know who done it?"

Marion nodded. "He claims it was Cleveland Pettigrew, an' that makes some sense. The two that got kilt was no older than Ruben here an' he doan know who they was, but Pettigrew is a ol' hand. He worked for the Pinkertons years ago. Was part of the bunch they sent after Sam Bass. For some reason, he just disappeared for a year or two, then showed up' on the wrong side a the law with Courtney Bellmont an' Matt Zimmerman when them boys was raisin' hell up in Nebraska. Pettigrew was right fond of lever action shotguns as I recall. Makes sense that he could easy have come to know the Waxler bunch. They run up in that neck a the woods. Homer thinks he mighta put one in him, but he ain't sure. Anyways, Pettigrew got away."

"Seems to me," Arliss said, "that ol' man Waxler knows who you boys are and was tryin' to settle the score."

"That's what I figger," Marion said. "The only reason nobody come after me is that I doan set in one spot like Ruben here or Homer. If I did, I reckon somebody woulda tried me by now, too."

"What are we gonna do, Marion," I asked him.

"We're gonna go to the Sweetwater," he said. "I ain't et nothing but jerky an' biscuits since day afore yesterday. I need a beefsteak or some chicken."

* * * * *

Marion went after his chicken an' dumplin's like he hadn't et since just after the war. I had, so I just ordered a piece a pie. Like most pie they made at The Sweetwater, it was a little sour for my taste. Sometimes a fella has to do with what comes his way, I reckon.

Marion was too busy shovelin' it in to say much 'til he chawed his way to a halt. The waitress brung him a refill on coffee, an' he drank about half a that afore he even seemed to notice that me an' Arliss was at the table with him. He leaned back, give a little belch, an' looked at me.

"Well," he said, "ya think we oughta go for a little ride, Ruben?"

"Willie's gittin' fat agin," I tolt him. "Wouldn't hurt him none to git some exercise."

"When's that baby a your'n due to show up?"

"The doc says around the middle a November," I said. "Miz Clary claims it'll git here a little afore that."

"Still gives us about a month," Marion said. "If we're gone that long, we won't never be back."

That comment put us all to thinkin' some. Finally Arliss spoke up.

"I don't see that you boys got much of a choice," he said. "You hide from a wounded bear, he'll come an' git ya. Only way outa that is to check yer load an' git after him."

"We wounded that ol' bear," Marion said. "They ain't no doubt about that. I figger a head count a the one I done for in the saloon, then them five you got, then the brothers an' that slinger at the jailhouse, then the one that Homer got when you run their horses off, then the seven that Bill Cole took with him, plus the two ya kilt here an' the two that Homer done for makes what? Twenny? Twenny-one?"

"Good Lord," I said. "It is really that many?"

Marion nodded. "Yessir," he said. "That's a passel, an' it don't count none that Bill mighta wounded that was still able to ride off. That many a them, one a us kilt an' one a us shot up. I reckon that ol' man Waxler's bunch has shore been whittled down some. You can bet he's restless in his sleep right now. Them wasn't just hayshakers he sent after us neither. Oh, they wasn't all pistoleers an' shootists for damn sure, but they wasn't just clodhoppers. Whoever he's got left has got to be some nervous. He's probably got two or three with sand, but most a his remainders'll be common, I reckon. That ol' bastard has got his pride, Ruben. He won't quit. Not never. He'll keep sendin' boys after us 'til they ain't nobody left ta send."

"You need a better horse than that roan for the trip," I said.

Marion tilted his hat back a little an' eyeballed me. "You fatmouthin' my horse?" he asked.

I grinned at him. "I'm just sayin' that you need a horse that can keep up with Willie. That roan cain't."

"That roan," Marion said, "is the horse I got."

"Harmony's got a horse that she might loan ya," I said. "Big ol' long-legged sorrel that even Willie cain't git away from. Used to belong to a fella name a Arkansas Bill Cole."

Marion's eyebrows went up. "You got Bill Cole's horse?" he said.

"That sorrel got snake bit. Bill give him to me to lead on down the trail while he took Homer's wore-out gray an' went after them fellas that kilt him. Bill had a growth in him an' was dyin' from it. He didn't wanna go out in no sick bed."

"Aw hell," Marion said, pullin' his hat back down low. "That's why that ol' dog come to help us. Lookin' for salvation. By God, boys, I reckon he found it. I'll be damned."

The three a us set quiet then, an' finally Marion spoke up.

"We'll leave day after tomorrow, Ruben," he said. "You git us enough chuck to keep a-goin, but no more than we can carry on horseback. Ain't no use in takin' Arliss. He won't be able to keep up."

Arliss give a little jerk. "By God," he said, "I'd hate to be a burden to you fellers!"

Marion smiled an' shook his head. "I ain't talkin' about you, ya ol' cob," he said. "I'm talkin' about Ruben's pack animal. Arliss the mule."

"Arliss the mule?" Arliss said, lookin' at me right sharp.

"That's what I named him," I said. "He's a terrible good mule, Arliss is."

"You named a durn mule after me?" Arliss went on.

"He put me in a mind of ya, Arliss," I said. "He's little, he's got short legs, he's kindly slow, he's older than dirt, an' ever time I speak to him, he switches his tail."

Arliss was starin' at me, his face kindly red like. He started to say somethin' but stopped an' just closed his mouth.

"He's ugly too," Marion said. "Farts a lot."

I couldn't stand it. I hit Marion with my hat an' purty much went south. Arliss got up an' stomped off. Marion leaned over in his chair an' let it happen, wipin' at his eyes with the back a his hand.

CHAPTER THIRTY-ONE

I didn't know how I was gonna tell Miss Harmony that I was fixin' to strike out after bad men agin, an' I was some glad she was sleepin' when I got back to the house. I fussed with it a lot over the night, wakin' up as much as I slept. The next mornin' I got up a little later than was usual for me. Her daddy was gone to the forge, an' she was in the kitchen fixin' a mess a biscuits. I give her a little hug, an' kissed her on the cheek. She smiled at me an' poured a cup a coffee an' set it on the table. I took a seat as she put cream in it for me.

"Marion's back in town," I said. "He brung news that Homer come up agin three fellers tryin' to kill him. He got two of 'em, but one of 'em shot his leg up purty bad. His knee ain't gonna work much no more."

Harmony stopped what she was doin' an' just stood there, lookin' at me. "When are you leaving?" she asked.

"Tomorrow, I reckon," I said.

She nodded. "I'll make some more biscuits," she said. "Tell Marion I said to take the sorrel. That roan of his won't be able to stay up with Willie."

"I hate to go," I told her.

"I hate for you to go," Harmony said, "but I also don't want both of us looking over our shoulders every minute of every day either. You could have no better companion than Marion, Ruben. I know you're afraid. I also know that you're not afraid for yourself, but for me and the baby. You have to put that away. There's not room for it where you are going."

"How did you git so smart?" I asked her.

Harmony smiled at me then. "Just one of my many virtues," she said.

* * * * *

I spent the mornin' goin' over my possibles for the trip, cleanin' my guns, checkin' Willie over real good, an' gittin' what we'd need an' ways to carry it without Arliss the mule. Verlon checked that Willie's shoes was all right, an' replaced one of 'em. I was glad for it. A little after noon I walked into the office an' met Hank Buford comin' out, shakin' his head an' grinnin'.

"What's so funny?" I asked him.

"Althea Parsons was just in," he said.

"She don't miss a day, does she?" I said. "What's wrong this time?"

"She wants her neighbor boy, that Lambert kid, arrested."

"That boy ain't but seven or eight year old," I said. "He rob the bank?"

Hank laughed. "Winda peekin'," he said.

"At Althea?" I said. "That's a brave kid! Sight like that would strike most folks blind!"

"I wouldn't have the guts to look," Hank went on. "I told Althea to keep her curtains pulled. They was laws agin public indecency an' she wouldn't do much good in jail."

"You didn't!"

"Yessir, I did," Hank giggled. "She just got to faunchin' at me. I speck she'll file a complaint on me or somethin'."

"I'll put it with all the other complaints she's filed. Winter's comin'. Be good to have lots a kindlin'."

"I seen Marion Daniels this mornin'," Hank went on. "He said you an' him was gonna hit the trail tomorrow. You want me to come along?"

"I'd be comforted to have ya," I said, "but you got a job to do here."

He nodded. "You go on, Rube," he said. "You got stuff to do today to git ready. Me an' Emory can tend to things. We'll take care a the town, you take care a yerself an' spend yer time on that. You are hereby relieved a duty, unless ol' Althea goes on a rampage or somethin'."

I slapped him on the arm. "Yer a good man, Hank," I said.

He grinned at me. "Can I have a raise?" he asked.

"Not until we git this upcomin' complaint agin ya took care of," I said. "It goes bad an' I may havta fire ya." I headed down toward Arliss' place.

* * * * *

As I passed by the Sweetwater, I seen Marion an' Arliss at a table. I went in an' set with 'em. Arliss looked at me an' shook his head.

"A durn mule," he said, then took to grinnin'.

"I tolt Harmony we was goin' north, Marion," I said. "She tolt me to tell you to take that sorrel so you can keep up with Willie. It was her idea. I never said no word about it."

"Right nice of her," Marion said. "I reckon I should. Gonna be some strange to me though. I don't believe I set on any horse but the roan in ten years. I'm fair used to him. He can pull a wagon outa a ditch, but he cain't outrun a hog. We may have some runnin' to do, Ruben. I gotta admit, I'd like to have Homer with us on this. Him an' that Sharps is some comfort."

"I got a Sharps that I finally fixed," Arliss said. "Forty-four ninety. Yer welcome to it if'n either one a ya can use it."

Marion shook his head. "Not me," he said. "I ain't got the patience."

"I never even fired one," I said.

"Well, the two a you boys is just shit outa luck then, ain't ya?" Arliss said, twitchin' his mouth like he done when he was bein' a smartass.

Marion looked at me. "Ya know," he said, "one a the nicest things about the other Arliss is he just does his job an' keeps his trap shut. I think I'm gonna miss him more than Homer."

The waitress come' then an' they both ordered dinner. I got a chunk a apple cobbler with cream an' a bowl a sugar.

* * * * *

When they finished eatin', we went down to Arliss shop. He went in the back room an' fussed around some, then come out carryin' a lever action rifle.

"Since neither one a ya want to mess around with a Sharps," he said, " an' since Marion carries that coach gun a his, Rube, you leave that Yallerboy a your'n with me an' take this." He handed me that rifle. It was longer an' some heavier than my Yellaboy. "That is a Winchester

'76 Centennial," Arliss went on. "Where yours is a 44/40, that'un is a 45/75. Bigger bullet an' damn near twice the powder. The barrel is eight inches longer'n than that rifle a your'n, so it'll feel some muzzle heavy. Boy, this thing kin reach out an' git 'em. Kill a buffler with one shot. It's sighted in for around a hunnerd yards, but it'll do it's job as far as yer bare eye can find a target. 'Bout a six-inch drop at two hunnerd, maybe a foot an' a half at three hunnerd. Leave a terrible hole comin' out of a man. I got about twenty-five rounds on hand for it. I'll load ya up fifty more tonight."

It was a helluva gun, no doubt about that. I worked the action some an' they warn't nothin' to it.

"Smooth," I said.

"Better than new," Arliss said. "Loadin' gate is real easy, keep it at ten or under. Trigger breaks at about two pounds like crackin' glass. I put some work into it."

"I'm right partial to my Yellaboy," I said, "but this here is a gun an' a half. I'll treat it good."

"You treat it however you need to," Arliss said. "It's only wood an' metal. You just come back with it. Will ya take some advice?"

"Prob'ly," I told him.

"Leave that durned ol' Schofield top-break behind, too. Lemme fix ya up with a pair a Colts. That Smith and Wesson load for them top-breaks is underpowered compared to a Colt .45 or 44/40. I got two .45's that is in good shape in the back. Lemme set ya up with a cross draw where ya carry that scattergun. Carry two Colts instead, an' strap that little shotgun to yer saddle horn."

Marion spoke up then. "Good advice ain't worth a damn unless ya take it," he said.

"I ain't never shot a Colt much," I said.

"Plenty a day left," Arliss said.

"All right," I said. "Gimme a box a .45's an' I'll leave my gunbelt here so you can fix it up for me."

"Good," Arliss said. "I'll git ya one a them guns."

"I'll git it later," I said.

"Well, what the hell you gonna shoot?" he asked.

"If Miss Harmony can loan Marion a horse, she can damn sure loan me a gun," I said.

* * * * *

I went out an' shot that Colt a while. Its balance was more in the hand than toward the muzzle like the Schofield. The barrel come up more on the recoil, but was also easier to git back on target. It felt unusual to me, but I didn't hardly mind it after I shot it a few times. When I got done with it, I went back down to Arliss' place. He tossed a gunbelt up on the counter an' looked at me.

"Try that on," he said.

It was rigged some different that most. Under my right hand was a holster on a short drop for a Colt. On my left side an' toward the front some was another Colt holster in a heavy slant toward the buckle. On the belt between them two was a pouch for extra bullets to go with the fifteen cartridge holders along the backside. Behind the crossdraw, where a drop holster woulda gone in a normal two-gun rig, hung the holster I carried that little shotgun in. Beside the rig, he put another scabbard on the counter for that sawed off double that would tie to my saddle horn.

"If ya need to," Arliss said, "you can carry both pistols an' yer scattergun, all at once. Left hand for the shotgun, right hand for both them Colts. Plus ya got a extra pouch for rifle ammunition. It'll be some awkward an' a little heavy but, by God, you'll have everthin' ya need. Ain't no room for your knife though. Guess you'll have to carry it in your teeth."

"Jesus, Arliss," I said, "this here is somethin'."

"Should set fair in a saddle, too," he went on. "Nothin' you'd want to carry on patrol, but it might come in handy on yer trip."

"Lord, I hope not," I said.

"Me too, boy," he said. "Me too."

* * * * *

I went down to the store an' got some dry beans an' flour an' jerky an' such. Without Arliss the mule, we wouldn't have the luxury a carryin' canned goods. Too much weight an' size for how we had to travel. I did git us some peppermint sticks, an' some a them maple an' cinnamon candies for Willie. I went home then an' et supper an' set with Harmony. She looked over my gunbelt an' asked where I was supposed to carry the dynamite.

* * * * *

I was in the livery at daybreak the next mornin', hangin bags a biscuits an' bacon, an' such on both horses, fixin' up my roll an' slicker, loadin' up my saddle bags with necessities. When I got done, Willie looked more like a camel than a horse. Marion showed up with the sun an' put a mess a his possibles on that big sorrel. By the time it was full daybreak, we was ready to go. I walked out with Harmony a ways an' we said our goodbyes, then the Marshal an' me mounted up an' went off.

Me an' Marion, back on the Nodaway trail.

CHAPTER THIRTY-TWO

We crossed the river at Jeff City an' got north a ways afore we stopped. We come across a little feeder crick that prob'ly found it's way to the Missouri sooner or later, an' pitched camp. The grass was fair still an' I hobbled the horses after I brung 'em back from gittin' a drink. Marion had a little fire goin'. The day had been right nice, even a little hot, but come the night an' a light breeze, an' things was fair cool. I fetched up some downed branches from the trees along the crick an' brought 'em up about the time Marion got bacon goin'. We et it an' biscuits sopped in the grease, an' I fished out a couple a them peppermint sticks after I threw a little more wood on. Marion leaned back agin his saddle an' commenced to suckin' on that peppermint. We set quiet like that a spell afore he spoke up.

"I could git used to that sorrel," he said. "Kindly makes my roan seem like a plowhorse."

"He gits around right smart," I said. "Since I got Willie, he's the only horse I come across that could outrun him."

"Hell, Ruben," Marion went on, "he oughta be able to. He's a hand an' a half taller than yer buck."

"That doan mean nothin'," I said. "Yer a hand an' a half taller'n me an' I can outrun you."

Marion chuckled some at that. "By God," he said, "you couldn't a done it twenny year ago."

"I speck not," I tolt him. "Twenny year ago I still hadn't figgerd out how to walk."

"Goddam smartmouth kids," Marion grumbled, an' pulled his blanket up.

I set there watchin' the fire spit little sparks into the dark for a time. It was good to be back on the trail.

* * * * *

By the middle a the next mornin' it was some brisk, an' clouds come in from the northwest. I got my slicker out to cut the wind an' put it on, an' pulled my hat down 'til it bent my ears so I wouldn't have to chase it. We come on a herd a mix-breed cattle, standin' in little knots with their tails to the wind. I eased Willie up closer to that sorrel an' Marion stood up in his stirrups an' studied them cows.

"I doan much like the look a that," he said. "Them steers know somethin' we might take heed of."

I agreed an' we both touched spurs an' headed toward a line a trees in the distance.

Willie left that sorrel behind when we took off, an' it musta been four or five hunnerd yards afore Marion caught up to us. He come on grinnin', low in the saddle, goin' by us at no more than a walkin' pace difference. He had me an' Willie by fifty yards or so when we come into some scrub oak an' thorn trees. Dodgin' an' cuttin' around them trees was hot biscuits to Willie, an' we passed the sorrel purty quick. Then we hit another open flat, an' here come that big red horse agin, easin' past us in spite a Willie doin' the best he could. It went on like that for near two miles I reckon, until we come into that line a big trees an' stopped. The horses was blowin' an' me an' Marion was pantin' an' grinnin' at each other like 'possums.

"Now that there was a bunch a foolishness," he said, gittin' down.

"I know it," I said. "Runnin' the only horses we got across unfamiliar ground coulda turned out bad. I thought for a while there that you wanted to race."

"Not me," Marion said. "I durn near wore them reins out keepin' that sorrel checked in like I done."

I nodded. "Ol' Willie wanted to go," I said, "but I wouldn't let him. Ain't no point in riskin' a horse just 'cause he wants to run a little bit."

Marion looked at the sky for a minute then turned toward me. "Ain't we a fine pair a liars," he said.

* * * * *

We found a cut bank on the west side of a small creek in them trees an' took shelter agin it. There was not a single bird in the sky. That wind had come up somethin' awful, makin' them trees squeal an' groan at each other. One big ol' oak down the way just give up an' fell over, it's roots throwin' dirt an' clods up that the wind plumb blowed away. The horses got to wantin' to run from it an' we had to tie both of 'em real secure like, our slickers flappin' an' poppin' with the force of the passin' of the air, leavin' little welts wherever a piece a slicker hit bare skin.

It never did really rain. It kindly misted for a spell, them little drops near burnin' a fella's face if'n he was to raise up outa cover to where they could hit him. We stayed there, squattin' agin that bank for the rest a the day in a cold camp, hopin' the world just didn't plum blow away. Come dark it eased up an' I built a fire. It was too late to put no beans on to boil. I made coffee an' Marion got out the bacon.

It might not a rained much on us, but it shore rained somewheres. The next mornin' that little creek was durn near in our bedrolls an' two feet deeper than the trickle it was when we come on it. Marion took his scattergun an' struck off while I got a fire goin'. Purty soon I heer'd a shot an' in a little bit another shot, an' directly he come walkin' back with a hen pheasant an' a fat rabbit.

"That godawful wind must a scrambled their brains," he said. "Flushed this hen right by my feet, an' the rabbit was settin' thirty yards off. I walked up about fifty feet away an' did fer him. He just set there an' waited on me."

He skin't 'em an' I fried 'em. I ain't partial to pheasant none, but that ol' cottontail was some tasty.

* * * * *

The sky cleared as the mornin' went on, an' by the end of the day we had made near another forty miles. We coulda done better, but we didn't wanna wear our mounts down too much, although Willie an' the sorrel both seemed to take it well. We camped outside a Brunswick a mile or two early enough I got some beans boilin' with a couple a chunks a that smoked bacon. It went right well with the last a Harmony's biscuits an' we made a good meal of it. I give both horses a piece a that maple an' cinnamon candy an' the sorrel seemed to favor it as much as Willie did, once he remembered what to do with it.

* * * * *

The weather stayed good, although cool, the trees all kinds a red an' yella an' brown where they was once green, an' in three more days we come up near Clearmont in the middle a the afternoon. We'd been out that way afore when all this mess started up, an' Marion turned away from the direction a town when we come on the railroad right-of-way, an' headed east followin' it. I looked at him.

"Where we goin'?" I asked.

"You want a good meal?" he said.

"Like a buzzard wants a dead hog," I said.

"I thought we might pay a little visit to the Thorson place," Marion said. "See if everbody there is still grateful we didn't hang that boy a theirs or put him in the pen for thirty years."

My brain had plumb misplaced the Thorsen folks I reckon, but Missus Thorsen's cookin', come back into my mind real quick.

"Am I gonna have to run that boy Agner down agin just to git us somethin' to eat?" I asked.

Marion shook his head. "I'll do it," he said. "This sorrel is some faster than that midget yer settin' on."

* * * * *

Mister an' Missus Thorsen greeted us like we was long lost relation. We'd been jawin' with them for just a few minutes when their boy come in from doin' goat chores. He seen us an' didn't hardly know whether to grin or run' in case we had changed our minds about cartin' him off an' had come back to finish the job. Marion took a minute to explain why we was in their neck a the woods'. Right off, they offered to feed us an' the horses, an' give us a place to toss our rolls in their nice barn. We took 'em up on their hospitality.

We led the horses down an' dropped saddles an' such. Their boy said he'd feed an' water 'em for us, an' tolt us to go on back to the house. Missus Thorson was floggin' the kitchen for all she was worth when we come back in, an' Mister Thorsen give each a us a glass a some blackberry wine he'd made. I got to say, I liked it quite a bit better than the wine I'd had when I took Miss Margie out for that fancy dinner. It was sweet-like on a fella's tongue, an' warm, too. I drunk two glasses afore I realized I was a little dizzy from it. By that time, Missus Thorsen had warmed up some pork roast for us with chunks a carrots an' potaters, an' some a her big ol' rolls with butter. I et durn near too much, but I lost that dizzy feelin'. Then Mister Thorsen brung out some more wine he'd made outa wild grapes an' blueberries, an' I took right to it. Dark come purty early it seemed, an' me an' Marion went to the barn an' laid our rolls out on a pile a straw.

I slept right good. The next morinin' my head did hurt some though, an' I was terrible thirsty.

We worshed up in the trough as best we could an' tried to make ourselves presentable afore we went up to the house. Missus Thorsen had breakfast ready when we come in. There was little thin slices a meat that had been fried up to where it was crisp on the edges. With it was the durndest pancakes I had ever seen. They was terrible big around an' as thin as a corn husk. She give us some syrup she'd made outa water, wild honey, sugar an' blueberries. I'm tellin' you I had never afore tasted anythin' like it. It was terrible good an' them crisp little pieces a meat set them pancakes off plumb fine. I commented on how tasty everthin' was, an' Mister Thorsen tolt me that the meat I liked so much was goat. Goat! I never in my life figgerd I'd be eatin' on no goat.

Their boy, Agner, come in from chores as we was drinkin' coffee an' set with us. I noticed Marion studyin' on him some. Purty soon he spoke up.

"You folks hear anythin' about that Waxler bunch lately?" he asked.

Mister Thorsen shook his head. "Not much," he said. "Seems like they have quieted down."

"How 'bout you, Agner?" Marion went on, turnin' to the boy.

"I was makin' a delivery down in Grant City a week or so ago," Agner said, "and I heard they had gone back up north, but I don't know where."

"You reckon you might be able to find out for us?" Marion asked him.

"Yessir, Marshal," the boy said. "I might. I could go to Worth County around Sheridan an' ask over that way, then back over to Nodaway County up by Hopkins an' see for ya. Maybe over to Clearmont an' Burlington Junction."

"I hate to ask ya to do it," Marion said, "but me an' Marshal Beeler here is knowed by these fellers. I doan wanna let 'em find out we're back up thisaway. There was four a us Marshals involved in this mess. Waxler's bunch kilt one of us, bad wounded another, and has twice made unsuccessful attempts on Marshal Beeler's life. These are some truly bad men, Son, an' I want you to know that afore ya git in this."

"I make deliveries all over around here," Agner said. "Folks is used to me comin' and goin'."

"How long might it take ya, do ya think?" Marion asked.

"Three days," Agner said. "Maybe four."

Marion looked at Mister Thorsen then an' raised a eyebrow. Mister Thorsen nodded.

"All right," Marion went on, "but you listen to me, boy. You be as easy about it as you can be. You doan take no chances, an' you don't git too curious an' tip nobody off. You be as careful as a crow, goddammit! I doan want you on my conscience. You hear me?"

"Yessir, I do. I'll find out what I can, and I won't say nothin' about you an' Marshal Beeler bein' around."

"Things git off center," Marion said, "you cut an' run for home. I ain't got one bit a use for no hero."

"I'll take the wagon," Agner said. "It'll be slower, but that's how I usually get around. It won't seem suspicious."

"Good idea," Marion said, "but give a thought toward tyin' that chestnut a your'n to the back in case you find out you get a need for speed."

CHAPTER THIRTY-THREE

I swear, I don't know how come Mister Thorsen didn't weigh five hunnerd pounds. While Agner was gone, Missus Thorsen come at us with food like nothin' I'd ever messed with afore. Ever meal we et was a big'un, an' ever time we come in the house, she was throwin' fried pies, or cookies, or preserves an' bread, or somethin' at us. It was right hard to pass up. If I'd a stayed there a month, Ol' Willie woulda fell down when I got on him. An' what Missus Thorsen done for us, Mister Thorsen done for the horses. They got all the grass they could eat plus grain in the mornin' an' a grain an' goatmilk an' molasses mash in the evenin'. Me an' Marion tried to help out around the place, but Mister Thorsen wouldn't have no truck with it. So we just et, hung around, et, cleaned our guns, et, oiled our leather, et, an' then had somethin' else to eat. An' then, a 'course, ever evenin' out come some other kinda wine. You can say what ya want to about heaven, but I reckon heaven'd have a helluva time standin' up' someplace like the Thorsen's.

It went on like that for four whole days 'til Agner come back. When he got home, his momma started throwin' eats at him like chuckin' rocks at a turtle. It took him most of a afternoon to git over it, an' then he found us down at the barn. I was feedin' bits a that molasses candy to a goat that put me in a mind a Arliss the mule when he come in.

"You doin' all right, Agner?" Marion asked him.

"Yessir, Marshal," he said. "I have found some stuff out. Last place I went to was Hopkins. That's up close to the Iowa line. There's a blacksmith up there that did some shoein' for me last spring. After I paid him, I gave him a bottle of wine. He told me that the Waxler bunch wasn't nearly as big as it usta be and that they'd pulled back up east and north of Corning about ten miles to a place they have up there."

"I doan know where that is," Marion said.

"North a Hopkins about ten miles is Bedford," Agner said. "About ten miles north of there is Gravity. North a Gravity around fifteen miles is Corning. Their place is ten or twelve miles east an' north of there."

"You figger the smith was tellin' ya the truth?"

Agner grinned. "He's fond of my father's wine," he said. "There was a free gallon of the blueberry in it for him. And another one the next time I get up that way."

"That'd make me tell the truth," I said.

* * * * *

We left some a our truck stashed away at the Thorson's place the next mornin' to lighten our load a mite. After a breakfast that was plumb scary, me an' Marion struck off to the north.

* * * * *

We figgerd it was near fifty miles to where we needed to be, so we went some easy on the ride, thinkin' to do it in two days. We avoided towns an' come to evenin' a hour or so north an' a little east a Gravity. Missus Thorson had sent along some kindly triangle lookin' puffy things she'd baked that had cherries in sweet syrup fillin' the inside. We had bacon outa the skillet with coffee an' them baked triangles for supper. The taste a that salty bacon' them sweet cherries was awful good. She packed up a half a dozen of 'em. We et 'em all.

"Swedish folks is from Sweden ain't they?" I asked Marion.

"Reckon they would be," he said.

"I wonder if all them folks eat like that Thorson family does?"

"Sweden is a far northern country, I hear," Marion said. "Long cold winters an' lotsa snow. A feller has to eat some more durin' cold weather if'n he wants to keep a-goin. Maybe that's it."

"They shore got a nice place," I went on. "I doan know how it supports itself though. Ain't but one cow, a couple a steers, a pig or two, an' only three or four horses. Wonder how they make any money?"

"That big shed out back a ways out from the barn is how," Marion said. "There's a full rocked-in cellar underneath it. Them woods an' cuts out there is loaded with wild grapes an' blueberries, black berries an' wild cherry trees. Ol' man Thorsen an' me talked about it. He sells goats an' kids to eat, goat's milk to drink, and four ta five hunnerd gallons a wine a year, at near ten dollars a gallon. He's got a clear profit around seven dollars a gallon after he pays for the sugar an' such an' hires kids ta pick the fruit an' grapes. That's thirty-five hunnerd a year right there, not countin' them goats."

"Lord," I said. "That's a fortune."

"It is," Marion said. "He makes the wine in that big shed an' stores it in that cellar. His boy does the deliveries to towns all around here. Got quite a business."

"I gotta admit I have come to like wine," I said, "but it is a sneaky drink."

"Like a fox outside a henhouse," Marion said.

* * * * *

We come onto Corning early the next afternoon under a clear sky with a light breeze from the south that was pleasant. We didn't go inta town, but headed west a little ways to miss it, then come back north. After we went on a spell, we got careful to stay offa ridgelines an' kept to cover as much as we could to keep from gittin' spotted too easy. It was near dark when we decided we'd missed the place. As we was pitchin' camp, I caught the littlest whiff a woodsmoke.

"Waxler is south of us, Marion," I said. "We come too far."

"That right?" he asked me.

"Yessir. I just smelt a little of his smoke. Burnin' red oak I think."

"Can you foller yer nose after dark?" he said.

"Long as the breeze holds up I can," I tolt him.

"Git the jerky out, Ruben," he said. "We'll have a cold camp bite ta eat, an' go find the place."

* * * * *

There warn't no clouds an' about a half moon that night. Didn't take more than two hours to come on the house. We was laid up on the side of a hill three or four hunnerd yards from a low set cabin made outa logs. It was fair sized with a big porch.

With it was two corrals, a barn, an' what musta been a bunkhouse. They was ten or twelve horses in one a the corrals. The place was total dark, but Marion noticed one sentry walkin' around. We pulled back over the crest a the hill a ways an' got out our bedrolls.

"Lemme sleep for a couple hours," Marion said. "Then I'll set up an' let you sleep as long as you can. Come mornin' we'll take a daylight peek an' see what we can see. Now ain't the time to git in no hurry, Ruben. That wine'll still be back at the Thorson place when this is over."

CHAPTER THIRTY-FOUR

Durin' false dawn the next mornin' we left the horses tied an' headed back up to the top a that hill on foot an' took a peek at the place in daylight. It was better put together than I figgerd when we was lookin' at it in the dark. It was set down in kindly a bowl like, shaped some like a horseshoe, with hills behind an' on both sides of the house an' barn. The hills warn't over tall an' was covered in scrub. A few cows was rangin' around, prob'ly some more on the off slopes we couldn't see. A trail led from the front of the place out through the break in them slopes in what was the open end a the horseshoe, an' off toward town. We was too far away to see faces or nothin' like that, but it was easy enough to notice a couple a fellers wanderin' around, comin' outa the bunkhouse or goin' to the convenience.

Next to the bunkhouse was a small shack. Just as the sun come full up, a feller come outa it an' started beatin' on a piece a some kinda metal. Eight or ten boys come out a the bunkhouse then an' got plates a food from him. Some set out on buckets or stools outside while they et, an' some went back inside. Two fellers come outa the house then, one standin' straight, the other'n kindly bent over. The bent one took a chair on the porch, while the other one went to the cookhouse an' brung him back a plate. Marion got out that telescope a his an' stretched it out. He looked down at the place for a minute.

"That's Waxler on the porch, Ruben," he said. "He's on crutches instead a canes. Prob'ly easier on the ol' bastard. We'll lay up here for a spell an' git the routine a the place some. Judgin' by the feller's eatin' an' them what come outa the house, we got at least ten on hand. Most a these boys is likely not much more'n warm bodies. Saddle tramps and drifters that found a place to squat."

A fella carryin' a rifle come up from back by the barn then, stopped by the porch for a minute, an' went over to git a plate. 'Bout that time, another one come from over past the corrals, checked in with Waxler, an' went off to the cookhouse.

"Nighthawks," Marion said. "One more than we seen last night. Good thing we didn't git froggy."

In a little bit a feller carryin' a long gun come limpin' outa the house. He leaned it up' the porch rail an' set beside Waxler, puttin' his right foot up on top a box. Gray pants, a dark blue shirt, an' a one gun rig on a deep right-hand drop. It was too far to see what he was packin'.

"That'd be Cleveland Pettigrew I guess," Marion said, lookin' through that scope. "He's one that'd stay in the house. Judgin' by that limp a his, maybe ol' Homer did git one in him. Must not a been too bad though. Ain't had enough time for a solid wound to heal."

He passed me the telescope than, an' I looked things over through it. "What we gonna do now, ya reckon?" I asked.

Marion pulled a piece a jerky out an' chawed off a bite. "Ruben," he said, "we are gonna wait for a opportunity."

It was a nice mornin', cool with just a few clouds. Waitin' seemed like it might be right restful. I musta drifted off some, layin' there up on that hill, 'cause, all of a sudden, Marion was slappin' me on the shoulder an' I couldn't recall what mighta caused him to do somethin' like that. I looked down at the place an' seen two ol' boys on a buckboard pulled by a team a horses, headin' out on the trail toward town.

"We'll take the long way, Ruben," Marion said, backin' down the hill. "Let's go to town an' cut these two strays outa the herd."

* * * * *

We'd saddled the horses afore we left camp so it didn't take no time at all to tighten our cinches an' git on the way. We swung east a mile or two, then turned back south, stayin' away from the trail, an' let that sorrel an' Willie out a little bit. Them horses wanted to have another race, but we kept 'em at a lope 'til Corning come in sight. We circled it an' come in on the opposite side a where that wagon should show up, then drifted through town an' hung around a hitch rail at a general store, watchin' for them fellers to come in. I slipped my little scattergun off the saddle an' into my roll so as not to attract too much attention. Down the street a ways was a saloon. Farther down an' on the other side was a courthouse an' jail.

"I reckon this is the county seat," I said.

"Looks like it," Marion replied.

"No help there, I speck," I said. "Any local law around here is most likely in Waxler's pocket."

Marion smiled. "You ain't so dumb," he said.

We walked down the street a ways an' back, not wantin' to just hang around the rail in one spot. We come on a restaurant an' I stayed outside while Marion went in an' had a piece a pie. When he come out, I went in an' had one. Them folks coulda used a lesson or two from Missus Thorsen. I had just got outa the place when Marion struck off toward where we'd left the horses. I went along an' seen that wagon come in an' tie up at the same rail where we'd left the sorrel an' Willie.

Them fellas went in the store for a spell then come out an' started loadin' sacks a beans an' flour an' such in that buckboard. They got it half full or better afore they finished. We watched 'em dig around in their pockets an' count change. Then they headed for the saloon. I looked at Marion an' he nodded at me. I left him then, an' foller'd them boys inside.

* * * * *

It warn't much of a place. The bar was just a countertop faced with rough pine. I got me a beer an' set at a table over on the side, away from the doorway. Them two stood at the bar an' had a couple a shots. One of 'em was maybe thirty an' skinny, in a broke down greasy hat, wore out boots, an' packin' a Colt in a deep holster on a short drop' his right leg. The other'n was younger an' beefy, but soft. He didn't have no hat an' had a Remington conversion stuck down inside a belt that was holdin' up some tore up blanket pants. Them two was less than fearsome.

After they had their shots, they compared what money they had left an' flipped a coin. The skinny one commenced to grinnin', got another shot an' throwed it back while the young'un stood there lookin' pissed off. I got up an' went to stand beside 'em. They looked at me an' the barkeep walked over.

"Two more for these boys here," I said, an' dropped a twenty-dollar gold piece on the bar. All of a sudden, I had two new friends.

I eased 'em over to the table an' we jawed a little about this an' that while they had three or four more shots a whiskey, thankin' me for my hospitality ever time. They was gittin' on down the pike when Marion come in. He walked over, set, an' looked at me.

"You reckon these boys can help?" he asked.

"I doan know," I said. "I ain't asked 'em yet."

Marion turned to 'em. "You fellers know a ol' boy name a Clovis Waxler?"

Them two looked at each other for a minute. Finally the young one spoke up.

"Maybe," he said.

"Maybe?" Marion said. "You either do or ya don't. Now do ya or doncha?"

Them two commenced to lookin' at each other agin.

"Aw, hell," Marion said, lookin' at me. "These two hayshakers doan know shit, Leroy. Goddammit, we was supposed to be there two days ago, an' you waste time on these puppies. Waxler wouldn't let a couple a tramps like these git within' a mile a his place. These two ain't got a pint a ambition nor a ounce a brains between 'em."

"We know him," the skinny one said.

"Bullshit," Marion said.

"We do!" the young'un near holler'd. "We got his wagon right down the street. We're fixin' to go back to his place with it. What do you want from him?"

"It's what he wants from us," Marion said. "He's the one that hired us. You boys git yer asses up an' let's git on out to his place. He's expectin' us. Light a shuck! We ain't got all day."

Them two jerked theyselves upright an' weaved out the door, grumblin' at each other. Marion looked at me an' grinned.

"Leroy?" I said.

* * * * *

They clumb up on that wagon, the heavy one takin' two tries at it, an' went on down the road. I got that little shotgun out an' put it on my belt, then throwed a leg over Willie an' trotted him to ketch up to Marion. We laid back from 'em a ways for a couple a miles, an' come on a spot where the trail narrowed some in between two low hills that had post oak an' cedar growin' on 'em. Marion touched his horse inta a trot an' passed the wagon, then turned that sorrel sideways so them boys had to stop the team. I moved up beside 'em, an' lifted out the shotgun about the time Marion showed 'em his Colt. The skinny one took exception.

"What the hell do you think yer doin?" he said.

"Savin' yer lives, boys, if'n you pay attention to me," Marion said. "If not, the two a you can die right here. Afore ya git froggy, take notice a that shotgun my pard has got pointed at ya."

They swung their eyes to me an' give up. I could see it in their faces.

"I'll have yer sidearms, fellas," I said. "Easy like, just drop 'em to the ground."

It took the young one a couple a tries to git that conversion pulled loose from his belt. To tell the truth, I felt kindly sorry for him. After them guns was on the ground, Marion spoke up agin.

"Pull yer wagon over there by that little copse a cedars," he said, "an' git down."

"Yer fixin' ta kill us ain't ya, mister," Skinny piped up. "Yer gonna shoot us daid!"

"I got no reason to kill you boys," Marion explained to 'em. "I'm tryin' to help ya. You do just what I tell ya to do, an' yer gonna be fine. You buck me, an' I will shorely make sure the 'yotes around here git their fill. Pull the wagon over."

They was scared enough a Marion an' that little shotgun a mine that they done what they was tolt. Once they was off the wagon, I covered 'em while Marion loosed the team from the harness. He left the bridles on em, an' cut the rains off short. Them boys watched the whole thing an' begin to figger out they might survive. Marion faced 'em an' spoke up.

"Fellers," he said," here's the deal. My an' my pard are U.S. Marshals. There's a total a ten of us out this way on a special mission. We are all here to do for ol' man Waxler and his bunch. Eight of us are surroundin' the house right this minute. The two a us are stationed to keep any that might git loose from comin' into town. That means you boys. You go north, them marshals will kill ya. You come south an' we'll kill ya. That means you can go east or west. There's two horses for ya so you ain't afoot, an' in my pocket are two twenny-dollar gold pieces, one for each of ya. I'd say that's a fair deal. What do you think?"

"Sounds right fair to me, Marshal," Skinny said.

"How many hands has Waxler got at his place?"

"Nine or ten an' that feller what got his leg shot a little."

"It's seven er eight, Will," the other one said. "We ain't there no more."

I could see Marion tryin' not to grin. "Any of 'em, pistoleers?" he asked.

"Most of 'em is just hands," the young'un said. "A couple is purty fair though. That feller with the shot leg is rough. Mister Waxler brung him an' some other toughs in when a bunch a his hands got shot an' Jack an' Jim was found hung."

"Boys," Marion said, "my bunch has kilt around two dozen of 'em. That feller with the shotgun over there kilt five of 'em in one night. He done fer Youngblood, too."

Them boys looked at me like I was breathin' fire.

"Either one a you figger on buckin' us?" Marion asked.

They shook their heads.

"All right then," he went on, reachin' into his pocket. He handed each of 'em a gold piece an' pointed to them horses. "Now git," he said.

Them two swung up on them horses an' took out at a dead run, headin' east. Marion looked at me an' smiled.

"C'mon, Leroy," he said. "We got to hide."

CHAPTER THIRTY-FIVE

We went up near the top a that hill beside the wagon, tied Willie an' the sorrel on the offside slope an' out a sight, an' settled in to wait for somebody to come along lookin' for them fellas we run off. Nobody come. We set there, waitin' an' watchin' the rest a the day an' not one traveler showed up. We kept a cold camp that night, not wantin' no fire to show, et some jerky an' slept in shifts, one of us settin' up all the time watchin' that wagon an' such. By mornin' I was some tired of it, an' I speck Marion was, too. The horses was restless, bein' tied all night like they was an' without water.

It come up a cloudy day an' a little chilly with a fair north wind. Marion went down the slope an' hid behind a couple a fat cedars while I set up a ways in some weeds with that Winchester Arliss give me. We stayed like that all mornin'. On toward noon, I seen a couple a riders comin' south an' yelled down to Marion about it. He tolt me to stay hid an' cover him. It took a little while for them boys to git to us. When they noticed the wagon they come over. One was just a kid in pants an' suspenders over longhandles an' a bent up ol' hat with near no brim, with some kinda a handgun in a top flap cavalry holster. He set a lanky bay horse an' acted like he was cold. The other fella was quite a bit more.

He was older with a full beard an' a black slouch hat, wearin' a long drover's coat an' settin' on a real purty paint horse that tossed its head quite a lot an' chewed the bit. His spurs was silver lookin' an' shiny. When they seen the wagon an' come over toward it, he loosed the front of his coat an' opened it. He was carryin' at least one Colt in a crossdraw an' was some suspicious, behavin' like the kid warn't even there. Marion didn't move. Neither did I.

They stopped by the buckboard an' got down, the older fella just holdin' his reins out to his side while the kid took 'em. He walked around the wagon once an' looked it over, spied that cut up harness, an' said somethin' to the kid. I took a bead on him then, an' Marion, gun drawed, stepped out from behind them cedars, about thirty feet from the wagon. Without no hesitation at all, that older fella dove to his right to get behind that buckboard an' went for his gun, all in the same motion. Marion fired twice then, an' that fella didn't make it. His paint bolted at the sound of the shots an' took off runnin' north. The kid, still holdin' the reins to the bay, just stood there with his mouth open. Marion yelled up to me to shoot the horse.

I switched targets then, leadin' that paint a little 'cause a him runnin' away from us like he was. 'Cause I was up on a hill like I was, I sighted a few inches high. I touched that Winchester off, an' the kick of it rocked me back some. I levered another round in an' took sight agin, but the horse warn't there no more. He was back a few yards from where he woulda been, down on the ground an' kickin'. I aimed' an' fired. The kickin' stopped.

When I got down to the bottom a the hill, Marion had took the kid's ol' rusty Colt from him, an' the boy was settin' on the ground, shiverin' an' still hangin' onto that bay's reins. I tied the horse to a wagon wheel an' watched the kid while Marion went over to the body. It was face down on the ground, that drover's coat splayed out around it. He pulled the coat offa the body an' tossed it to the kid.

"Put that on," he said.

The boy got into that coat an' pulled it up tight around him.

"Take it easy, son," Marion went on. "We ain't gonna hurt ya none. What's yer name?"

"Wesley Bains," he said. "Folks call me Wes."

"How old are ya, Wes?" Marion asked.

"Thirteen I think," he said. "I doan righty know for certain."

"Where'd ya git them bruises from up on your face and neck, son?" Marion said.

"Them fellers hit on me now an' then," he said. "I got em' all over me, purty much."

"How'd you come to be with this bunch?" Marion asked him.

"I was with my daddy," he said. "He rode for the Waxlers since I was little. He an' some a the other fellers went off with Jack an' Jim back in the summertime an' none of 'em ever come back. I didn't have no place to go, so I jest stayed an' done chores an' stuff for eats an' someplace to sleep."

Marion glanced at me then, an' I knowed the truth when it come at me. I'd kilt this boy's pa. It rocked me some, an' I hated the thought of it.

"Didn't ya ever git any schoolin'?" Marion asked.

"Nossir," Wes said. "I cain't read nor write nor nothin' like that."

"Wes," I said, "would ya like to? Would ya like to go to school an' git paid to work an' take care a yourself?"

"Me?" he said.

"Yes, you," I said. "Would ya like that?"

"Lord, mister," he said, "I never figgerd I ever could. It'd make me right proud to learn my letters an' numbers. I can work. I feed the stock an' sweep an' such. An' I can cook some. I know how."

"There any open water near here?" Marion asked.

"Yessir," Wes said. "Back up toward the Waxler place a little an' over to the west a couple a hills is a little pond a runoff. They's deers out that way a lot. Ain't very far."

"Why doan you take Ruben here over there and make us a camp. I'll be along in a minute."

"I can do that," Wes said. "What do I do with Kelly's coat?"

"Kelly don't need a coat," Marion said. "You do."

* * * * *

Lord it was good to have a fire. We set up close to a nice little pond, well sheltered from the wind. I got beans goin' real quick, an' we had them, bacon, an' frybread. That boy pounded it down like he'd just discovered food. After he got filled up, I give him a peppermint stick, an' he got to grinnin' somethin' fierce, havin' never et one afore. Halfway through that stick, he went off to sleep, huddled inside that drover's coat.

"What the hell we gonna do with him?" Marion asked me.

"Ain't you never wanted to be a daddy?" I said.

Marion glared at me. "Quit that," he said.

I grinned at him. "Ol' Arliss asked me one time if'n I'd care to apprentice gunsmithin' with him."

"This boy is a ways from that," Marion said. "He cain't even read. I wouldn't feel right about just turnin' him loose. Somethin' will turn up I reckon. He ain't the problem right now anyway. Ol' man Waxler is."

"When these last two doan come back, he gonna send some more to see what's happened, ya reckon?"

"I doan know," Marion said. "He's lost a third a his hands in the last couple days. If them boys from the saloon was right, he's down to six or seven now. I doan speck he wants to send out a couple more that won't come back. Then agin, he's got to be terrible curious."

"You think we can trust the boy to stay here an' keep camp alone?" I asked.

"We're feedin' him an' keepin' him warm when we coulda just kilt him," Marion said. "I believe we'd havta throw rocks at him to git him to run off."

"Let's leave him here tomorrow an' git back over to Waxler's place real early," I said. "Git the mood of it an' such. I ain't got much compassion for anybody that's still there. Maybe we can finish this shit an' git on home."

"Stay alert," Marion said. "I'm fixin' to take a nap."

CHAPTER THIRTY-SIX

The next mornin' just afore dawn, me an' Marion set up on the hill' lookin' down over Waxler's place. We was some closer than the first time, bein' about two hunnerd yards out, behind a little spread a post oaks an' hid good. When it was light enough to look around, they was only five horses left in the corral that we could see. I figgerd then that maybe some a them boys had spooked an' run off. The cookie come out an' beat on that chunk a iron a little later, an' only two hands showed up from the bunkhouse to git plates.

"Some of 'em took out, I reckon," I said.

Marion nodded. "When you went right to sleep last night after we et, I walked over to where we left that wagon for a look-see. The ol' boy's body was stripped a anythin' valuable, an' the saddle was gone from that paint with a ol' one left behind. Could be the fellers that done that, just took what they did an' kept on goin'."

"They is spooked, I bet."

Marion looked at me. "Reckon you could hit a feller down at the place from this far away?" he asked me.

"Ain't no wind," I said. "Arliss tolt me to aim about a half a foot high at this distance. I speck I could hit a man."

The door to the house opened then, an' Waxler come out on his crutches, Cleveland Pettigrew with him. Waxler set in that chair like a broke down ol' owl an' the cookie brung him a plate. Pettigrew just set there with his foot up on that box an' a long gun his across his lap.

"That his lever shotgun ya reckon?" I asked.

"Most likely," Marion said. "He's partial, I hear."

"I'd prob'ly be able to hit him at this distance," I said.

Marion shook his head. "Naw," he said. "Not him."

We watched another minute or two an' a fella with a rifle walked up from the barn.

"He's the only nighthawk out this mornin' I think," Marion said. "An' he's the only one I seen with a rifle. Knock him down."

I stretched out on the ground, set that Winchester across a limb layin' there, an' took my sight. He warn't much mor'n a speck, an' I foller'd him as he walked to the cookhouse. While he stood there waitin' for the cookie to bring him a plate, I lifted that sight to a little bit over his head, emptied my breath, an' squeezed the trigger. When I got back on sight, he was sprawled out on the ground, his rifle in the dirt beside him, an' the cookie was standin' there, holdin' a plate an' not movin'.

Them two hands come tearin' outa the bunkhouse then an' seen the nighthawk layin' there about the time the cookie went for cover. They ran for the corral an' ducked behind the barn. In just a minute or two, they showed up', this time on horseback, cuttin' a fat hog for the hill on the west side, goin' for all they was worth. Pettigrew an' Waxler was both crouchin' down with they heads on swivels, tryin' to figger out where the shot come from.

"They doan know where we are, Marion," I said.

"Leave the rifle, Ruben," he said, an' stood up outa cover. "Rifle is too slow for close work."

He commenced to walkin' down the hill an' toward the house, then. I stepped away from him ten feet or so to his right, an' went along.

*****

We was about fifty yards away from the porch, long shot for a revolver, when Cleveland Pettigrew popped up with that shotgun a his. Afore he could git to full height, Marion drawed his Colt an' turned one loose. Pettigrew kindly jerked. Marion fired a second time an' Pettigrew dropped his shotgun offa the front a the porch an' went to his knees. He just squatted there, watchin' us walk up, blood showin' in two spots on his shirt. We was about thirty feet away when he fell over on his side. Waxler was settin' in his chair, starin' at us, his crutches on the porch floor, his clawed up hands graspin' at the arms a his chair. I dreaded the sight of him, an' the thoughts a how many folks he or his had kilt an' ruined over the years, just 'cause he'd decided he was king a somethin'.

"Yer them thar dirty sonsabitches what hung my boys!" he croaked. "Oh yew bastards. Aw, you dirty bastards." He focused on Marion then. "Well, ya kilt everbody else," he went on, grippin' at that chair's arms with long fingernails. "Now I guess you'll kill me!"

His plate was layin' on top a his lap, spilt all over his clothes, an' he had spit runnin' down his chin. I could smell him.

"C'mon you sonofabitch!" he holler'd at Marion. "Shoot me. Shoot me, goddam ya! What's the matter? Ain't ya got the guts to shoot a crippled-up ol' man?"

He was hateful, an' I couldn't hardly stand to look at him. He laid his ol' yella eyes on me then, spittin' all over hisself.

"How 'bout you, ya chickshit cocksucker!" he yelled.

"Believe I will," I said, an' touched that little twelve gauge off.

It took him fair in the chest, at least seven a them nine balls loaded in the shell. He fell back in his chair from the shock of it, an' commenced to dance like, flingin' his legs an' floppin' while he gasped an' choked. Marion fired then, an' the bullet took him above the left eye. Waxler come over quiet, an' slumped to his side.

Marion put his Colt back in the holster an' looked at me. "Go git the horses and your rifle, will ya, Ruben?" he said. "I'll see if the cookie has got anythin' left on the stove."

CHAPTER THIRTY-SEVEN

Afore we left the Waxler place we picked Wesley out the best a the five remainin' horses, another bay that was some more likely than the plug he had. We also found him a nice Heiser Denver high-back saddle in the barn to replace the ol' McClellan split seat he used. We never went in the house at all. When we rode off, the cook was peekin' at us from around the cookhouse door. I speck he went through the place purty smart when we got outa sight.

Wes was some got an' grateful for his new horse an' saddle, an' he fussed around fittin' that Heiser to hisself an' pettin' on his new horse while we broke camp. We took to the ride then, but kindly slow an' easy 'cause a the boy. He was fair wore down an' thin. I don't speck he never got enough ta eat. On the trip back down the Nodaway Trail, ever time we stopped, he et like he'd never got a look at food afore in his whole life. It was good to see him git a little confidence as we went along, nobody hittin' on him an' such. Neither one a us wantin' him to do nothin' we didn't do, too. I don't speck he'd ever been used fair by nobody.

* * * * *

We'd promised the Thorsen family we'd stop by on our way back. When we got near Clearmont, we went on into the town. Ol' Wesley's eyes was stickin' out like a bug when he run across all that civilization. We took him to a store an' got him a new pair a pants, two shirts, boots, suspenders, a winter coat, socks an' such, an' some saddlebags an' a bedroll. Then we went to a big ol' barbershop an' all of us got a haircut, with me an' Marion gittin' shaved, too. They had a fine bathouse there with five tubs, an' we all took a soak an' shower. Wes was in a world he never knowed existed, an' me an' Marion had a time watchin' him tryin' to shake a loop over all of it. Once we got outa there, we found a drygoods place an' got a better headstall an' reins for his bay, an' talked him into a new hat an' some winter gloves. He didn't hardly look like the same kid when we got done with him. Ol' Wes spent a lotta time grinnin' an' lookin' at his feet.

After all that, we went to a restaurant an' got him a beefsteak an' some pie, then spent the night in a little hotel, givin' him his own room all by hisself. He was some overtook by it, confessin' to Marion an' me the next mornin' at breakfast that he'd never slept in no proper bed afore, but just in blankets on loose straw at best.

We got out to the Thorsen place in the early afternoon an' innerduced him to everbody. Missus Thorsen got one peek at him an' headed for the kitchen. Agner took him outside to show him around the place, an' we told the folks about how he'd been raised an' how we come on him. They was some angered by the story an' right concerned about him, an' made us promise to stay on for a couple days to let him settle in some. Agner come back after a spell without Wes, sayin' the boy was right took by all them goats, an' wanted to stay outside an' mess with 'em for a while, special a pen a kid goats bein' raised up in the barn.

I swear, that boy growed in the next two days. Between Missus Thorsen poundin' food down him ever time he come in reach, everbody treatin' him so good, an' him gittin' used to the fact that he was worth a little bit to somebody, he opened up like a durn flower or somethin'. It was a treat to see. An' Lord, he did take to them goats.

On our last night there, after he went to bed in a little room they had in the house, the three Thorsen folks asked me an' Marion if'n he could just stay on with them. Missus Thorsen said that she'd been a school teacher when she an' her husband met, an' she could learn him his letters an' numbers, an' that, 'cause they was gittin' on some, another family member on the place would be right welcome. Me an' Marion knowed that they'd treat him real good an' all, an' agreed to it. The next mornin' Wesley made us both swear we'd come back an' see him sometime, an' had tears in his eyes when we rode off. To tell the truth, I did too. I don't know about Marion. He kept up a good pace for a ways, not lettin' me git up beside him to where I could see his face.

CHAPTER THIRTY-EIGHT

Our horses was good an' rested and we didn't dally on the way back to Deer Run. The sorrel throwed a shoe outside Chillicothe a little ways, but that was the only problem we had on the trip. The weather was gittin' right cool of a night an' I admit I enjoyed settin' around a fire in the evenin' an' givin' my back to the dark. We got to the house late in the afternoon a the third day, an' Marion took the horses on down to the barn while I went inside. Harmony was settin' in the kitchen with a pot a beef stew bubblin' on the stove.

We hadn't been gone terrible long, but it seemed to me she'd about doubled in size. She levered herself up offa that chair an' grabbled onto me some, an' we stood there swayin' back an' forth as was our way, both of us lettin' a tear or two loose, bein' glad to be back with one another an' all. She poured coffee for me that had a little chicory in it, an' we set there lookin' at each other an' grinnin'.

She tolt me she'd been feelin' purty good, but was gittin' some tired a bein' so slow ta do things, an' was kindly wore out carryin' herself around.

"When does the doc figger the baby'll show up?" I asked her.

"He believes I have about another three weeks," Harmony said. "Miz Clary thinks about another week or so."

"Who's yer money on?" I said.

"Clary," Harmony said. "But that could be just because I'd like to be able to put this baby down on the bed without having to lie down there with it."

* * * * *

Marion headed out the next mornin' an' I went down to see Arliss an' give him the whole story. Hank Buford was in the office when I dropped by to let the boys know I'd be back to work, an' I had to tell him everthin', too. It was early afternoon afore I got back to the house. Me an' Harmony had some a that beef stew for dinner, an' it was time for me to go to work. To tell the truth, I hated to go off an' leave her, but her daddy was there an' that give me some comfort. She said she was doin' fine, an' she was, I speck. Harmony had lots a color in her face, an' moved around purty fair for as big as she was. Gittin' up an' down outa chairs was some effort for her, but she was stout.

* * * * *

I reckon it was about two weeks later when Marion come up to the office on that roan, an' clanked inside. He unbuttoned his coat an' looked at me.

"You a daddy yet?" he asked.

"Nossir," I said. "But it cain't take much longer or Harmony ain't gonna be able to git around without a wheelbarrow."

Marion grinned at me. "Pappy Ruben," he said. "Just the thought a that make the hairs on the back a my neck stand up."

"Don't you criticize me, ya ol' stump," I said. "There ain't a woman that'd have ya, nor a kid that wouldn't run from ya!"

Marion chuckled some. "You gittin' yerself a fambly an' everthin' like ya are," he said, "I thought you might want a extra twenty dollars or so a month comin' in."

"For doin' what?" I asked him.

"Bein' a deputy U.S. Marshal. They call it deputy 'cause it ain't no full time job. But if'n a warrant needs to be served or somethin' like that out this way, there might not be nobody like me around for a hunnerd or more miles ta do it. They could git aholt a you on the telegraph an' send you out. Might not have ta do nothin' for two or three months at a time, but the gov'ment will still send you that twenty ever month. They need ya, an' there's some kinda foofarah goin' on in Deer Run where you cain't git away, yer job here comes first. You can git away, an' they pay ya two dollars a day while yer on Federal business extra over the twenty a month."

"Don't sound too bad," I said. "Lemme talk to Harmony about it."

Them words warn't more than outa my mouth, when Harmony's daddy come up outside on horseback. I went out.

"Looks like it's time, Rube," he said. "I'm goin' for the doc. You tell Miz Clary."

* * * * *

Harmony had took to the day bed in the little parlor downstairs by the time I got to the house. The doc come in a little after I got there an' went in, shuttin' the door behind him. In a few minutes, Miz Clary showed up with Missus Holman from the ladies store on her heels. Clary went in with the doc an' Missus Holman got a pot on in the kitchen an' fetched a couple a clean sheets an' such into the parlor, while I brung in wood. Marion, Verlon, an' me set in the livin' room an' looked at each other.

It was around midnight when the doc come out. He tolt us everthin' was goin' right along an' left. Missus Holman put a pan a water on the porch so it'd git cool. Ever now an' then she'd come out, soak a rag in that water, an' carry it back in the parlor. Harmony started to holler ever so often about the time the dawn come, an' the doc showed back up. He went in for a few minutes, then come out an' looked at me.

"Shouldn't be too long," he said. "She's fine."

Around ten o'clock, Harmony started yellin' right regular for a spell, an' the sound of it like ta tore my heart apart. Purty soon though, she settled down an' Missus Holman come out, askin' for some clean towels. I got 'em for her an' she went back in the room. About a half hour later, them two women an' the doc all come out, smilin' at everbody.

Miz Clary walked over to me, her eyes shinin'. "Go on in, Ruben," she said. "Harmony is waitin' for you."

Marion tolt me later that I went through that door like I was afeared they was a bobcat on the other side. Harmony was layin' there in the bed, lookin' some wore out, but smilin'. She had a wad a sheets or somethin' held up agin her. I went over an' set in a chair beside her an' she looked up at me.

"Hello, Daddy," she said.

It come over me then, just like that. Tears commenced to runnin' down my face. Harmony pulled some a them covers back an' there was this little ol' red face next to her, a tiny little hand with it, all balled up in fist.

"Oh, my," I said.

"Here's your son, Ruben," Harmony whispered. "Here's our son."

"Mercy," I said. "You done so good. Would you look at that? Would you just look at that."

I kissed her on the cheek then, an' we set for a spell, smilin' at each other an' such. After a time I spoke up.

"What do ya reckon we oughta call him?" I asked.

"Oh, he has a name," Harmony said.

"What is it?" I asked her.

She smiled at me. "William Cole Beeler," she said. "Is that all right with you?"

I was rollin' the thought a callin' my boy after Arkansas Bill Cole around in my head when the baby give a little squawk.

"Miss Harmony," I said, "I think that there is just fine. He was my friend, ya know."

* * * * *

Author's notes:

I would love to know what you think about the TRAIL series. Ratings and reviews are a great way to applaud (or boo) an author. Please consider leaving a review on any of the retailer sites where my titles are found.

For more information regarding other titles, please visit my website http://www.ironbear-ebooks.com.

(Keep reading for the first 3 chapters of CALICO TRAIL.)

Preview

CALICO TRAIL, Book 3

Copyright 2012

By David R Lewis

CHAPTER ONE

The winter after little Bill was born was some harsh. It warn't terrible cold or anythin' like that, but Lord, we had a mess a snow. It just kept stackin' up most all winter long. Them with stock to care for had a time, an' there was some cows an' pigs lost to it. Even a couple a old folks passed on while tryin' to dig out an' such, an' a lot a supply wagons was slow in comin' 'cause a the roads bein' so covered up an' all. I purty much had my hands full doin' what I could to keep the town goin', an' my deputies, Emory Nail an' Hank Buford, didn't git off no easier than me. On top a that, I was a daddy an' all, an' that was a helluva change in my life.

Harmony took to bein' a mother some easier that I took to bein' a father, I reckon. I done what I could to lighten her load, an' so did her daddy, Verlon, but it was some fretfull havin' a baby around. Seemed like to me that little Bill had a sense about him of just when to git to squawkin' or somethin' at the most inconvenient time. He'd start up in the middle a the night an' most always wake me up afore Harmony would hear him, my ears bein' tuned to the trail an' all. I'd git up an' fetch him to her so he could git a bite to eat an' such. As time went on, I come to notice a difference in the way he'd holler if he was hungry or just wantin' somebody to fuss over him. Them times, I'd walk him around, or go downstairs an' lay him on the davenport for a minute while I stoked the stove or somethin'. It got to where, after a while, that him an' me kindly worked it out between us an' he'd purty much settle down whenever I picked him up. I even got to be a fair hand at changin' him, but I left that to Harmony when I could. She seemed to handle it better. Sometimes what come out a that boy would set me to gaggin'.

He didn't lack for friends much. Miz Clary come by whenever she could to mess with him an' make sure he was bein' attended to in a manner fittin' her standards. She most always brung somethin' for him, knittin' him little booties an' such, an' even a pouch with a head flap to stick him in if Harmony wanted to take him someplace out in the cold. For his first Christmas I built him a cradle from some hard rock maple that hung in a stand an' could swing back an' forth to give him comfort. Arliss carved him a little-bitty Colt out a hickory an' showed up with it all wrapped up in tissue paper with a little red bow on Christmas day. Harmony got a kick outa that an' allowed as how little Bill was a mite young for firearms. Arliss give it to him anyway an' Bill grabbed a holt of it, like babies do, an' waved it around a little afore he lost his grip on it. Arliss pointed out the fact that, 'cause the boy had took it by the barrel an' not the grip, he wasn't no smarter than his daddy an' we probably should put it up 'til he was old enough to git some proper instruction on the use a handguns. Bill could be troublesome, no doubt about that. Now an' then I'd threaten him about givin' him to the Injuns, or feedin' him to the hogs, but it didn't seem to make no difference to him. I loved little Bill as much as I loved his momma, an' it was a treat watchin' him git to know me an' recognize his daddy among all others.

Seemed to me that he got a little bigger ever day. By the spring, he set where he was propped up an' lookin' around, studyin' on things. I'd watch him watchin' stuff, seein' things for the first time an' all. I could durn near hear them little wheels turnin' in his head as he come across somethin' new, an' almost everthin' was new to the boy. What a wonder that musta been for him, discoverin' the world all fresh an' such. Sometimes I'd ketch Harmony watchin' me while I watched little Bill an' smilin' in that sweet way she had. The truth of it is, I was happy. Oh, life ain't all sugar cookies an' rainbows, but I was anchored in a family, my family, an' I took some fine pleasure in that.

* * * * *

Spring broke sudden like after that winter, an' everthing greened up durn near overnight. All that snow cover had done the ground some good, I guess. It was early April an' Deer Run was boomin'. We'd added several more families an' another church was goin' up. I worked some on the finish carpentry when I could to help out an' such. The new preacher was a younger man named Clayton Beech. He was more "love yer neighbor" than "fire an' brimstone," an' seemed to be a good fella. Part of the roof of the Red Bird Saloon had fell through from the snow load of the winter, an' when they started fixin' it, they went at the whole inside, too. Brung in a bunch from Jeff City to do the job, an' it looked like it was gonna be some fancier than afore, the way they was goin' after it.

I went to the office on a real nice afternoon an' run across Hank Buford comin' out as I was goin' in.

"Hey, Boss," he said, "how's that baby?"

"Mean as a snake," I told him. "Caught him chewin' on a table leg this mornin'. He got halfway through it afore I could pull him off."

"I was you," Hank said, "I'd git Verlon to build a iron cage to put that boy in afore his teeth sprout. Won't nobody be safe."

We stood there grinnin' at each other for a minute. Then Hank spoke up agin.

"There's a telegraph on the desk for ya," he said. "I'll be down at the Sweetwater for a bite."

That message said that I was needed for some marshallin' business over near Dunston in Calico County, an' that Homer Poteet would be comin' to see me about the job. I should look for him to get details. I hadn't seen Homer since afore he got shot by Cleveland Pettigrew in that Waxler mess, an' I was some curious about how he was doin' an' how bad he'd been hurt. I put that telegraph message up an' went outside to start my rounds an' durned if I didn't see Homer Poteet ridin' up the way on a likely lookin' blaze-face sorrel with four white socks. He stopped in front a me an' brimmed his hat.

"Homer Poteet," I said. "I just got a telegraph that said you was comin' to see me. When ya gonna git here ya reckon?"

"Hell, Rube," he said, "ya cain't depend on me. Might be another day or two afore I show up. That good lookin' woman a yourn' ever quit pinin' over me an' have that baby?"

"You'll find out at supper tonight, I reckon," I told him.

Homer swung down offa that sorrel then an' come toward the porch. He had a leather an' steel brace on his right leg that looked to me to be troublesome an' he limped quite a bit, but he didn't seem to be slowed up much. He followed me inside an' we set.

"How's yer leg?" I asked him.

"I done fer them two fellers Pettigrew had with him, an' got one in him, too, but he shore done me worse than I done him. The doc wanted me to let him cut it off, but I tolt him that I'd go under afore I be one-legged. They brung in a feller from Jeff City an' he cut on it some an' left instructions. I done some exercises I was supposed to an' he come back a time or two, checkin' up on me an' such. Then he had this brace built for it. I'm still gittin' used to it an' all, but I git around purty good."

"It cause ya much pain, does it?" I asked him.

Homer nodded. "Fair bit," he said. "But less than it did. I got some laudanum I carry, but I doan use it none if I can help it. It does for the hurtin' alright, but I'll tell ya what. A feller takes too much of it an' he can easy git to where he craves it even when he ain't hurtin'. It kinda got on top a me for a spell. Got to where it was on my mind most of the time. That ain't no way to live, Rube. I got the best of it, but it durn near had me, boy. I come close to bein' a dope fiend, an' that's the straight of it."

"Gotcha a new horse, I see."

"Yessir. I didn't know how far down my ol' gray really was. This gelding I got now is purty fair. You still got Willie I guess."

"I do," I said.

"You still got Arliss the mule?"

"Him, too," I said "He runs loose over at the forge with the chickens."

Homer grinned. "I reckon he ain't had his back scratched for a spell, has he?"

"Not since you done it," I said. "You shoulda been here when Arliss the gunsmith found out about his namesake Arliss the mule."

"I bet that bandy-legged little shit got plumb insulted," Homer laughed, "an Arliss the gunsmith prob'ly didn't like it much neither!"

That hit me sideways an' it took a minute for the two of us to settle down.

"I didn't know you was a Marshal," I said.

"Deputy," he said, "like you. Marion is out in the territory runnin' after somebody. They doan know when he'll be back. When he is, I speck he'll look us up."

"What do they need us for?" I asked him.

"Jeff City got some complaints from over near Dunston in Calico County," he said. "You seen any a these red cattle with white faces?"

"A few," I told him. "Purty things. Built stocky an' meaty like."

"Comin' thing the way I hear it," Home went on. "Them an' those Black Angus ya see now an' then. The days a the Texas cattle drives is fixin' to end I reckon. Prairie grass is sufferin' some from drought an' them ol' range cows is thinnin' out. The beef on these new ones is a damn site better, but they cain't be just left ta run loose like them ol' longhorns. They take some care. Call 'em Herefords. The breed come from England, or Scotland. Someplace like that across the waters. There's a ol' boy come over from England name a Merrit Treadstone. Sir Merrit Treadstone, whatever the hell that means. He showed up Calico County way a year or two ago with more money than the devil. They say he's buyin' up everthing he can git his hands on to ranch them Herefords. Sellin' a few bulls an' cows to other fellers out in Oklahoma, Nebraska, Ioway, an' such for big money, keeping stock back for his herd, sellin' off steers at high prices for Hereford beef in Kansas City an' Sain't Louis. Fixin' to build hisself a empire or somethin'. Folks is complainin' he's tryin' to take over the whole durn county, an' then some. Marshal's Service wants us to go take a peek."

"How far is it?" I asked him.

"Less than a hunnerd miles, I speck," Homer said. "Calls it the Calico Cattle Comp'ny. A extra two dollars a day an' expenses, if ya wanna go."

* * * * *

Homer come to the house that evenin' for supper to visit with Harmony an' Verlon. He enjoyed the meal an' made over little Bill somethin' near shameful. After he went off to toss his roll at Miz Clary's place, I tolt Harmony about why he'd come to town.

"Ruben," she said, "you can't let Homer go off on this all alone. He's not up to it yet. Plus, you have been cooped up here all winter. I know your nature. You need to get out from time to time. I married you without the intent of trapping you or binding you to me. You were a wanderer when we met and, in your heart, you still are. If you don't go, you will be a mess worrying about Homer every day and missing the space you need now and then to be happy here. The baby and I have a lot of support. You go on and you come back, safe and sound."

Two days later we had all the chuck an' possibles we needed an' took out a little after daybreak. Me an' Homer, on the Calico Trail.

CHAPTER TWO

Homer an' me didn't hurry none, tryin' to make it easy on the horses, especially mine. Me workin' in town mostly an' it bein' early spring, Willie had been some idle for a spell, an' then had been after that new grass about as hard as he could. He had a couple a problems. He was feather-footed 'cause a bein' not rode much, an' he was spring fat. He was strong in his mind, figurin' he knowed more than I did, an' he was overweight an' soft. After a hour or two a him tossin' his head an' gittin' after the bit, hoppin' an' fussin at me, I tolt Homer that I'd be back in a while, give Willie a touch a both my dull spurs, hissed at him, an' turned him loose.

That little buck was a mess. He squealed an' durn near left me settin' on thin air when I let him git after it. If it hadn't a been for my saddle horn, I'd a rolled right offa his butt. He could run an' he knowed it, but he was some optimistic about how long he could keep goin'. Warn't more than a few minutes 'til Willie figger'd he'd slow down. I wouldn't let him. I give him another mile or so about as hard as he could go afore I let up. He had enough left to git upset with me an' try to buck a little. When that didn't do no good, he got plum mad at me an' figured he'd just go back home.

Willie had never been hard to git along with, but when he got to actin' like that, my ruff come up. I cannot abide a barn-sour horse. I tolt him that he could go anyplace that he wanted, as long as he'd back up to git there. Horses don't care for backin' up much, it's a unnatural gait for 'em. If they is made to do it for too long, it gits after their hocks an' can cause swellin' an' such. Ol' Willie lost his taste for it purty quick. I trotted him in a circle a little while, then kept it up at a easy canter. It helped cool him out a mite an' straightened out his attitude. After he settled in I got off of him an' give him a half a biscuit I'd stuck in my jacket pocket afore we left home. By the time we got back to where Homer was, ol' Willie was plumb humble. Homer grinned at me.

"Git his mind right, did ya?" he asked.

"He's settled some," I said.

"Take it slow today, I reckon," Homer went on. "Make a early camp."

Prob'ly should," I tolt him. "Be easier on the horse. He ain't been rode much for quite a spell. He'll be sore tomorrow."

Homer grinned at me. "You ain't been out no more than he has," he said. "Gonna be interestin' to see who rides who in the mornin'."

As it turned out I was the one that got on top, but I didn't like it much.

* * * * *

By late afternoon we crossed the river at Jeff City an' got outa town a ways afore we made camp. Homer had brung some cans of them beans with him, an' even a tool somebody had come up with to git the top a them cans off. I'll tell you, it was some easier than hackin' at 'em with a huntin' knife. We heated them beans up in the can an' I fried up a little bacon. Harmony had sent along some balls a corn meal she fixed that had onion an' wild garlic cooked in 'em. She'd never made 'em for me afore an' they was right tasty.

"Corn Dodgers," Homer said.

I looked at him an' he went on. "Or Hushpuppies is another name for 'em. Depends on where yer from, I guess. My momma usta fix these things whenever we'd have catfish. I got used to 'em. Sometimes she'd make 'em without the salt an' onion an' such, an' put dried blueberries an' cinnamon an' honey in 'em. Good to chew on when a feller was workin' out in the cold. Give ya a little boost like."

We tossed our rolls after we et an' I passed Homer a peppermint stick. He spit out his chaw an' stuck it in his cheek like a cigar.

"I noticed you ain't carryin' yer Yallerboy no more," he said.

"Nossir, I ain't," I tolt him.

"Winchester '76 ain't it?"

"It is," I said. "Centennial 45/75."

"Purty good rifle," Homer said. "Shoot two-thirds as far as my ol' Sharps."

"Arliss put one a them adjustable peep sights on it for me a couple a months ago," I said. "It'll reach out there a ways."

I waited for him to say somethin', but he didn't. He did commence to snore, though. I swear, Homer an' Marion could both go to sleep so quick they'd beat their eyes gittin' closed. Me? I'd most always lay there for a spell, thinkin' about this an' that.

There come a little rain the next day that slowed us down a mite, an' then Homer's sorrel throwed a shoe. We got into Columbia late in the afternoon an' found a smith. He put new shoes on the horse all the way around an' let us stretch out in a empty stall for the night. They was a restaurant a couple a blocks away an' we et there that night an' had ham an' eggs there the next mornin'. They sold us a dozen biscuits to take along an' we was back on the trail a couple a hours after daybreak. I give Wille a bite a one a them biscuits afore we left an' he took right to it.

Homer swung up an' grinned at me. "I shoulda brung Willie back a piece a pie or somethin'," he said. "I doan know what I was thinkin'."
* * * * *

We made it to Mexico by late afternoon. It was kindly a bustlin' town. We found a livery down by the rail yard an' left the horses there, then got some purty good fried chicken and found a roomin' house. We got a double room an' Homer took off about as soon as we got settled. He said since we was in Mexico, he figger'd they was a senorita out there someplace with his name on her. He never did come back to the room that I noticed, but he was at the livery when I went down there the next mornin', leanin' agin his horse. When he seen me, he put a leg over the saddle.

"Ain't we gonna git no breakfast?" I asked him.

Homer didn't say nothin' back to me, but just turned that sorrel an' headed off at a walk. I got Willie under leather an' took out after him. He hadn't gone a half a mile afore I caught him, settin' head down and swayin' quite a bit. I fell in behind him an' left him alone. Looked to me like Homer didn't feel too good.
* * * * *

We didn't make mor'n twenty miles that day, but it was shore some nice country. Easy rollin' hills an' heavy grass. A little stream showin' up now an' then. Gittin' on toward late afternoon, we had to detour from time to time 'cause a fences bein' put up with that bob-wire. Now an' then we'd see a few a them Black Angus cattle strung out makin' dark spots agin the green grass in the sunshine. Except for havin' them fences in the way, I don't believe I ever had a nicer ride. Gittin' on toward evenin' we was about five or six miles outa Dunston an' made a early camp by one a them little cricks. They was a small bunch a them red cows with white faces grazin' off a ways, lookin' as purty as they could. I got out some beans in a can an' bacon while Homer picked up sticks a firewood. I had just got the skillet hot when Willie tossed his head an' fussed a little. Homer looked off down the way across that grass an' studied on things for a minute with them eyes a his.

"Hide yer badge, Rube," he said. "Four of 'em comin' on a trot. Fair horses. Prob'ly ain't no stockpushers or hayshakers. We're just passin' through, ain't we?"

"On the way somewhere else, I reckon," I said.

Homer nodded, went over an' hid his Sharps under his roll, an' come back an' set. I started heatin' up the beans an' put some bacon in the skillet, while he made coffee. The bacon was near done an' the coffee boilin' when them fellas showed up. They rode in an' stopped close, about thirty feet from the fire. We looked at them an' they looked at us.

"Howdy, boys," I said. "Coffee's hot if ya got cups. Sorry, but we're a little short on bacon."

The one in front, settin' on a handsome black geldin', let his horse step forward. He was older than me but younger than Homer, carryin' a 1875 Remington in a crossdraw. I had always admired them Remingtons.

"You fellers is on Calico land," he said.

"My sister had a calico dress," I said. "Didn't know it had nothin' to do with dirt. Learn somethin' ever day, I guess. How 'bout that coffee?"

"This here dirt that yer squattin' on belongs to Mister Treadstone," he said.

"By God, he has done hisself right fair," I said. "He's got hisself some fine grass. Purty cows, too. It a no on that coffee? Got some brown sugar if yer sweetooth is actin' up."

He set up some straighter in the saddle. "Yer tresspassin'," he said.

"We are?" I said. "Homer, did you know that? We're tresspassin'."

"Never give it no thought," Homer said.

"I 'spose you two just didn't notice that bob-wire," the fella said.

I grinned at him. "I mighta," I said. "Lemme check my horse for cuts."

A little snicker come from behind him. "You men havta move on," he said. "Ya cain't stay here."

Homer spoke up. "We'll git outa yer way in the mornin'," he said. "Camp is made, I'm tired, tomorrow is soon enough. You run us off now, we're gonna be out here on unfamiliar ground in the dark. I just got that sorrel. I run him up agin' some a that wire in the night, he's gonna git hurt. He gits hurt, I'm gonna have to cut some a that wire. I cut that there wire, an' some a them good lookin' cows might git out an' run off. That there would be yer fault, pard. I'd hate to see you git in trouble 'cause a nothin' more than bacon, beans, an' a night's sleep."

That fella an' Homer looked at each other for a spell. "Alright," he said. "Tomorrow mornin' you two be gone. I'll be back to check."

Homer smiled at him. "All by yerself?" he asked.

That fella reined his black around right smart, an' the bunch of 'em left at a canter. Homer turned to me.

"I bet you a dollar agin a donut that them four ain't the best that Treadstone's got," he said.

CHAPTER THREE

We got into Dunston late the next mornin' an' rode down the main street. They was a couple a saloons, a handsome eatin' place, a bank, a barbershop an' bathhouse, a general store, a drygoods store, a little grocery place, an' a sheriff's office an' such. We stopped at the restaurant, tied the horses at the trough, an' went on in an' set. Purty soon this good-lookin' little gal with red hair come over an' brung us coffee and a smile.

"Gentlemen," she said, "the special today is beef roast. Have you ever had Hereford beef?"

Me an' Homer allowed as we never had an' took her word on everthing. She come back after a while with a big ol' bowl a mashed potatoes, a bowl a sweetcorn, an' two plates with a couple a big slices a beef on each one under gravy, an' baked carrots along the sides. I'll tell you what. That there was the best beef I ever et. I couldn't git over it. Homer neither. We tolt the waitress so, when she come with more coffee.

"A gentleman named Treadstone raises the cattle near here at a place called the Calico Cattle Company," she said.

"If he's half as good as his beef, he's a heck of a man," I said.

"At least his beef is good," she said, and walked away.

Homer smiled. "That there," he said, "was some less than what a feller might call a ringin' endorsement."

We had no room for pie or anything. When the waitress come back to git money, Homer asked her if she knew where the Royce Taylor place might be.

"Why would you be asking me about something like that?" she said.

"I figger'd you workin' here an' all, you'd be acquainted with most folks," Homer said. "An' seein' how you feel about Treadstone, I thought you might be wise enough not to tell anybody else that two United States Marshals was here in response to Mister Taylor's complaint about the Calico Cattle Comp'ny."

"You men are marshals?" she asked.

"Yes, M'am," Homer replied. "This here is Ruben Beeler. My name is Homer Poteet."

"I have heard those names before, Marshal Poteet," she said, her face comin' over a little pink.

"It would be kind of you not to mention us to anyone," Homer went on. "Word like that gittin' out could put lives in danger. 'Specially the two that's settin' here at this table."

"My name is Susie McGrill, Mister Poteet," she said, smilin'. "Mister Taylor's place is about three miles west of town. There's a wagon road that runs that way. He's probably puttin' in corn about now. White house with a small white barn and some corn bins. And I shall not say one word about the two of you."

Homer stood up an' handed her two dollars. "Keep the change, Miss Susie," he said, "an' the secret."

"I have no idea what you're talking about," she said, smilin' at him. "You two cowboys come back an' see us now, Mister Smith."

"M'am, that'd be Homer. Just Homer," he tolt her. "Right pleasin' thing, meetin' a handsome lady like you."

* * * * *

I held onto my grin 'til we got outside, but then it got the best of me. Homer looked at me an' grimaced.

"Why Homer, just Homer," I said, "I am just so thrilled to be in yer comp'ny, I don't know what to do with myself. Mercy me."

Homer snugged his hat down real low in front. "I reckon that's enough a that, Rube," he said, an' struck off for his horse.

I let him git a little ahead a me, an' followed him on outa town. When he turned west on a little wagon road I eased Willie up beside the sorrel.

"You ain't gonna slap leather agin me or anythin' like that, are ya Mister Smith?" I asked him.

"Goddammit, boy," Homer grumbled, "I cain't take you nowhere."

"Well now, Homer," I said, "I don't understand why you ain't in a better mood, you makin' a brand new friend like ya done."

"Keep it up," Homer said.

"Knowin' now that yer so fond a redheads," I said, "I bet you are plumb thrilled to be settin' on a sorrel horse, ain't ya?"

"Rube," Homer said, "I believe I enjoyed yer comp'ny a lot better when you was a wide-eyed kid that knowed how to keep his mouth shut."

"Speakin' of enjoyin' comp'ny," I went on, "I reckon there's a livery someplace that'd rent you a little buggy or a gig so you an' Miss Susie could take a little night air together."

Homer took a swipe at me with his hat then, but Willie spooked an' jumped away. If I hadn't a been ready I'd a come off.

"You could, by God, spend a little time mindin' yer own business," Homer said.

"I am mindin' my own business," I tolt him. "If'n you was to take up with a woman I could give Harmony the bad news. Then maybe she'd quit settin' up nights starin' out the winda, waitin' for you to return to her an' pay attention to her own business. That way, I wouldn't have to walk that durn baby all night."

Homer nodded. "She did take it hard, me leavin' her with you, didn't she?" he said.

"Red swole up eyes ever mornin'," I said. "Pitiful to see."

Homer grinned. "Bullshit," he said, an' touched spurs to his horse. That sorrel was purty fast.

* * * * *

In a little while we come up on a place on the south side of the road with a white house an' barn, an' a couple a corn cribs. There was a feller in a field workin' a team a big ol' mules an' a two bottom plow an' planter comin' our way. We waited for him. When he got fair close he shucked his reins an' faced us from about fifty feet. They was a Remington conversion tucked in his belt.

"You boys may as well go on back," he said. "My word is final. I ain't sellin'. Not to Treadstone nor nobody else. You can tell him that agin'."

"Never met the man," Homer said. "We're lookin' for a feller name a Royce Taylor. You him?"

"What if I am?"

Homer brimmed his hat. "Mister Taylor," he said, "The Marshal Service mentioned that you maybe could use a little help. That's why we're here."

Mister Taylor took off his hat an' wiped his brow on his sleeve. "Can you drive a team a mules?" he asked.

"Druther not," Homer said, smilin'.

"Well, go on up to the house," Mister Taylor went on. "Martha's got some sweet tea. I'll finish this row an' be on up that way. Good to see you fellers."

* * * * *

Martha Taylor was a plump little woman with a sweet smile that, once we tolt her who we was an' what her husband said, stuck us on their porch an' got us each a glass a tea from a crock wrapped in a wet rag settin' in the shade. It was plumb good. After a little bit a small talk, she left us alone. In about twenny minutes, Mister Taylor come walkin' up from the barn.

"Hate ta take ya away from follerin' them mules around," Homer said, standin' up an' stickin' out his hand.

"Ground's a little too wet anyway," Mister Taylor said. "You know who I am, I guess."

"Yessir," Homer said, finishin' the shake. "I'm Homer Poteet. This here is Marshal Ruben Beeler."

"Nice to meetcha, Mister Taylor," I said, shakin' with him. He was a thin man an' not tall, but he was ropey an' some stout, I reckoned.

"You boys are on my porch drinkin' my tea," he said. "I guess you better call me Royce."

'Bout that time, a little girl with yella hair come out of the house. She was wearin' a blue gingham dress an' carryin' a plate a sugar cookies. She was brave enough to hold the plate out to Homer an' me, but too shy to say anythin'. We each took a couple an' thanked her. She smiled at her feet an' went back inside.

"Yer daughter I 'spose," Homer said.

"A twin," Taylor said. "Her sister died of the fever when they was four. Mandy is seven now."

"That's a hard thing," Homer said. "A wound like that doan never really close."

"No, it don't," Taylor said. "Walk with me to the barn, fellers, an' we'll have a snort. I'd be right proud to share a little corn whiskey with Homer Poteet an' Ruben Beeler."

* * * * *

For more information regarding other titles by David R Lewis, please visit his website at http://www.Ironbear-ebooks.com.

Made in the USA
Las Vegas, NV
14 January 2021